SIREN

Annemarie Neary

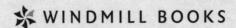
WINDMILL BOOKS

1 3 5 7 9 10 8 6 4 2

Windmill Books
20 Vauxhall Bridge Road
London SW1V 2SA

Windmill Books is part of the Penguin Random House group of companies
whose addresses can be found at global.penguinrandomhouse.com.

Penguin
Random House
UK

First published by Hutchinson in 2016
First published in paperback by Windmill Books in 2017

www.penguin.co.uk

A CIP catalogue record for this book is available from the British Library.

ISBN 9780099592587

Typeset in 11.1/15.48 pt Fournier ITC Galliard Std by Jouve (UK), Milton Keynes
Printed and bound in Great Britain by Clays Ltd, St Ives Plc

For Conor

Peel off the napkin
O my enemy
Do I terrify?—

From 'Lady Lazarus' by Sylvia Plath

Belfast

Róisín sensed the danger long before she'd had a chance to think it, when it was just a quivering of something in the air outside the room. Not quite a sound, not quite. Then from the other side of the wall, a thud, a gasp, a dull thump like a fist in a pillow. They broke off from kissing, and she felt his sharp intake of breath as if it were her own. He scrambled off the bed towards the window.

'No, no,' he was murmuring. 'Fucking no.'

He found his shoe, began battering at the glass. But the men were in the room now and the window wouldn't break.

It didn't sound like much, just a dart puncturing a board. But it got him. As his body slumped backwards from the window, Róisín lurched across to try to reach him, but one of the gunmen had her by the hair. She kicked and scrabbed and punched at him, but he flung her out on to the landing like she was nothing.

She crouched there with her head wedged tight between her knees, her body trembling. She watched through the veil of her hair as the men clattered past her and down the stairs: dirty-white runners with blue side-streaks, then desert boots. She heard the metal scrape of their guns against the wall, the heft of their breath, a shout from down below to get those hoors the fuck out of there.

When she was sure they were gone, she scuttled back towards the bedroom, but Lonergan was there now, beamed up from nowhere, leaning against the frame of the door.

'Lift's waiting,' he said.

She turned and saw Dolores there too, wincing against the vinegary light with her skirt undone and her legs bare. Her hair was frizzed up, her kohl-rimmed eyes even blacker than before. And round her mouth the lipstick smears of dead kisses.

In the queasy corners of her vodka head, Róisín was beginning to realise what this was. She glanced between Lonergan and Dolores, but neither met her eye.

'We can't just *go*,' she said to no one in particular.

When they didn't answer her, she pushed past Lonergan to reach the room. But his hands, still cold from outside, gripped hers. She kicked out at him, spat, screamed. But he was deft at the side-step, the duck and weave. He took her by the back of the neck and spoke right into her ear.

'It's over now,' he said. 'You done good.'

She couldn't move her head, and he had her arms

clamped tight behind her back, but she struggled hard to land a kick.

'You really want to go in there? You want to see?'

But that wasn't where she wanted to go at all. All she wanted now was to go right back to the beginning of the night and make a new one. With no Dolores, no disco dancing or vodka or men with crew cuts. All she wanted now was to be a girl in a sunny field. She tried to tell him that, but her stomach heaved and sank and all she could manage was a kind of whine that made her feel ashamed.

He brought her in there anyway. From the window there was the orange wash of street light and the faint blue glimmer of a far-off TV, but the room itself was dark. She shut her eyes in case he flicked the switch, so he couldn't make her see. There in the dark, she could hear the sound of her own breath, nasal and ragged. She felt him bending down, heard his leather jacket creak, and then she felt a streak of something warm and wet across her forehead. The room dissolved, and Róisín with it, and as he dragged her down the stairs, she heard the screams of someone she'd already ceased to be.

Lamb Island

1

Boyle is sitting in the island's only pub, scratching his initials into the worn surface of the table with the sharp end of a compass. Outside, a gale is whipping the life out of the stubborn string of prayer flags tied to the crooked tree. A pair of plastic chairs rattle across the tarmac until the wind hoists them up over the drystone wall and off in a canter across O'Driscoll's field. By now, it's nearly evening and the light is draining slowly off west until the sky vanishes, then the sea, and the last thing visible is the white plastic jumble of those chairs lodged, feet up, in the gorse.

He's been nursing the same pint for two hours now, and no one's said a word to him. Not that he minds the solitude – there's sanity in that. It's the malice that gets to him, and all their thick talk. He has the ear cocked, and bit by bit he catches their drift. There's a new one coming to rent Johnny Yellow Murphy's bungalow out at Reen. He feels the first curdle of excitement he's had all year at the prospect of something new to look at. Out by the South Harbour on an elevated spur more sea than land, Murphy's house is stroked all night by the lighthouse beam. Boyle has squatted twenty years in the abandoned school that grips the rocky hill above it. He has watched the tenants come and go. The house is nothing special – just a pebbledash bungalow on a rag of silky, rock-strewn grass. But Boyle has the perfect view, and it's a shame to waste it. New woman, new story.

'New York,' says Murphy. 'A Yank, taking it for a month. Fuck knows what she's doing here in March. Painting, mebbe.'

Boyle feels their eyes on him.

'What you think, Pete? Painting the mist, or the fucken stones, what?'

'She'll not be painting you, Murphy, anyhow,' says Pete, and they all laugh.

Boyle knows they're aiming all this at him, but he won't rise to it. He lets the acid come, and spits it into his sleeve. Then Theo the Dutchman arrives. He lets in the rain, nods at Boyle and says it's a foul night, which it is right enough. For a moment it looks like he might pull up a chair, sit down and shoot the breeze. But he changes his mind, and goes to sit with the others at the bar. Next thing he's asking Murphy what the new woman calls herself.

Murphy's back sinks into a fat curve, revealing a strip of cod-coloured flesh. 'Her name's Sheen,' he says, and smirks. 'Tell me, says I. Would that be the furniture polish, or the hairspray?'

'It's probably Sheen-agh and you took it down wrong,' says one of the Ruas. 'Or Sheila or –'

'Mebbe,' says Murphy, but he's clearly not that interested. 'She's on her own. Time out, she said.'

'Sure what would she paint in that?' says the other Rua, gesturing to the rain-spattered window that faces on to the blind sea.

'Jesus, catch up,' says Murphy. 'Some people just like being in the back of beyond, I suppose. Use your head, Barry. Fucked if I know.'

Boyle waits to see what more he can pick up. He's learnt to snatch a shred of sense from them wherever he can. Murmured confidences, jokes half-cut, the odd something tossed against the wind. Soon they're forgetting themselves. Louder and louder they drink. Wetter and wetter the talk of money and plans. Pleased as punch to have a Yank goose lay golden eggs till summer comes. And then the Dutchman's mobile rings. Right away, he's on his feet, moving away from Murphy and the rest of those gobshites at the bar. He's heading for the door. But as he passes, Boyle hears just enough to make him wonder. 'They're saying she's American, so –'

Boyle scrapes back his chair and scores a screech from the tiles, but nobody looks up. Outside, there's no sign of the Dutchman. The gale has blown itself out and the sea is sighing. The hedgerows are drenched, and Boyle is nearly up at the ridge before he knows it. He's hardly drunk on the one pint, but he feels like he's glided up there. There's not a catch in his breath – just a green haze in his head at the thought of a new one coming. He stops a moment and looks back down the bluff. The light-house beam doesn't stretch that side of the island. The whiskey glow from the pub is all there is. Beyond that, there's nothing but the dark water, the silent skerries. And in the distance, the mainland glittering. Reaching the top, he has the old feeling again, the hip-hop over-and-back in the pit of his stomach. A flash of the last one – white throat curving away from him, hair stream-ing off behind.

When he gets to the other side of the ridge, the light-house beam catches him, whitewashes him. He breaks into a half jog, shortening his stride on the last gritty stretch up to the abandoned school, shut down for want of island children. The building, salt-blackened and licheny, can scarcely be seen from the road. Even the leak-ing roof is more moss than anything else. Most of the windows are gone, blocked up now with hardboard. But there is still one, high up in the gable end. He could perch up there at the top of the stepladder and look down on the whole world if he wanted to. He'll be able to look down on the new one, anyway, mark the exact second she moves in. He feels a little rush of joy as he unlocks the padlock on the metal door they installed ten years ago to keep him out. He casts an eye about the place. As he left it. Safe and sound.

To the right of the fireplace, THE WORLD, all pas-tels and failed states, is locked at 1989. The seven times table, written out in seven childish hands, is pasted un-evenly on to a foxed sheet of green manilla. A half-torn frieze tracks waist-high along the walls and shouts out that A is for Apple, B for something long forgotten. There's a Brigid's cross above the door, and a knobbly-kneed crucifix hangs skew-whiff over the sand and water trays, next to a chart with pasted-on mugshots – JFK and Dev and the Pope before last – People You Should Know.

Each winter, Boyle has burned a little more of the school. The desks are all gone now, the teacher's table, too. He is working his way through the books. Sometimes he treats himself to a bale of peat briquettes and sits cross-legged in front of them as they burn down to a pile of dust studded with hot orange gems.

He swipes aside a Frisbee from the bottom of the games cupboard. Pulls out the last bottle of whiskey. He pours two fingers and knocks it back, and then two more. The whiskey speeds around his veins. It eases him, but the feeling doesn't last. Another two fingers, then another, until finally he realises something else is necessary to make things right. He is getting excitable at the thought of this new one coming, a light returning to the bungalow below. A fire, he thinks, might settle him. He arranges his last three peat briquettes, tepee-like, on a bed of kindling. Throws on *Progress in Irish*. The flames flare and the pages curl and, for a while, the fire is almost enough to satisfy him. But it fades too quickly and he is left flat. The new one is coming on the last ferry of the week and he is ragged at the thought of all the hours till then.

The water plinking into half a dozen buckets tells him that the rain is on again. He's just thinking about making a dash to the outside jacks for a piss when it comes. Whack

whack whack. A fist on the old metal door. No one ever comes to that door. Not since the trouble over the last one. But there it is again. Whack whack whack whack, and then his name, 'Boooooooyle.' He grabs a poker from beside the fire. Props it against the wall. Out of sight, but reachable.

'Hurry the fuck,' says the Dutchman.

Boyle unhooks the first of the chains. How long are you in this bleeden country? he thinks. It's up, you wanker. Hurry the fuck up. There are still two locks to go, two keys to work in, two chains to slide off. For all he knows, the Dutchman might have gone by the time he opens it. For all he knows, he might still be there though, and half the island with him. When he's worked his way through the locks and opened the door, the Dutchman is standing there, alone and dripping wet. He just walks straight in, without being invited. His eyes eat the room and then he turns to Boyle and comes straight out with it.

'I've had a call from Lonergan,' he says.

'Oh yeah?' Boyle tries to sound light about it, but his mood is gearing up up up, and God only knows where that will take him.

'He thought you might be interested in a bit of work.' And then his eyes are off again, zigzagging over the room, taking in the half-dead fire, the empty bottles. Boyle follows his gaze to the buckets, to the peeling transfer of a Nativity scene on the one good window, to the gas camping lamp that punishes everything with its blue-white light.

He feels his mood crank halfway to a rage. 'He's been asking for me, has he?' Rising slowly. 'Bit fucken late. I could have done with him when the Guards were all over me. He might have been a help to me then.'

The Dutchman is making a tour of the room. 'He'll be in Skibb tomorrow for a funeral.'

'Gobshite.'

'Like I said, Boyle, there's a bit of work going.' The Dutchman heads for the door. 'He'll see you at eleven. Field's café.'

Boyle is just fiddling with the locks again when the thought strikes him. 'What about you, Theo? Why didn't he ask you?' He calls it out into the night, but the Dutchman is gone, and the lighthouse beam is sweeping his retreating figure off the surface of the night.

Once he's on his own again, Boyle thinks of all the other things he should have remembered to ask the Dutchman. How much he'll be paid, for one thing, and when the next boat is due in at Goat Point.

After the transatlantic flight, the short hop across to Cork feels like an anticlimax. The B&B Sheen booked online is on the edge of an industrial estate not far from the airport. It smells of burnt toast and bacon, and even the kitchen chairs have frills. The woman of the house has dairy-farm cheeks and a solid, comfortable shelf for a chest. Sheen seems to be the only guest, and she finds herself the focus of all the woman's efforts: tea in a squat brown pot, a fan of brightly coloured tourist brochures advertising medieval banquets with complimentary Prosecco, a miniature village, a wildlife park. Sheen finds the woman's chat, its unpredictable ups and downs, impossible to follow. She is suddenly exhausted.

The bedroom is small, damp, peach-coloured, and its only window looks on to a black hillside. She takes out the map and runs her finger along the crinkled coastline until she finds Lamb Island. Six miles offshore, ferries twice a day. Already, she has memorised its shape and the scant details she could find: a pub, two harbours, the man who makes ice cream with goat's milk, the devastated fishing fleet.

A knock on the door, and the woman of the house is back with more tea and a plate of bright pink biscuits dusted with coconut. She remembers those biscuits, the base soggy, the marshmallow firm enough to stuff a cushion – Mrs McKeever, her mother's friend from down the street. And though that memory is benign enough, it brings with it other, darker things.

'I suppose you'll be moving on in the morning,' the woman says, cosying herself on to the edge of the bed.

'I'm heading west,' Sheen says.

The woman screws up her nose at that. 'I wouldn't bother with the Ring, if I were you. Fierce weather forecast. Mind you, there's some lovely new places in Killarney if you fancy a bit of luxury. Seaweed wraps and hot stone massages.'

Sheen doesn't mention the island. In the years since leaving Belfast, it's always been her way to censor the first thing that comes into her head. The next one is nearly always good enough, even if it isn't actually true. On her own in the small peach room, she is impatient, unable to settle. Eventually, the lack of Wi-Fi forces her out into a light squall and the endless cul-de-sacs of a half-finished business park. Everything is shut, if any of it was ever open. And then she remembers it's a Saturday, and the world of days and weeks and weekends begins to take shape again. At a parade of shops that breaks the long run of pebbledash houses, she stops to buy an A4 envelope and a book of stamps. The takeaway next door is nothing like the chippers she remembers from Belfast days. It sells felafels, kebabs, veggie things in wraps. A shop beyond is painted red and white. Polski Sklep.

The first thing you get rid of is a name like that if you don't want to stand out. Róisín. Roe-sheen. Little rose. When she first arrived in New York, Róisín dropped a syllable and was transformed. She relished the soft whisper as the new name slid between her teeth. Once she'd got used to it, she went shopping for a better past. She picked up jumble thrown away by people who took themselves for granted: a teacup with a rim of faded gilt, a one-eyed rag doll, a book of Spanish songs. She gave them each a place, a time, a relative, and built a new story for herself.

Sheen became a different kind of Irish person, from a gentler, mistier place. By the time she encountered Tom, she had a Donnelly visa and East Coast vowels, but Tom loved the Irish part best. They met at one of Lauren's parties and, though the DJ played jazz standards all night long, Tom only seemed to hear an Enya track. His Ireland was Ey-er-land – a folksy homestead decked out like a Third Avenue bar. It amazed her that he could be so naive, though it suited her too. He took her at face value, and so she learnt to hide the things he wouldn't want to know. Until Ma died, that is, and her defences failed and he began to realise that everything she'd told him was a lie.

She is relieved to find an internet café wedged between the takeaway and a small boutique. The girl who takes her money is the spit of one of the waitresses at that Russian place on Lexington, and the man at the only occupied computer is an African in a sharp suit and snake-skin loafers. She is amazed – it feels like someone has opened a window on the country and let some fresh air in.

Sheen scrolls down through her messages. She won't be at that yoga class, or need the boiler serviced, or see that Gainer exhibition that she and Lauren planned so carefully. Her ears feel funny, like she is swimming under-water. She grips her nose and blows to free them. But nothing else changes – there is still no reply from Lonergan.

When she returns to the B&B, the landlady is bustling in and out of the garden with armfuls of garishly pat-terned bed linen.

'Any more thoughts about your travels?' she shouts in from the gleaming grass as she pegs out the wash.

Sheen is tired of questions. She longs for the deep duck down of sleep, to slash time and wake on Lamb, with Lonergan almost within reach.

'Oh, I just want to get away,' she says. 'See the countryside, I guess.'

'I might have known,' the woman says, hitching the laundry basket higher on her hip. 'A mountain top, I suppose. Or an island.'

2

When Boyle wakes, it's already light. The whiskey from the night before has dried him out and his head is tight. But then he remembers about the new one coming, and the day rears up in front of him. He washes in one of the mini basins out the back, working up a decent enough lather from a sliver of cracked green Palmolive. He takes care with his clothes. Wears his best trainers and ties back his hair. Even after all that, he still feels like shite. He goes back out to the washroom, splashes a bit of water up around his face and smacks his cheeks back to life.

Down at Molly's shop, he loiters by the chill cabinet with its cheese triangles and plastic slices of Galtee. He picks up some poison-blue Powerade to drink on the boat. The refrigerator cools his head. To prolong the effect, he buys some Ice Blast chewing gum and stuffs two sticks of it in his mouth at once.

Molly nods at him. For a moment, he thinks there might be conversation, a comment about the new one coming, or even about the Easter Céilí. But it's Saturday and Molly does the Simplex crossword on a Saturday. Even though he stands there a bit longer than necessary to pack his small canvas bag, she doesn't look up again – just writes her little letters in her little squares, then sucks the end of her pencil.

He is on the pier a full half hour before he needs to be. It's a bright blue morning – a world away from the night before. Everything is sharp for once, and the waves are racing raw across the sound. He finds a quarter-inch butt in his jacket pocket. Lights it, draws hard, then spits a fleck of sour tobacco from the tip of his tongue. They have the ferry off her moorings. She's already tied up at the end of the pier, squatting against the slap of a neap tide. He can see them on board, O'Sullivan and the son, with a flask of something and the sun glinting off the tinfoil from their sandwiches. They don't acknowledge him. They don't say, 'Would you not like to come on board a few minutes early, Boyle?' like any decent person would. Not until another punter arrives – a lone wolf, Gore-Tex hiker. And then they're all action – fenders and ropes and whatnot.

He doesn't like to watch the island slip away from him, so he sits with his back to the receding coast and breathes in the familiar smell of diesel crossed with fish. Once you're off the island, you lose control of how things might pan out. There are as many bastards on an island as any-where else, but at least you know who they are.

On Lamb, he is used to being *persona non grata*. He has grown accustomed to the downward spool of his life since they found the last one's shoe. Just over a year ago, on a day when the balloons from the New Year party were still hanging limply over the pub door. She'd been missing since November and this was the first trace of her since.

She'd been working with two others on a research project from the university in Cork – flora, fauna, whatever. The other two were hopeless cases – lezzy haircuts and tree-trunk legs – but Jennifer Ryan was something else. The university had taken the house on a three-month rental, and in September when the wild flowers were over the other two returned to Cork. Word was that Jennifer was winding things up, collaborating on some report or other with the marine station on Sherkin, but by that time she was also fucking the Dutchman.

At first, there was no reason to think there'd been foul play. The house had been cleared. Everything gone but some sea-life posters, a driftwood mobile and a clatter of golf umbrellas in a pot by the door. There were those who said would you blame the girl if she'd jacked in the studies and taken herself off somewhere else? Sure what kind of life is that for a woman, scrambling up on the high cliff after scraps of sea lavender? But her family said there was no way Jennifer would just up and leave like that. And although they might not have known the woman quite as well as Boyle did, he knew they were right. And then they found the shoe, an impractical type of item – high heel, bronze metallic leather – on the beach at Reen below the high cliff path. They questioned the Dutchman all right, but he had an answer for everything. And then they turned to Boyle.

He could see himself how he'd make an excellent villain.

A squatter, and a watcher, and a craver after women he couldn't have. And because he had watched her and drawn her and painted twenty-two versions of her in different parts of the island, because he had wanted to get inside her knickers, so they all said, and was jealous of the Dutchman who had, he was the one they blamed. And on Lamb Island, they don't forget.

The sea is glimmering as the ferry sets off. Even the mournful Slea islands, flat as cowpats, look friendly enough for once. It has already dulled to grey by the time they reach the Gascanane, where, even on the calmest days, the sea burbles. Apart from the hiker, there's a shower of O'Driscolls on board. Molly's there too with her flask of tea. When the ferry reaches Baltimore, two people carriers are waiting on the pier. The rest of the passengers hop in, but nobody offers Boyle a lift. As he starts to walk away, Molly raises an arm in his general direction but her mouth doesn't actually come out with anything. The vehicles sweep past him as he heads up the pier road towards the edge of the village. Up past the lines of dinghies, still covered in their winter tarps, past the craft shop with the shell mobiles and the French café with the black-and-white flag. He passes the castle they tarted up for the millennium, then stops outside the holiday cottages they painted tango and magenta to put two fingers up to the drizzle and the sharp Atlantic winds. He throws down his bag and starts to hitch.

The first driver to stop for him is an old biddy in a headscarf. She has left her shopping money, a curled twenty, in the tray between the seats. Right away, he thinks of Jenka in the room above the Eagle, where the ham-coloured curtains match her off-white, off-pink thighs. She's a decent stick, Jenka, but she's not a charity. He feels bad for swiping that twenty but he can't help thinking of the relief it would be. The next lift is a peaty-looking farmer who only takes him as far as the boatyard. Third time lucky: a young fella heading in to Pearce Hickey's to pick up his wedding photos is the one to take him all the way.

In Skibbereen, Boyle squints at the brightly painted shops. Orange and yellow and fuchsia pink. There are window boxes everywhere, ready to be filled with objectionable flowers when summer comes. He scans the cars crawling through the main street to see if he recognises anyone he doesn't want to see. But it's all much as usual. Near the weedy river, a boy in an Arsenal shirt is practising kick-ups. Outside Cecilia's Home Bakery and Select Delicatessen, a group of teenagers with knotted hair sit on their rucksacks while they wait for the bus to Schull.

As he approaches Field's, the smell of sweet buns and coffee is distracting. He is suddenly ravenous for cream, sugar, jam. The racket in the café is something else. The hiss of steam, the clatter of pots and cups and trays, a stream of bilge music from the sound system. He spots Lonergan standing at the back wall of the café with his collar up, inspecting a bruise-coloured painting of a headland. Meanwhile, a couple at the next table are matching him to the picture on the front of their morning paper. 'Government on the Brink,' it says. 'Man of the Moment'.

Still capable of scanning a room without turning his

head, Lonergan takes in Boyle. 'I'm tight for time with this funeral and you're twenty minutes late. So if you're having a coffee you'd better get it down you quick.'

'That's nice.'

'I'm in a rush, Boyle.'

'Everybody's pin-up, these days.' Boyle nods towards the couple at the next table, fumbling now with coats and beanies, gathering the scattered pages of their weekend paper, about to scuttle off.

The waitress who comes to take their order ignores Boyle completely. She addresses everything to Lonergan. She wants a slap, he thinks, though he knows he looks shabby next to Lonergan, whose skin is pink and whose nails are clean. What would he be now? Fifty? More? He doesn't have a lot of hair, but the few strands he does have are neatly swept to one side.

Boyle reaches up to tighten his own ponytail. It feels thinner than he remembers. He looks down at his trainers and notices they're dirty, yellowish. As for his tats, the Spiderman from his teens has begun to crinkle and sag. Even the CND, on his wrist from way back, has turned blueish now.

Lonergan doesn't consult him. Just orders two black coffees.

Boyle calls after the girl for sugar and cream, and a doughnut while she's at it.

'One of the long lads,' he says. 'With the squeeze of jam along the side.'

The waitress screws up her nose. Bitch. It hadn't occurred to him that, despite the Palmolive, he might reek.

'Help yourself, Boyle,' says Lonergan. 'How about a bit of tart while you're at it?' He smirks, then folds his arms on to the shiny pine table. In his Crombie coat he looks like a drug dealer, which is unfortunate when he's meant to be a politician.

'I hear you've a job for me,' says Boyle.

Lonergan makes a funny sideways movement with his head. 'Oh, I wouldn't call it –'

'That's what Theo told me.'

The waitress is back now with their coffees. She puts the doughnut on the table between them, with two forks. Is she taking the piss?

Lonergan waits for her to set everything down.

'Super,' he says.

She smiles at him as she moves off.

Boyle picks up the doughnut and levels it into his mouth. The cream squirts out over his fingers.

'Not a job exactly,' says Lonergan. 'I suppose I'd call it a favour.'

And Boyle can hardly get the comeback out quick enough for jam and goo. 'Is that because jobs cost and favours don't?'

Lonergan laughs, kind of. 'It's because jobs are official and favours aren't.'

'Spit it out then.' Boyle finishes the last of the dough-nut and wipes his fingers on his jeans. 'What unofficial job do you want me to do? The house again, yeah?'

That was a decent gig, easy work with regular pay. Check no birds have come down the chimney, empty the mousetraps and air the place. He could do with the cash or whatever else Lonergan might chuck his way. A pair of trainers, a bottle or two, a few grams for himself.

'Theo does the house. I want you to keep an eye on a female, not a house. Could you do that for me, Boyle?'

This last while, Boyle has had a drought when it comes to females – not counting Jenka twice a month, more or less, in that room above the Eagle. He could watch a female all right. The waitress is back, and asking if she can get them anything else. Lonergan shows her his teeth. Pretty good, these days, fixed.

'That's OK, love,' he says. 'Just bring the bill.'

And you can hear his accent coming through in the vowels. Brang the bull.

When she's gone, he looks straight at Boyle. 'Well?'

Lonergan is used to getting what he wants. Boyle wonders what he wants this time. That's as interesting as anything else. As for himself, he's cautious about watching females these days.

'I didn't think females were your poison, Lonergan,' he says, to give himself time to think. Sweet. It's a while since he's had the craic.

'But they are yours.' Lonergan waits a moment for the comment to find its mark. 'I could get Theo to handle it for me, of course, but he'd be in there right away. Wham bam and, before you know it, I've got a problem on my hands. But you, Boyle. We all know you've had to learn patience the hard way.'

It's a new idea to Boyle that he might be a man of patience. But he wonders, too, what Lonergan knows about the Dutchman and isn't saying. These days he's finding it harder and harder to pick up things that aren't said outright. It's a skill you lose when you're not in touch with people.

'She'll be turning up on Lamb any day now. Her name is Róisín Burns, but she's going by Sheen these days.' He raises his eyebrows. 'I hear from Theo that she's rented that house out your way, the one the Ryan woman stayed in. I'd like her to decide, off her own bat like, that it's not worth her while being here.'

'Where do you want her to go?'

'I couldn't give a shite, Boyle. I just don't want her in my fucken hair. Not with those O'Neills kicking off, and the election and all the rest of it. She's not here to lick my arse, and I doubt she's here for the scenery.'

'Old friend of yours?'

He doesn't answer that. 'How you go about it is up to you. But use a bit of cop on, yeah? A bit of subtlety?' He reaches into the leather briefcase resting on the floor next to him and takes out a small padded envelope. 'There's a few bits and pieces here will help you out. Plant them in her house and she'll not hang around for long.'

Boyle reaches for it, but Lonergan stops his hand. 'Jesus, not here. Wait till you're back in your hole before you open it.'

I don't like your tone, Boyle thinks but doesn't say. He nudges the package back through a little puddle of spilt milk. 'What's all this to me?'

'Hundred quid?'

'Fuck off.'

'I didn't think money was your thing, Boyle.'

'Two hundred.'

Lonergan joins his fingers together and rests his elbows on the table. 'Everybody wants something. Sometimes it's a surprise when you find out what it is.' He is sounding philosophical, which Boyle finds mildly interesting. Lonergan has never been a philosopher. 'Money, information, sex. Some want to remember. Some want to forget.'

Jesus, Boyle thinks, is that the best you can come up with, a fucken song lyric?

Lonergan reaches into his coat. 'But if money's your thing, Boyle, you can have your two hundred.'

What he takes out is not a stash of notes, though, but a small, flip-top phone still attached to its charger. When Lonergan passes it to him under the table, Boyle thinks of the spy movies his da, old Dr Boil, used to watch on a Sunday afternoon. He has the urge to rip the piss, but when he sees the face on Lonergan, the long jaw of him, he thinks again.

'You're to ring me when she arrives. And before I forget, the key's in the envelope with the other stuff. Let her know I'm on to her. Keep in touch, Boyle. I want the blow by blow.'

'What about a few quid up front? To keep the wolf from the door.'

Lonergan looks at him like he's a ball of shite, but he reaches into his inside pocket again, peels a fifty from a thick fold of notes and slides it under the sugar bowl. 'I want her gone, yeah?'

Boyle walks out of the café, turns right past the rows of brightly coloured confectionery on the sweet counter in the shop, past the newspapers with Lonergan's face on them, then out into the clog of traffic. As he heads up the street towards the Eagle, he looks back through the plate-glass window and into the shiny-piny mauve-and-yellow café. Lonergan's still there where he left him, but he's not on his own any more. The other man has his back to the window, but Boyle would know the Dutchman anywhere.

It doesn't seem real until she's on the ferry, the wind whipping her hair across her face, her stomach queasy from the smell of fuel. Sheen stands on the deck and tugs her down jacket round her as the engine churns. She has studied the geography. She knows where the islands are – some just flitters of rock, others that might hold a roofless house or two. And Lamb, far out beyond the rest, a last bastion against the ocean.

But the flat blues of the map have come to life now. This sea is all roar and heft and muscle. The prospect of being surrounded by it day and night is daunting – trapped out there on a rock, and the ferry gone till morning. As they pass the last winking beacon on the mainland, she feels a rush of panic. Behind her, the tumble of holiday cottages and the single-bell church are already child's size. Once they've passed the first trail of islands, the swell thickens. She grips the cold guardrail as they plunge into the valley of a wave, then rear up out of it again. Hair drenched, she licks salt from her lips as she holds on tight and squints for sight of Lamb. Someone is yelling and she turns to see the skipper waving wildly at her from the bridge to get the fuck below.

She carries in a blast of outside, struggling down the steps into the cabin with her huge suitcase. The passengers turn as one to scan her, then turn away again. One man whispers something to another and they both laugh. She is a spectacle. She sits at a bench of her own away from the others and steadies herself. The locals communicate at long distance, lobbing scraps of conversation back and forth above her head. Two men poring over the racing pages are having a lopsided exchange that has nothing to do with horses. And then, an enormous lurch. Through the misted window, she watches the swell half swallow the small ferry before pitching it on to the crest of the next wave. The smell of fuel is growing stronger, and she thinks she might be sick. If there are islands out there, they can't be seen for the dense sea mist. She shuts her eyes a moment and the nausea eases.

When the sea flattens, a woman in a tight headscarf produces a flask of tea. She lays out some plastic cups, a Tupperware container of sugar and a small carton of milk, then lifts one of the flimsy cups by its rolled rim and hands it to Sheen. She is in.

'You're too early for the birds,' says one of the racing men. 'They'll not be back this way till May time.' He sucks in his tea. 'And the pottery's shut.'

'Oh, I'm not a tourist,' she says.

'You're writing a book, so,' says the woman, who says her name is Molly and that she runs the island's only shop. 'Your *Year in Provence*?' The men snigger into their tea.

'Or you're a painter. Come on. Take us out of our misery. We've a bet going.'

'Just some time out.'

'Isn't it well for you?' Molly says. 'A lady of leisure. You haven't much of an accent, by the way.' She makes it sound as though Sheen is already a bit of a letdown. 'You're from the States, right?'

In the early days, Sheen would spend hours studying the way her flatmates spoke, examining the shape their mouths made when they pronounced foreign words like sidewalk, sneakers, eggplant. She's pretty sure that after all these years her accent is good enough for most people.

'Yes,' she says, 'New York.'

But maybe even now it's possible to hear a trace of Belfast in the way her sentences still curl up sometimes at the ends if she doesn't watch them. And then there is the tightness in her mouth that comes from all the clamping down on things she's learnt to keep well hidden.

She is grateful for the shelter of her new name.

3

Back on the island, Boyle makes a little ceremony of opening the envelope. He lights the fire, pours himself two fingers of Paddy. But when he tears off the Sellotape and slides the contents out, he feels a nip of disappointment. Is that all there is? A yellowed scrap of newspaper folded postcard-size – a blank, black-and-white cartoon face – and an A4 photo of a teenage girl with a violin case strapped to her back. From the girl's vacant expression as she looks over her shoulder, she doesn't even realise the photographer is there. It gives him a thrill to think of that, a ripple in his groin, but the girl herself is ordinary.

He's about to shove the contents back into the envelope when he realises there's something else in there. Small, blunt, hard, it drops down on to the tiled floor with a clink. He's never seen one in real life before, but who doesn't know what that is? He picks it up, rubs his finger across the tip. That would scare her off all right. That alone would probably do the trick.

Waiting for her to arrive, the hours pass like sludge. Now and then, he nods off, and each time he wakes the sky is that bit darker than before. By dusk, he is stoked and ready for her. He arranges a paint-spattered stepladder beneath the one good window. When the time comes, he is up on top of it, watching the little red-and-white ferry struggle cartoonishly against the swell. It lingers outside the mouth of the harbour, as if to catch its breath, then plunges in towards the pier. Will Hannie pick her up in the taxi or will she be too busy watching telly? Or will Murphy do the honours himself, barrelling down the pier in the four-by-four like a fucken king?

The ferry docks just as the light is fading. Murphy has been waiting for her on the pier. He steps forward as soon as he sees her, reaches for her bags. A big man with a slick of hair pasted across the top of his balding head, his gaze sweeps her, head-to-toe in one. Sheen doesn't feel much like talking, but Murphy is all chat.

'I'd say you could murder a coffee. How about a decaff skinny latte down at Cat's?' He makes speech marks with his fingers. 'She's a new machine in. I'm a grande Americano man myself.' He lugs her ridiculous suitcase into the boot of the car, then opens the passenger door for her. 'Well? What's it to be?'

'I'll pass on the coffee, thanks. Still feeling a bit yuck.' She smiles, to be friendly. 'I guess I'm just a landlubber.'

When he fails to rustle up any more conversation, he switches on the radio. A woman with a twangy voice is singing out about a big old moon and laying a blanket on the ground. The land rises sharply up from the harbour, and Murphy's four-by-four struggles on the climb. When they reach the top, she recognises the shape of the island from the map – the back-to-back harbours, the ridge that runs the length of the island like a spine. No sooner are they up there than a band of rain sweeps towards them, battering the windscreen so that the metronomic wipers have no effect at all. She has already worked out that Lonergan's place must be somewhere in the middle of the island. On the map, there is just the one through road, so it can't be hard to find. She is dimly aware of the tourist spiel Murphy is giving her – pirates, orcas, shipwrecks – but her mind is on the move. Now that she has come here, her heart is thudding and her lungs feel scraped inside out. As the sun drops into the ocean like a big orange tab, she is still between worlds.

Boyle doesn't allow himself any more to drink. He wants to be sharp, to remember exactly how she was the first time he clapped eyes on her. He prepares himself, pulls a hoodie down over his head, then tops it off with black oilskins and a pair of boots. He brings the key, though he won't be using it. Not just yet. He waits up on the ridge, facing out to sea, until he hears Murphy thundering up the boreen. His giant headlamps swoop and dip across the hedgerows. Boyle avoids the road, takes a shortcut through the bracken. He is there at the gate when they arrive – half hidden by greenery, but visible to anyone with the sense to know he'd be there. The clunk of a car door. Once, twice. The boot clicks open. Boyle's throat clenches when he hears her voice. There's a bit of a warble in it. He thinks of Cameron Diaz. He hopes she's a blondie. Jenka is a blondie. And Jennifer Ryan was a blondie, too – a gold so pale it was almost silver. While they're bringing her stuff in from the car, he makes his way to the front of the bungalow, to the large rectangular picture window that overlooks the South Harbour. They're at the side now, and Murphy is bleating on about the forecast for the rest of the week. For a moment, he's scared they'll keep on walking and come upon him crouching there. But they stop, turn back. Next thing, the engine starts and Murphy's gone. She didn't invite him in. Fair fucks to her. He's surprised she got rid of him that quick. Murphy loves showing people round, banging on about the view and the slate floor and the fucken killer whales.

The silence makes her ears buzz. The house feels raw, a plaster skim away from its breeze-block shell. She wonders how long it's lain empty. There is little in the way of comfort: a rag rug in front of the sofa, two side lamps with dusty, dented shades, a framed photo of an over-detailed jellyfish.

She scans the room, and is suddenly sad. It should all feel more momentous. When she takes out her cell, she finds the screen is cracked. She rubs it on her sleeve, flicks her nail against it. She could ring Lauren maybe, or

Renzo, but what would she say? That she's scared, that she's not sure she should be here? Better to leave New York in its place: the sublet apartment, the unpaid leave that was a breeze to get in March.

In need of noise, she flicks through the TV channels: news, golf, cartoons. A woman with reliable hair is reading a late-night bulletin. A lorry has jack-knifed; there are talks in the North. She aims the control and flicks it off again. And in the silence, old memories start to elbow their way back in. The whine and thud of silenced bullets, a woman bound and gagged. And Lonergan, in an upstairs room above a Belfast pub, telling her she can never come back.

Those words of his eddy around her, but she tries to head them off with practicalities. She lays the suitcase on the floor and runs the zip around. She pauses a moment to admire the perfect patchwork of denim and cotton and fleece – her packing has always been immaculate. She double-palms a bundle of ironed tops and sets them on the pine table. She has packed for cold, for rain, but she has packed for trouble too.

She empties the cabin bag of press cuttings and print-outs and photos. She separates Ma's letter and the accompanying two statements, and slides them into the envelope she bought yesterday. The originals are back in New York, in a sealed package in the gallery safe, but it gives her strength to know she has copies here. She opens the oven she has no intention of using, and slots the envelope in between two black baking sheets that no one else has ever used either.

It's only when she has unpacked the props for Sheen that she starts to feel her confidence return. Gathering her hair into a loop, she fixes on a diamanté clip. She reaches into the bag, and from a fold of bubblewrap extracts a small blue glass bottle. She places it on the empty mantelpiece, where it looks like something left by aliens. It was one of the first things she bought when she came to New York – a yard sale, somewhere in Queens. And though the scent is long gone now, back then it held a trace of rose and musk. She told herself it was from Venice, even though the sticker on the bottom said 'Made in Hong Kong'. She kept it wrapped in matching tissue paper, and conjured out of it a mother. Someone with long black hair and twinkling, high-heeled feet. This mother wore a wasp-waisted dress with a swing in its skirt. She went dancing and had lovers. She was a world away from Ma.

She takes down the oversized jellyfish, replaces it with a framed school photo – three rows of grinning girls. She has no idea who those schoolgirls really are – she bought that photo years ago in Goodwill – but the one whose schooldays she has borrowed is in the back row, two in from the left. Even now, the girl could be a younger sister. Sheen is pale, thin-faced. Slightly vaguer than the others, slightly less there.

Boyle crouches at the uncurtained window and watches her unpack. Rain seeps in at the corners of his hood and trickles down his neck. She can see nothing out that window. Not with a skim of rain on the glass, and himself well clear of the lighthouse beam. But he can see her. She is no Cameron Diaz. She is not remotely blonde, though she's pretty enough. Dark and lean, with the kind of stringiness you find in a woman who likes the gym. He wonders what age she is. Late thirties? Forty or more? The hair is a bit short for his liking. A woman should have hair that reaches down her back. As for her shoes – all wrong. Beige suede booties with heels on them? They'll not last long on Lamb.

Right off, he can see that she's a different kind of woman from the last one. She has every bloody light in the place on, for starters. It shows up the scrapes on the magnolia walls, the bare look of that navy sofa. Shabby, he thinks, but that's Murphy for you. She's opening the wrong cupboard. And what's she plugging in now? Is she made of money? He feels like a benevolent god, crouching out there in the nettles, watching her make mistakes.

The beam from the lighthouse wipes the grass. Just as it approaches him, he ducks and it passes over. He lifts his head, to get a better look. He wouldn't have had her marked out for an American. Not tall enough, or tanned enough, and those teeth are not really that white. Her legs are fine, though. She has breasts and all the necessary. But Jesus only knows what links the likes of her to Lonergan. He reaches into the pocket of his jacket and rubs his thumb along the little jagged mouth of the key. She has two suitcases, each with a ribbon tied to the handle. He has no time for ribbons. She sits herself down. Pulls off boots and socks. One clunk. Two clunk.

Her feet are pale, small. She stands on tippy-toes as she walks across the floor. Those tiles must be cold. Her feet, cold. Next, she's at the fireplace. Ripping up sheets of newspaper, scrunching it into balls. Then she's back at the bags. Everything out on the table, piled up on the floor. Jumper, book, shoes, jumper, jumper, shoes. What a load of junk. Teabags, bottles, torches – one, two, three. Why three torches? And matches – two large boxes. And then something else catches his eye. A photograph, framed in black. She tries it up against the wall. Then takes it down again, staring into it.

From the way she's gazing at that photo, he's guessing those were good times. Better, anyway. And, God, does he know the feeling. God, how he misses the good old better days. There is a picture in his head. A diamond sky, and a fella with a mandolin. The wood on the fire, spitting and crackling. His head half-cut on whatever was going that night. Lamb was a kind of paradise then. But he forces himself back to the present, squinting through the raindrops on the window until the new one turns her back on him. When she walks out the door he feels a little rush of grief. How come they always walk away?

But a moment later she returns. And there she remains, just looking out into the night. Looking straight at him, if she only knew it. These are the precious moments, when it's all fresh and new, when you can see her clearer than you'll ever do again.

She comes right up against the window then, like there's no barrier between them at all. She makes blinkers of her hands, goggling out into the night. There is a mole on her neck and her shirt is open three buttons down. The breasts are small, but they have a nice bit of shape to them.

And then, just like that, the light goes out and he realises that if she looks down now he can be seen. His heart gallops to his throat so fast he almost vomits it out. He thinks he hears her gasp. Does she sense she's being watched? Is she sharp like that? Maybe, being from the city, she is. But she has moved away from the window now. He can hear her thrashing around in there, knocking things over. The beam of the lighthouse sweeps across the picture window. She's overloaded the electrics with all her bloody lights. He thinks he hears her whimpering and then he understands. The new one is afraid of the dark. He says the words out loud. She's afraid of the dark. And he knows in his gut that fact will some day come in useful.

Why would you drag yourself away from bright lights, big city to come here? Why would you come to an island that's pitch black at night if you're afraid of the dark? You'd have to have something you wanted desperately. The thought intrigues him. But the lighthouse beam is on the move again. You only need to find the fusebox, he whispers to her. You only need to flick the switch. It's in the back porch, he tells her, just inside the door. But she's got one of the torches now, swiping it wildly at the window. Boyle ducks, grazes his cheek on the pebbledash. It's time he was going, but he just can't resist one more look at her in the shared blackness. He raises his head, just enough to see her coming straight for him behind the jaggedy beam of the torch. No matter what Lonergan wants, he's tempted to have this one for himself.

After she finds the trip switch, she stands a moment beneath the harsh overhead light, soaking it up. She has a sudden stark vision of herself; not the silvery reflection on the dark windowpane, but a vivid snapshot of someone real and rash and stubborn. Someone who could be with the yoga girls tonight, eating sushi at that place in Brooklyn with the black slate walls. Someone who should know better.

She turns on the side lamps, pulls the sofa as close to the fire as she dares, and starts to rig up a bed. She piles on sweaters, but she still can't get warm. At first the lighthouse beam is reassuring, but soon she is moving to the back of the house to escape it – into the back bedroom, where at least there are curtains. It is profoundly cold in there. The duvet and pillow feel damp; even the air is sour with it. All she wants is sleep, but as soon as she shuts her eyes he is there.

He came back into her life when she was at her lowest ebb, in the unlikeliest of places. It was Happy Hour at Renzo's, and she and Lauren were sitting at the high chrome bar. Recently, she'd been through hell – the break-up of her marriage coming just two months after her mother's death – but she was trying hard to be good company that night. Lauren and she had spent all day preparing for the Podolsky show, a glassmaker from Kiev who specialised in shallow, tear-shaped bowls with graceful stems. They'd emptied the gallery to make way for the team of painters who would coat the walls in white emulsion, and now they were discussing how best to display the bowls. Perspex columns, they'd decided. Perspex columns bathed in light. She remembers watching Renzo loading cocktail glasses with chunks of psychedelic fruit. The brash colours of his Hawaiian shirt matched whatever syrupy concoction he was mixing at the time, and the light glinted on the shaker as he poured the liquid out. The midweek crowd weren't particularly interested in the TV. There were no ballgames that night, no Serie A playbacks either. It was background noise, that's all. And the irony is that she was just about to leave. She was actually reaching for her jacket when she glanced up at the screen. Perhaps it was the voice that attracted her attention. Who knows? But when she saw him it felt as though the world was ice.

Lonergan had shed the donkey jacket. It was a suit, these days. A crisp white shirt. He was so at home with the camera that he didn't even bother to face the interviewer. He was standing outside a building with steps and a colonnade – it could have been anywhere – addressing himself to his unseen viewers, to a SoHo bar, to Róisín Burns or whoever she'd decided to be now.

The accent was the same, hard and nasal, but Lonergan had acquired a tone of self-importance, as if he'd grown to expect the things he used to have to grab. He sounded as if he thought he'd earned his microphone, his swivel chair and desk. But even as her heart was shrivelling, she couldn't understand why he was still so terrifying when she was standing in the middle of a whole new life, and he was just an image on a screen. Something the interviewer said displeased him. His reaction was almost imperceptible, but Sheen recognised the deadening of his eyes, the slight flattening of his upper lip. She strained to hear, but whatever he was saying was drowned out by the cheers of a group of guys yahooing at the other end of the bar.

And then he was gone. Without even realising it, she'd stood to face him, but now her legs were weakening. She felt around for the edge of the stool, and Renzo brought water in a misty glass. It was ice cold, and she gulped it down. Lauren kept apologising about the hours Sheen had had to work that week.

'Take a cab home,' Lauren said. 'Just charge it, honey. You look wiped out.'

But Róisín had been wiped out long ago. Sometimes she found it hard to remember the person she used to be. There was a picture taken the summer before she'd had to leave Belfast. And maybe that was the last time she'd known normality. Róisín was standing with her sister, Maura, on the beach at Portstewart, with the sea sucking the sand from in between her toes. She was wearing that Indian skirt, her favourite at the time, the one with little mirrors embroidered into the hem. Maura was looking right into the camera, but Róisín was taken when she wasn't looking.

She didn't see herself as superstitious, but this fleeting glimpse of Lonergan felt ominous. It planted a kind of anxiety in her. Her life as Sheen already seemed frail, vulnerable. And there he was, just when she was at her weakest.

But that night in Renzo's wasn't the start of it. The start came later. Almost three months to the day after Ma died, a package arrived from a firm of Belfast solicitors. The curt covering note advised that the enclosure had been sent per the instructions of Mrs Joan Burns (deceased). There were just three items inside: a letter to Róisín from Ma, and two handwritten statements from men she'd never even heard of about the death of another man she'd never heard of either. But the power those statements gave her couldn't be ignored. Power made her brave. That was the start.

4

She wakes to the sound of static somewhere in the distance. Eyes still shut, she trawls the layout of her old apartment until she remembers that what she's hearing is the sea. She blinks, and finds the room is flooded with a pure and perfect light. Although the layout of this house is similar to home, the outlook couldn't be more different. Instead of looking down into the dizzy street, this view leads across bright green grass to the ocean. The island reminds her of the place where Tom's folks live. It is beautiful, of course. But she isn't here for beauty.

She opens the window and lets in the sea, and the sound of it is a kind of compensation for the night just gone. The room is filled with its heave and sigh. A small boat phut-phuts along the shore, dropping a line of pots. It is followed by a whirl of shrieking gulls and in the distance a clutch of darker birds is dive-bombing a scumbled patch of water. There is only one other building in sight: a greyish concrete structure just visible to the left, perched in an elevated position above the bay. The place looks derelict, with flayed walls and a patched roof. It is an eyesore, and she turns her back on it. She is good at that.

As for the bungalow, it is small, cold, basic. She can walk from one end of the main room to the other in twenty paces, her city shoes clacking on the slate floor. There is a mobile made of shells and driftwood hanging at the window, the kind of thing Tom's mom used to make in her Shaker kitchen in that place in Maine. They went whale-watching there once, Tom and Sheen – so far out to sea the shore was just a greyish line. They cut the engine and sat there for an hour or more before the flat sea began to tremble into a quivering circle – a footprint, Tom said – the sign that a humpback was about to breach. And when finally it did heave out of the water in a perfect arch, she was astonished that any wild thing would reveal itself so completely.

She takes out a mug and clangs it down on the stainless-steel draining board. At the back of a cupboard she finds a crumpled carton. Lyons Green Label. She opens it, sniffs the slightly stained bags. On the shelf below, a sticky sprinkling of something that might be sugar. She flings the teabags in the bin, scrubs at the residue stuck hard to the Formica. She unpacks the little bag of foodie items that Renzo gave her because he simply wouldn't believe she could exist without them. And then she checks the items that Murphy left. The 'welcome pack' he called it. There is bread, but no butter. Bacon, but no milk. She pulls off her night things, throws on her running gear. A quick shop for basics, she decides, then

47

down to work. Once she has laced her shoes, she has almost forgotten her fitful night – the cold and damp, the unwelcome thoughts. She stretches, lunges, breathes deep. She is back in control.

Boyle hauls himself up to the top of the stepladder. He squints out the window, and sees that her bedroom curtains are still drawn. She's late up, and there'll be nothing in that fridge. But then he spots her on the road below. She is wearing a terrible shade of pink, heading up towards the ridge. She turned right. Ha. She'll not do that again. Left is bad enough, but right is almost vertical. She's moving out of sight, but you'd not lose her in that get-up. You could spot her a mile off in that. He feels a surge of excitement at the prospect of meeting her at the top, when she is weakened from her climb. He has five minutes at least, maybe six or even seven. He scrambles down the stepladder when she passes out of sight, kicks over an empty metal bucket in his rush, sending it rattling across the room.

He rinses his mug and stacks it safely away in the stationery cupboard, next to the materials he uses for the mobiles he sells to the craft shop in Schull – the Tupperware box of blunt, sea-scoured chunks of glass, the tins of blasted tufts of blue nylon rope, the bleached Tayto crisp bags. He caresses the smooth back of a shell for luck. He takes it slow, heaves three or four deep breaths, and he's still out on the road in plenty of time. Four minutes and thirty-six seconds, to be exact. Pulling the hood down over his forehead, his view of the road is narrowed like a blinkered horse anticipating the race ahead. Already, he can feel the slow curdle of excitement. Will she stop, or will he have to step into the middle of the road? How will it be, that first meeting? It's crucial to get that right. Vital to establish who's the blow-in and who has seeded.

By the time Sheen leaves the house, the weak sun is gone. A steady drizzle has started to obscure the bay. Two roads stream up behind the house. Left is steep, right no less so. She heads right, making her way up the green springy strip in the centre of the road. Her limbs feel stiff, as though she crossed the Atlantic in the hold, and running is an effort. The grey bunker she spotted earlier looks even grimmer from up close. Its unpainted cement has been blackened by damp. Despite its dereliction the post-box set into the wall seems still to be in use. 'An Post', it says, but visible beneath the green paint are the embossed initials of a long-dead king.

As she runs, she examines each gate and tests it against the image she has memorised, a photo of Lonergan taken with his two young sons against a screen of sparkling sea. The three of them are standing at a steel gate tied with bright blue rope. 'Lonergan in his Lamb Island hide-away', the caption said. In their unlikely Arans, the boys look more wholesome than seems necessary, even for a politician's kids. The article that accompanied it made her stomach turn. The deferential interviewer who questioned nothing: the mackerel fishing, the Easters spent on Lamb, the fluent Irish, the sensible wife who is rarely seen with him in public. All those rewritten years.

She struggles on up the hill, past a pair of silent cows in a rocky field, past a long-abandoned car laced with rust, filling a gap in the hedgerow. Out in the bay the clouds whip across a nervous sea straked with black plastic barrels that have been tethered together in lines. She envies Lonergan his ease, his way with lies. She has examined those eyes in image after image for any hint of doubt, and found nothing. She envies him those tousle-headed sons too, the children she will probably never have now. She hates the wave of self-pity, and beats it back. And yet there's no disputing it. He has all this, and what does she have?

A little way along, she spots a place marked Cormorant House. She guesses that's the bird-watching centre, but there doesn't look to be anyone around. In fact, so far, she's seen no one at all. Gradually, her strides ease. Her breathing evens out, and she begins to feel like she can do this.

Waiting makes him jumpy. Boyle on the hilltop, and the woman labouring towards him, already half-defeated. He imagines the charm he dredges up from somewhere, the smile she gives him in return. He checks his watch and forty-two more seconds have passed. She can't be taking this long. She must have turned back. Unless, that is, she's caught in the blind spot where the road doubles back on itself, and coils out of view. His breath is tight. And then he hears her on the road below him, the squeak of rubber soles on damp grass.

A moment later, there is a blur of pink on the lush green centre of the road. She doesn't stop. Doesn't even look his way. She weaves past him, almost stepping into the ditch to avoid him, and runs slowly on up the hill. He turns and watches her. Before he knows it, she is gone.

He feels a rage begin to grip hold of him, although this is not how he wants it to be. He doesn't want to have to be angry or cruel. He wants to be the hero. He wants to look after this one, to keep her safe. She is acting as if she's still in the city, but there are no such things as strangers here. There is never a time when you can just pass on by. That's the first thing she will have to learn.

From up on the ridge, she sees that most of the buildings are concentrated at the North Harbour where the island narrows. They look across the sound towards the mainland, and the night-time display of diamond-cluster villages set low along the coast. In the sound itself, there must be a hundred islands. Most are clumps of evil-looking rocks or small flat puddles of land, but one or two seem populated. The next island along, for instance, has a little knot of houses by a stubby pier.

Sheen runs on, towards the roughly painted white sign on a distant roof: 'SHOP'. It takes her about ten minutes to reach the scattering of houses that passes for a village. There is a boarded-up chip van, and a Portakabin with a large plastic sign: 'Lamb Island Pots'. Down at the harbour a couple of benches, painted brave Mediterranean blue, face out to sea. A set of matching tubs contains an assortment of weeds and strangled geraniums. A glass-fronted message board carries a bright yellow flyer, an ad for a B&B. She stops a moment for a closer look. Times of Masses. GP clinic. A 'Missing' poster, with a bleached-out face. There are posters like these in every subway station in New York. She has often wondered if the people pictured are ever found, how many of them have simply decided to disappear. It seems out of place to see a thing like that on Lamb. She can just about make out the name. Jennifer Ryan, last seen on Lamb one November day.

She pushes open the door of the shop and a bell jingles. Molly from the ferry is behind the counter, filling something in on the newspaper. She glances up, then looks back down again. 'At the jogging already?'

Sheen pauses at the door to catch her breath. 'It's so lovely here.'

'Ah, you'll miss the city soon enough.'

But Sheen doesn't fall for the trap. 'I doubt it,' she says, and Molly looks satisfied. 'Though it's a shame about all those things out in the bay. I guess it must be a fish farm?'

Molly makes a fierce little scribble on the newspaper. 'Isn't it well for you, here for the scenery. Some of us have livings to make. Nature's all very well and good till you have to get by.'

Flustered to have caused offence, Sheen blurts out something about the noticeboard outside, the 'Missing' poster. 'That's so strange. I mean, it's not the kind of thing you expect to see, in a place like this.'

'Ah she was only here for a while. Another nature-lover, always haring off after bracken and weeds.'

After that, Molly is all business, and the message is clear. She should learn to shut up and keep her opinions to herself about things that are none of her business.

Sheen trawls the two lines of shelves and the small refrigerated section. She picks up a few essentials – milk, butter, cheese, tomatoes, apples, pasta. She is just about to sling the basket up on to the counter when she spots a headline on the newspaper rack.

'O'Neills Pile Pressure on Lonergan'.

And, just like that, her equanimity deserts her. She is Róisín Burns again, and Jacinta is lying bound and gagged in front of her. And because she is out of her depth, and frightened, and keener to save herself than Jacinta, Róisín does nothing. How much longer did they keep her alive? Was she dead by the time Róisín arrived in New York? In her worst moments, she has tried to imagine where they might have dumped her – a bog, a culvert, out at sea?

'He's a regular,' says Molly, following her gaze. 'Though I really couldn't tell you if there's any truth in what they say. He doesn't mix in much. Hangs out with the blow-ins on the other end of the island. Doesn't bother much with the rest of us. He's a big cheese now, anyhow.' Molly's eyes, sharp, quick, are scanning her face. 'He might be even bigger, soon enough. If they win the by-election coming up and the government falls, there'll be no stopping them. I'd say he'll be here for the Easter, so if you're that interested you can introduce yourself.'

'I'm not interested,' Sheen says, more abruptly than she intended.

Molly looks at her strangely. 'Fair enough.'

When Boyle reaches the gate of the new one's house, he hesitates a moment, then walks straight through. At her door, he takes a quick glance around to make sure he's not been spotted. He holds the key steady, then slides it in, two quick twists to the right.

He stands on the slightly stained doormat and breathes in deep – the smell of shouldn't-be-here, the smell of not-allowed. He feels better for being in the house without her knowing. He scans the narrow hall. There are three pairs of unsuitable shoes on prissy parade beneath the coat rack – he can't resist a sharp little kick that sends a slingback skittering.

He begins with the kitchen cupboards. Empty, empty, empty. They make a hollow sound when he pats them shut. In the last one, there are some poncey-looking herbal teabags and, on the shelf below, a little cluster of unopened jars, all packed in cellophane tied with a raffia bow. Moutarde verte and teriyaki. Chili relish and wasabi. Jesus wept. Who eats this shit? And down below, the kind of crap you might find at the Vincent de Paul: a frilly-edged plate, a single doll's shoe, a blue glass bottle. The fuck this one's on holiday. Who brings this crap on holiday?

In the living room, an oil painting the size of a large paperback is propped up against the sofa. He lifts it, casts his eye over it. Rubbish. He picks at it with his fingernail, but the lump of paint he's working at doesn't shift. He fetches a knife from the kitchen drawer, scrapes at the rough surface until he's removed a sliver of red. He takes out a matchbox from his pocket and drops the paint chip in. Sweet. On the table, there is a little bundle of pens tied neatly together with a scrap of blue ribbon. He slides out a purple felt tip and makes a little scribble in the bottom left-hand corner of the canvas. There. He feels better for having left his mark.

Then, the thrill of recognition: that photo he watched her unpack the night before. Three rows of schoolgirls of assorted shapes and sizes. Some are already women, with great big jugs on them. Others are still little kids. They all wear the same get-ups: navy gymslips, white blouses. But some look tartier than others, with dangly earrings and lipstick and skirts that are way too short. He tries to guess which one she is. He's sure she's not one of the slappers. He chooses one of the littlest ones, a girl with mousey-blonde hair. He takes his marker pen out of his pocket, then draws a tiny heart on the glass, just above the sleeve of her white school shirt.

When he spots the laptop, he can't believe his luck. Even if she only picks up a pint of milk and a loaf of bread, and speaks to no one. Even if she just jogs down and back, he should still have ten more minutes, easy. He has a quick check out the door. He can see as far as the ridge, and there's no sign of her at all. He sits down at the table in front of it, side on to the window so he can keep an eye out. He selects a letter. K for kiss. He licks his index finger and places it slowly down on the key. The screen springs to life. No passwords. Nothing. Sweet. There's something already up there. All fresh, like she's only just left it. Even a quick glance says it's not about what happened today or yesterday or even the day before. No, the new one is writing about THEN.

He scrolls down the screen, and feels the kick in his gut he always gets at the start of something new. He scrolls back up again, and runs his eye down the middle of the page. It's a Sent email. And it's angry. Sent three months ago, but still being read. And that's interesting, he thinks. She'll not be sending any emails from here. You have to go to Cat's for the emails – the internet café she has upstairs from the pub. Sure there's no signal this side of the island. Nothing. Does she not know that?

As he reads on, he realises. No way is this one on holiday. No more than the last one was. Fair fucks to science. Thank God for mighty Microsoft. Hallelujah for your man from Apple. As for who it is she's sent this email to, the address is just a jumble of letters: bgl@nrp.ie.

He takes another felt tip from the bundle, a black one this time, and inscribes the address carefully on the inside of his arm. There. He'll work out later what it means. And then it's back to the email. In all the ranting and the raving, one name stands out. DOLORES. She's frightened of this Dolores, and he'd love to know why, because that would be a way in, wouldn't it? She's frightened of someone else, too. Even though she's pretending she isn't. She's frightened of YOU, whoever you are, he is, whatever. And she's trying to explain herself, making excuses for something YOU made her do, something YOU didn't realise, ask, or even care about. And it sounds like Belfast and hijacks and bomb scares and yesterday's news. He never cared much for the North, one side as bad as the other, grey miserable fuckers at the best of times. And then he realises that in among the accusations is a threat.

In Molly's shop, Sheen gathers herself. She unloads the metal basket and transfers her purchases to the drawstring bag. She hoists it on her back, then closes the door carefully behind her. As she jogs back up towards the ridge, the sun struggles out again. It casts a lemony glaze on sharp green fields.

This side of the ridge is sparsely populated, the land rockier, the coast more difficult to access. Just beyond the island's western tip, the sea is dotted with the black buoys of the fish farm she noticed earlier. Beyond that, the lighthouse is the last thing visible before the sea stretches out towards New York.

Distracted by the view, she finds she's made an unintended turning. She's no longer on the coastal path, but on the road that slices through the centre of the island. The bag's thin cords are cutting into her shoulders and she stops a moment to adjust it. She is just about to set off again when she notices a house nestled in behind a high, unruly hedge of fuchsia.

The chimney stack is raw cement, as though the painter's ladder didn't stretch quite far enough to reach it, but the rest of the house is painted a harsh gorse yellow. It's like something out of a kid's drawing: pitched roof with that single chimney, four squareish windows and a central door. The garden has long gone wild and the ragged hedge seems too close to the house for light or comfort, even allowing for the winds. The steel gate is like a thousand others: twice as broad as it is tall, fastened with a tight loop of blue rope. But on the mailbox, nailed American-style to the gate, there is a small white label with a tricolour sticker. 'Lonergan'. She feels like punching the air. Beginner's luck. A bullseye on her first throw.

The two upper windows look clear of the hedge, but otherwise the house is almost completely hidden. Although she knows that Lonergan's not there, her heart is battering. When she clutches the steel, her ring clinks against the metal. The sound reminds her that this is real, that there's a purpose here. There is a bargain to be made between the present and the past. And so she forces herself to clamber over the gate and into the wild garden.

The front door is mock-Georgian with a small frosted fanlight. There are plastic window boxes on the ledges of the bottom windows, empty but for some weedy soil topped with fag ends. Downstairs, the curtains have been pinched or pinned together.

She walks around to the rear of the house, where the back door's single pane of dirty glass looks into a kitchen with varnished, dark-knotted pine cupboards and a metal-legged table with four chairs. Through the kitchen door, a couple of rain jackets hang on pegs in the narrow hallway.

The sight of those jackets brings Lonergan forcefully to life. His face too close to hers, the spittle on his lip as he raised his hand to strike her. Already, she is tempted to abandon this whole enterprise. Her fear of him is disabling, she'd forgotten that. But she clenches her fists inside her pockets, digs her fingernails into her palms and tells herself she mustn't run. He's not here yet, but very soon he will be, and she must make herself confront him, face to face, if anything is to come of this. She stands there a moment longer and tries to imagine him in front of her. She rehearses her stance, the accent she will use. She even tries to summon up the words. And then she's had enough, and has to get away.

She walks quickly back down the path towards the gate as the first spits of rain begin. She is halfway over it when she hears the pant and skitter of a dog along the lane outside. Ever since an encounter in Central Park with a spoilt terrier that worried at her ankle, she is wary of dogs. She fears their intuition. While she is still perched half on and off the gate, it is there in front of her – squat and bull-headed with a burr in its throat, as if it's bitten into her already. And now that running is the sensible thing to do, she doesn't seem able to move at all. The burr becomes a bark, but the dog doesn't move any closer. She is careful to avoid eye contact as it squares up to her, bouncing on its front paws, and then she hears a voice.

'Heyyayay, Rambo. Hey, boy. Cool it. Heel.'

Meek as a lamb, the dog curls back towards its master, streaking its body along the man's calves. She slides down from the gate, trying to regain some dignity.

'I was . . .' she starts, before realising that she doesn't owe him any explanation.

The man is in his early forties – sailor's skin, lightish hair. Jeans and a thick navy sweater. His gaze is neutral, appraising. The dog and he both look at her and she looks at them and nobody says anything for a moment. 'You were spying,' he says. 'Checking out the celebrity. Seems everyone's a celebrity these days. Even this guy. All over the front page.'

She shrugs.

'I'm Theo,' he says. He walks towards her and shakes her hand.

'Sheen.'

'Well, of course, I already know about Sheen.' He smiles. 'Everyone knows about Sheen. That's what it's like when you live on an island. Not much goes down, so any little thing is a big thing. You, for example.'

Still anxious about the dog, she watches the lead wrapped tight around his hand as she tries to place his accent.

'I'm from Rotterdam,' he says, as if he's read her mind. 'Originally. And you?'

'New York.'

'Oh? I thought I'd heard you were from somewhere else.'

Her heart jumps, and it must be showing on her face, because he is looking at her closely now, his head to one side, waiting for a reply.

'What's wrong?' he says, and moves towards her. No more than an inch or two, but closer all the same.

But then he lets her off the hook. He glances at the animal, then back at her. 'Ah,' he says. 'I forget that not everyone is used to dogs. Don't worry about Rambo here, he's all bark.'

He bends to ruffle the dog's jowls, and by the time he's straightened up she has had a proper look at him.

'Shall we?' he asks. He gestures towards the harbour as he puts the dog on the lead.

She moves ahead of him. To cover her discomfort, she asks him if he lives nearby.

'Oh no, not here. I'm on the other side of the island. I've got a studio out on Goat Point.'

The dog seems unhappy to be on the lead. It starts to growl, and Theo bends to quieten it. 'This guy, he's like you. He likes to have a nose around.'

She laughs because it seems to be expected, then finds herself enjoying it. She hasn't laughed much recently.

'I make chairs. Green wood. They put my name in the guidebooks, but I don't get too many casual callers. Just try carrying a chair home over your arm. Not many bother. But if you're asking if I'm often here, if you could come up here and maybe run into me?'

She wishes she hadn't been caught. 'I didn't realise –'

'That this was private property? Of course not. Especially not with a gate. You didn't see the name on the mailbox either. Oh well.'

He is mocking her, but she can take that. Something about his faintly amused demeanour relaxes her.

They separate at the crossroads, and she breaks into a jog as she heads back over the ridge. The distance is further than she'd remembered, and the bungalow seems even more remote than it did the night before. The light is greyish now, the house greyish too. On the sea side of the house, a slope of lush grass studded here and there by large slabs of rock is all that separates it from the edge of the cliff.

5

Boyle is running short on time. She could be back any minute. He claps down the lid of the laptop, replaces the shoe. The last thing he wants is Murphy changing the locks. And that's when he sees the photos, laid on the windowsill like an ID parade. Some cut from newspapers, others downloaded.

Lonergan at a desk, a gold *fáinne* on his lapel to show his fluency in the Irish language. He is leaning towards the viewer. Patriotic, the image says. Scholarly. A man of the pen, not the sword.

And it's him again, standing with his back to the sea, a waist-high child either side of him. Behind him, an unpainted steel gate is tied with faded blue rope.

He looks like a Mormon in the next one. White shirt, dark suit. Hair brushed to the side. Dark green tie. Head and shoulders – an election leaflet. Fucksake.

He's astonished just how much she has on him. Impressed. What is she anyway? Reporter, biographer, number one fan? He starts to gather up the sheets, licking his forefinger like a teller at the bank. He might have himself a feed of fish and chips this weekend, a session on the mainland with his earnings. There might even be a bonus in a treasure trove like this one, a task so well discharged. He takes out the Nokia Lonergan gave him. He is just about to punch in the pre-set, and then he stops himself.

He thinks of the show she gave him at the picture window. He thinks of her smooth skin, her lean limbs, her satisfactory breasts. He returns the Nokia to his pocket. Maybe this isn't the way he wants to play it. Doesn't he deserve something for himself? He hasn't decided yet who's up to what, whose side he's on, which side his own bread's buttered.

When Lonergan first came to Lamb to claim the house that he'd been left – or so he said – he couldn't hide what he was up to in the North. You could smell the tension on him. And even though he seems to have forgotten all about that now, back then he was jumpy as a flea. The house itself was a wreck, little better than a cowshed. Since there was no land with it, nobody on Lamb cared less who got the place – or took it, maybe. Back then, he paid Boyle to do a bit of DIY – basic stuff that anyone could manage. He began to use the place, just now and then. And when the Troubles in the North no longer rang his bells, Lonergan diversified.

He can't be sure if it was Lonergan who started it, or if it was the Dutchman making use of old contacts back at home. He isn't even certain what exactly it is they're bringing in, these days. But their business is the ferrying of merchandise on to the mainland, the piloting of boats into quiet coves near Schull. For Lonergan, it's just a sideline. For the Dutchman, it pays the bills. Nobody bothers them, out at Goat Point. And nobody remarks on Lonergan. Easter, summer, Hallowe'en – he comes here regularly, and does just enough to pass muster with the locals. He spends a few quid on pints and toasted specials, turns up to the Regatta and the Easter fete. Sometimes he brings along his two little fellas in their wetsuits, but mostly he's on his own.

Now, why would the very woman that Lonergan asked him to watch, the woman who says she's from New York, have pictures of him all over her windowsill? There aren't many interesting questions that cross a man's radar on the likes of Lamb, but this is one of them. Boyle knows all the places that people hide things. The pot on top of the cupboard. Jewellery in the freezer, money in the gap between the wardrobe and the wall. But the new one hasn't bothered with any of that. Her life is open for inspection.

He enters the bathroom and goes over to the window. He tears a bit of the sticky film away – just an inch or two in the bottom right-hand corner to make himself a spyhole. A little eye-shaped hole for him to watch her through, if all else fails.

Next, he checks her room. He opens a drawer, takes out a pair of lacy knickers and rubs them on his cheek. He sniffs the cotton gusset. Detergent. Synthetic flowers. He pockets them anyway. In a plastic carrier bag behind the door, he finds a pair she's worn and shoves them in the other pocket to savour later.

In a drawer in the living room, he finds a clue he didn't even know he was looking for. Something she keeps wrapped in tissue paper that rustles like Christmas. He's not sure what it is at first, then decides it's a wallet – leather, cheaply made, with a large crooked harp on the front. He remembers these things knocking around, years back. Prisoners made them, up North. On the front there is a big blowsy flower. Embossed on the back are two words he knows from an old Phil Lynott song. '*Róisín Dubh*'. The little black rose. He lifts the wallet to his nose and sniffs. It smells of dirt, not roses. He opens it, hoping for a bit of luck, but there's nothing inside but a shiny penny and a slip of paper, 'With love from Da'.

Already, he can tell what this one is – she's a shape-shifter, a coverer of tracks. He feels the phone buzz in his pocket and closes his fist over it. Lonergan already? Let him wait. This is about the Wee Black North, about dirty old secrets and cover-ups. He glances down at his wrist where he wrote down the email address bgl@nrp.ie. And it's obvious now that the email is to Lonergan. This is about HIM.

As she crosses the threshold she catches his scent. Sour sweat, stale smoke. She glances over her shoulder, takes tiny noiseless sips of air. And her head is clearer than it's been in months. She wants this. She wants it for Ma, who demanded as much from beyond the grave. She wants it for the O'Neills, because she knows what it's like to have a mother you weren't allowed to bury. She wants it for Jacinta, abandoned on the floor of a safe house. But most of all she wants it for herself. To do one brave thing. One good thing. Tears spring to her eyes, but she blinks them away. She grabs an umbrella from the stand in the hall and smacks the wall with it. She makes so much noise that she is no longer afraid. Whacking at doors, walls, skirting boards. Advancing like the god of rain. And when she has beaten her way through the house and found that there is no one there, she sinks to her knees. She remembers the interview she came across online. Gemma O'Neill seeking justice for Jacinta.

'*Somebody out there knows what happened to my mother. If you've any decency in you, then tell us what you know about Jacinta O'Neill.*'

The right ending, that's what's called for. If he will give the O'Neills the peace they deserve, then that might be enough for her. If he will let them have Jacinta's body after all these years, she might still allow him his career – the glowing future, the wipe-clean past. But if he doesn't give her what she wants, it is comforting to know she has the means to bring him down.

As she pulls herself up from the tiled floor, a sudden squall has swept in from the west. The rain is battering the picture window where sea and sky have merged into a muddy shade of grey. In a rush of panic, she remembers the envelope. In the kitchen, she yanks open the oven door. It's still in there, exactly as she left it. No one has been here. Why would they be? He'd never think that she would come here after him. Passing by the school photo she hung up on the wall the night before, she notices a little inky smear of something on the glass. She moistens her finger with her tongue and smudges it away.

Back at the schoolhouse, Boyle sits at the fire and scrapes the poker through the ash, skiting up a spray of sparks. He is this woman's saviour – she just doesn't know it yet. But she will need him, that's for sure. Whether it's Lonergan or the Dutchman, or both of them at once, there'll come the day when she'll need someone there to face them down.

He painted Jennifer Ryan with her back to the sea behind an altar laid with wholesome things, things that console. Bread, oil, wine, fruit. Another time, he laid the altar with items he'd taken from her house. Hairbrush, perfume, ashtray. But the pictures he made of her aren't up on the walls any more. These days, he stacks them underneath the peg rail, in behind the old roof slates he might get round to putting back some day. After she disappeared, and they searched his place, the Guards said he must be a right weirdo, a right perve. What normal fella paints the same woman naked twenty-two fecken times? Naked, they said. Nude, he replied. He said he was an artist. A cat can look at a king.

Beside his bed, he keeps an old biscuit tin. Family Circle. Six varieties. He takes the flyer for the Easter Céilí and creases it in two. He puts it in the tin along with the other things he's taken from the new one's house: the light bulb, the paint chip in its little matchbox, and the two pairs of knickers, used and clean. There is comfort there, but his stomach is raw. He could do with a bowl of something bland. He looks in each of the presses in turn, but the cupboard is bare. Time for Molly's. He scarcely has the energy to drag himself there, but somehow he trudges up to the ridge, then flings himself down towards the scribble of houses that passes for a village.

Molly has one hand in the window display when he enters. She's been at her favourite job: polishing the cans of baked beans and stacking them into neat pyramids. She stands up straight when she sees him, rubs down her front and places her little pink hands on her hips.

'Now, Boyle,' she says, like he's some kind of halfwit. 'You're not to be annoying the new lady. Do you hear me? It's not on.'

He puts his face into neutral, the way he used to do when questioned by his father, Dr Boil, his turkey neck quivering in disgust at his crock-of-shit son. He doesn't look at Molly, but he can hear her tutting away. He scans the front pages. By-election up in Dublin. Lonergan's mug – right, left and centre. He clears a few cans off the shelves, then moves to the front of the shop and slams the metal basket on the counter.

'What's this?' says Molly. 'Are you planning on the Siege of Jericho?'

He looks to see what he's picked up. No wonder the

basket felt heavy, with six or seven cans of tuna in it. He doesn't even like tuna. Ready-made custard. Condensed milk. Ambrosia creamed rice.

'Would you not like a bit of variety, Boyle?' asks Molly, gazing down at the tuna. 'Beans maybe? Spaghetti hoops?'

They've long forgotten you can heat a can by shoving it into the hot ash of last night's fire. In the early days, they thought not having a cooker or fridge would get him out. They're daft like that, people. They think everyone wants the same as them.

And then Cat from the pub arrives, tits swinging, earrings flying.

'All right there, Boyle? Will you be at the Easter Céilí at all?' She comes up close to him, and right away she's tickling her nose with the side of her finger and he knows that means there's a whiff off him today.

'Oh, and if you're looking for a bit of work, we need the bench out in front painted before we're inundated with visitors for the Easter.'

Hasn't he got enough on his hands, watching the new one? But Cat's not the worst, so he does his best to come up with something civil. 'I hear the internet café's going great guns,' he says.

She looks surprised, but then she smiles. 'Well, you know. Progress, I guess. About time.'

'No man is an island,' he says.

Cat darts a glance at Molly as if she's not sure what to say to that. That doesn't mean he wants to join the Community. No fucken way. She's always going on about him joining the Community. Trying to make up for what Pete said about him to the Guards. No fucken way is he getting all pally with them at this stage of the game. Not after all their accusations. No fucken way.

Cat's bottom lip does a funny little twitch. 'You're welcome to use the computer, Boyle. It's probably free at the moment, in fact. Not many use it first thing.'

'Fair play,' he says. He swaps half the cans of tuna for three large tins of macaroni cheese, then adds a couple more of beans and Ambrosia creamed rice.

'Have you noodles in, Molly?' he asks, thinking of the sauces he found in the new one's cupboard and how he might bring her something to go with them as a welcoming gift.

She looks puzzled. 'Noodles, Boyle? Are you sure?'

But it turns out she hasn't got them anyway.

When Boyle arrives at the pub, Pete is outside the door, sawing away at a plank of wood supported by two plastic garden chairs. Hung between the two bent trees are several new lines of coloured muslin squares, flapping in the breeze.

'Jesus, Pete. Is that where she was the other night? Off to Skibb for more bloody prayer flags?'

Pete looks through him, and then Boyle remembers that Pete likes everybody to speak like the Dalai Lama, even in the pub.

'Were you wanting something, Boyle?'

'She said I could use the computer. She said to just go on up.'

Pete stops whatever he's doing and there's this silly

little dance at the door until Pete stands back and lets him through.

Upstairs is the room Cat calls the internet café, a weird womb of a place with dark orange walls and a spiderweb Red Indian thing hanging from the ceiling. He can hear Pete downstairs, mumbling into the phone. Checking up on him, no doubt. He supposes he should give Lonergan's phone a charge. He finds a spare socket at his feet and plugs it in. On the windowsill, there's a little pile of pebbles. Boyle picks one up and mimes skimming it at the computer screen. He sits on the rickety chair and flexes his fingers. Then he licks one and places it on the keyboard. This time, he chooses L. L for Lonergan. It takes him less than five minutes to find out five important things:

1. Lonergan's party is going to win a by-election up in Dublin.
2. If they win, the government will fall.
3. Unless, that is, they do a deal with Lonergan.
4. A family called O'Neill wants Lonergan arrested for something he did years ago in the North.
5. But the O'Neills don't have any proof, and Lonergan's admitting nothing.

Boyle reflects on how it's always important to know the context. That way, things start to make sense. He'd always taken Lonergan for an ambitious fucker, but he hadn't realised the stakes were quite so high. Before you know it, he'll be handing over the shamrock at the White

House, smarming over starlets and Goodwill Ambassadors. And if only half the stuff the new one says about Lonergan is true, he's a lucky man. Lonergan has never been in prison. He's as clean as a whistle and out to make the world a better place. Except he's not. Boyle can sniff a hypocrite from miles off. There's enough of them about.

The Dutchman – peace and love?

Not so.

His own father, Dr Boil, general practitioner – all-round decent stick?

Not so.

His own uncle, Father Malachy of the Wholly Catholic Church – pure as the driven snow?

Fuck no.

As for the new one – an American, just taking a bit of time out?

No way.

He's trying to work out what she's up to, piecing things together, taking mad stabs in the dark. He thinks he might be getting somewhere when Cat appears with a cup of tea. She bends over him to set it down on the desk. She smells nice and the skin on her inner arm is as perfectly white as the flesh of a freshly bitten apple. The colour distracts him because he has no word that really describes it properly. The only thing that would do it justice is a loving stroke of paint. But Cat's Cat. Practically a saint. Who wants to paint a saint? Maybe he's looked at that skin for too long, though, because when he glances up at her face Cat's giving him a funny look.

'Have you eaten, Boyle?' she asks.

Has he eaten? Does it matter?

'I could bring you up a toastie?'

In no time at all, she's been down the stairs and up again. She stands there a moment with the plate out in front of her and waits for him to take it. As soon as he hears her clumping back down again, he gets rid of the tomato because tomato gets too hot, and pulls out the stringy bits of onion because they stick in his teeth. When at last he bites into the salty melt, he realises how little he's had to eat that week, let alone that day. He's had no appetite since he heard about the new one coming. But once he realises he's half starving, he can't get that sand-wich into his mouth quick enough. By the time he's eaten it, he could murder another. He fumbles around in his pocket and finds a couple of quid – almost enough, but not quite.

He goes downstairs to where Cat is cleaning out the coffee filters. She jumps when she sees him.

'No problem, Boyle,' she says. 'Don't worry about the money. I'll just bring it up when it's done.' She glances at the plate. 'Just ham and cheese this time, so.'

He has a favourite website he doesn't get to visit often, and he spends a while on there, watching the ins and outs, the ups and downs, growing hot and hard, until he hears Cat calling up from down below. 'Are you done there, Boyle?'

He can't find his voice in time.

'Your toastie's ready, Boyle.'

She's on her way up. He clicks and zips, clears History.

And when Cat comes into the room, she's got someone with her and he can't believe his luck.

Close up, she looks paler and prettier than she does from a distance, or struggling with the hill, or under a bare light bulb in an empty room.

'We've a customer now who needs to use the computer, Boyle,' says Cat in her sweetie-pie voice.

The new one looks at him, but she doesn't linger on him very long. Her gaze slides across him to the window and the view. She's going on about how lovely it is, and what a pity it is about the fish farm, and do they get many tourists over for the Easter?

He knows why she's asking that, and he feels like telling her not to be wishing for Easter to come, because Lonergan will be down on her like a ton of bricks before she knows where she is. But he keeps her little secret all the same.

'It'll be getting cold,' says Cat.

What is she talking about? What's getting cold? He can't believe she doesn't have the manners to introduce him. That's the thing about women. They come across all right until they have to treat you like a normal human being. And then they fail.

But the new one doesn't fail. She stretches out her small pale hand to him, and her fingernails are like the inside of a shell.

'Sorry to bump you off,' she says. 'I'm Sheen.'

And that's the name for her all right. Smooth, she is, and glossy. She sounds like a real American up close. All drawly and take-your-time. He can't hear hardly any Northern in her voice at all.

'No bother,' he says, and rubs his hand on his shirt before shaking hers. He stands up and takes a good look at the top of her head before he turns for the door.

'Good to meet you,' she calls after him. 'I'll see you round.'

And I'll see you, he thinks. Eye spy.

6

He smells terrible but he looks familiar. And then she remembers him from her run – the tall stooped figure with the straggly ponytail standing right in the grassy centre of the road. As he gets up to leave and shakes her hand, she notices something inked on his forearm. At first she thinks it's a tattoo because the letters are quite regular. It trails off at an angle, though, and she can't quite decipher what she then decides is probably just a reminder to himself.

As soon as he's through the door and walking down the stairs, Cat sprays anti-bac on the keyboard, whooshing it on, then swiping it off with a cloth. She waits for the click of the front door.

'That was Boyle,' she says. 'Harmless enough, but a bit dodgy on the old hygiene. He's been here for years, in that kip on the hill up above you. Anyway, what can I get you? Tea? Coffee?'

But Sheen is busy piecing things together. She'd seen

the high window in the gable, the perfect vantage point for the black rectangle of her picture window, but she hadn't realised that anyone was living there. She noticed the hunger in his eyes as they zoned in on things most men don't even notice – shoulder, elbow, wrist – as though he'd been waiting for an opportunity to examine her close up. That scrutiny disturbs her – she has always striven to be unremarkable, to be the one that nobody remembers.

When Cat returns with a pot of coffee, she has brought two mugs as if they are already friends. 'So you're on your own out at Reen?' Her eyes flick to the ring that Sheen still wears, even though Tom does not. 'It's lovely out there when the sun's shining,' she says, 'but a bit bleak if it's not. You can drop in here any time you like. We have a guy with a guitar most Fridays. Quiz midweek.'

Sheen starts to explain about Tom, but it's all too raw and recent. In the end, all she says is that, yes, she's on her own. She was married once, but these things happen. 'It's good to have some time to clear my head. I've got the house for as long as I want, and a couple of months' leave from work, so . . .'

'Cool,' Cat says. 'That's great. I really hope you'll like it here.'

A customer calls up from downstairs and, as Cat goes to deal with him, Sheen is back in the final scene of her marriage. Tom had come home late. Really late. And he'd been drinking, something he rarely did. When he stumbled into the apartment, he headed for the galley kitchen ranged along one wall and bent to drink water straight from the faucet. As he turned to face her, tiny droplets were suspended in the hairs just visible at the open neck of his shirt. When he told her he was leaving, the reason he gave was brutal, brief, and somehow too ordinary to be the real one. The woman's name was Cally. They'd met at an offsite in Connecticut. They were in love. She noticed that the knuckles on his hand were grazed, as if he'd trailed them along a wall, getting here. She wondered if Cally would tend to them, like she would have done. And then, out of nowhere, she had the urge to hurt him, to wound him in some fundamental way. But Tom got there first.

'All the mystery, the secrecy, I just can't cope with that any more. Nightmares and no-go areas, Cally doesn't have them. I know where I am with her. What you see is what you get.'

She hadn't realised he knew about the nightmares – the blood, the fire, the little stockinged feet. She thought she'd hidden those. And as the night seemed to cave in on top of her, she heard him sliding out a drawer, rustling through their wardrobe. Everything he took with him fitted into a daypack. Tom looked like he was setting off on a hike just as her world was ending.

She shakes herself back into the present, forces herself to give the computer her full attention. And today, the news is all of Lonergan. Each day, it seems, the stakes are rising. 'New Republic Party Surge in Opinion Polls' is the lead story on the RTÉ website. She waits for Cat to go back downstairs before opening the link.

Political newcomer, Brian Lonergan, recently elected leader of the New Republic Party, is tipped to be a significant player at the negotiations likely to take place after the forthcoming Dublin East by-election.

Meanwhile, there are fourteen new messages in her inbox.

Lauren says that things are deadly quiet at the gallery. 'How's that nostalgia trip? Any artists on your island? Send pictures if there's anything you think I'd like.'

The yoga studio acknowledges her cancellation, and Renzo and Brad miss her. But they have news. 'Moving to Connecticut, baby. Yay!'

Did they ever mention Connecticut before? She doesn't think so. She is hardly gone five minutes and already things are changing. She feels suddenly forlorn. How she wishes they were with her now. They would tease her, feed her, make her laugh. They would tell her to come home.

There are book club choices, special offers, supper nights at Jazz O T. But there is still nothing from Lonergan. Easter is less than a week away, and she will be waiting for him. He would never dream she'd have the nerve to come here after him. She can hardly believe it herself.

Ma's letter had arrived on a day Sheen had taken off work. She'd spent the morning at the apartment, bagging into huge black sacks the clothes that Tom had never bothered to collect, until it all got too much and she went out into the bright blue afternoon to pick up a flat white at the Austrian café a block away. On her way back, she checked the mailbox. There was scarcely ever anything but junk and bills in there, and receiving an envelope with a Belfast postmark was rarer still. The envelope looked official, with a typed address and her name misspelt. Miss Raisin Burns. Inside, a covering note from a firm of solicitors and a smaller, sealed envelope with the words 'Insurance for Róisín' written sturdily across the front in Ma's hand. Ma's letter was in her usual blue pen in careful convent script, trending forward just a little, digging deep into the Basildon Bond. Sheen ran her fingers across the page and tried to conjure up a face, a lost voice.

Dear Róisín,
Your da always said you never know what way
the wind will turn, and by God did Kenny know
all about the wind and how it can change on
you. You know a thing or two about Lonergan,
Róisín. I realise that. But I know a thing or
two more.

The Ma she'd known had been ordinary – just a wee Belfast woman. Cooked ham, sliced pan, daily Mass. This Ma sounded like a completely different person. As though proximity to death had freed her up to become somebody else. The statements she enclosed were both written on jotter paper in blue ballpoint. Two former colleagues of Lonergan's had spoken to Da about an incident that had shamed them both. This was their written testimony. One man's handwriting was all loops and neat joins. It reminded her of the script she'd been expected to copy into her handwriting book in primary school. The other was awkward, angular, as though written with the wrong hand. But even on that initial reading she realised that the story they told would ruin Lonergan. Morally, it was no worse than everything she already knew about him. But this would damn him in the eyes of the party.

Don't play the hero, Róisín. Make sure you have your back covered. But when the moment's right, make your move.

She'd felt a sting of resentment when she reread the statements and Ma's own interpretation of those events, but she felt a sense of possibility too. For a long time that afternoon she hesitated. Since leaving Belfast, she'd avoided at all costs being forced up against the past. She stayed clear of Irish interest groups, ignored the obvious news sources, the societies and singing pubs.

To clear her head, she went out and had a walk among the skateboarders and Scrabblers in Washington Square Park. She thought about Tom and the fixed points of their early years together. How they used to bunk off work on the day the pool in Astoria Park opened for the summer season, or challenge each other to a six o'clock run on snowy mornings. She thought of the Christmas habits that were beginning to evolve into rituals: his mom's stollen washed down with sweet wine after skating; the stocking fillers wrapped in coloured tissue paper that Sheen collected for him throughout the fall. They should have lasted, Tom and she. But the half-life she'd been forced to lead since leaving Belfast had stunted her. And so the loss of Tom was down to Lonergan as well. By the time she got back to the apartment, she had made up her mind.

She opened the laptop and began to search for him. The real Brian Lonergan was easy to find, but she circled around him for a while, not quite able to approach him yet. In the meantime, she discovered that the world is full of Brian Lonergans. He was the captain of a Scottish golf club, the owner of a West End bar. He gave Ned Kelly tours in Victoria, played cello in the LSO. He'd climbed Kilimanjaro and lost at chess.

The real one had acquired a title to go along with the suit: Communications Director, New Republic Party. She started to build up a picture of him from web pages, and only after that did she start on the images. She came across a YouTube clip, the aftermath of some inter-governmental meeting in which the camera panned along a double line of balding men. Out in front, a former prime minister was showing his teeth and clasping the hand of a pinker, fleshier man. And there in the background, Lonergan. He was on-screen for barely five seconds, but she played him back over and over again. She forced herself to look at him, and not to flinch.

When she'd exhausted the Google images, the references to him on obscure sites, there still wasn't the slightest hint of who this really was. No bombs or dead soldiers, no abductions or harassed widows. No protection scams or armed robberies or kneecappings. Not a single day in prison. Lonergan murder. Lonergan convicted. Nothing. She searched for him alongside all the words that she herself avoided: soldier, Dolores, Belfast, bombing, commander, terrorist, republican, arms, membership, feud, breakaway, jail. Nothing. Blank.

She read Ma's letter again, the handwritten statements with their simple syntax. She added to it all the things she herself had seen, the things she knew. And the implications made her heart race. How could there be nothing known about any of this?

It was late afternoon when she found the little chink in his public armour. A recent entry, an interview.

He took my ma. Even if he didn't actually come to the flat himself, he did it. The dishes were still in the sink when I came home from school, the clothes still damp and ready for the line. A neighbour spotted them coming up the entry. Four of them, the usual hoods. She dropped the blinds, scared to see any more, but she heard the squealing, heard my ma being dragged, kicking and screaming down them steps that lead to Rebecca Street. I want people to remember her name, Jacinta O'Neill. She was a person after all.

Sheen had never been able to forget Jacinta. In her head, Sheen rehearsed all the things that she could tell this woman about her mother: the locket at her throat, the tape they used on her, the sour stench in the room where she was held. But those were truths she could never speak aloud. The shame was just too great. She was terrified of the exposure, the long trek back over old ground. And yet, as she returned to the screen and called up a gallery of images of Brian Lonergan, New Republic Party – a smiling, genial man in a suit, a father with his sons, a fisherman in flat cap and cagoule – she found that she could barely breathe.

Later, she lit a scented candle, ran a bath sweetened with lavender oil and vanilla. She knocked back a fistful of Kalms and went to bed, where she lay with the duvet wrapped around her and the blanket on. She tried to sleep, but her head wouldn't quieten. In the end, she ransacked the place for alcohol, the stronger the better, anything to obliterate her thoughts. Sheen had never been a drinker – she had never risked the abandonment, the loss of control – and there wasn't much of it around the place. Eventually, though, she found a half-finished bottle of tequila from God knows when. She forced it down in bitter little gulps. It deadened the pain and stoked her fury. Soon, she was light-headed – powerful and trigger-happy. Her thoughts were a maelstrom of mothers unburied or mourned at long distance – Ma, Jacinta. And Lonergan was to blame for all of it.

The next time she googled him, there was something new.

With a strong base in the West Belfast heartland, New Republic Party spin doctor Brian Lonergan is making a move for the leadership of the party. Supporters cite his talents as a party strategist over the last decade. He is also thought to have extensive business interests in the Republic and powerful support nationwide. Lonergan is expected to bid for the leadership tomorrow at the party conference in Dublin. Meanwhile, relatives of Jacinta O'Neill are escalating their campaign for release of information about the whereabouts of her body with a sit-in outside the offices of the New Republic Party announced for the weekend.

Just beneath the text, they had printed the familiar photo of Lonergan taken with his two young sons against that sparkling sea. It was easy to find an email address on the New Republic website. She drank and typed and drank. By the time she'd finished, her head was spinning.

She took out Ma's letter and reread it. 'When the moment's right, make your move.' She decided then and there that she wouldn't do that, at least not yet. Instead, she would use the knowledge that she had evidence against him to give her courage to ask for something. The demand she made of him was not extravagant. All she asked was that he let Jacinta's family have her body back. And he would do that, she thought. Because it was easy – just a word in the right ear would do the trick.

When she finished the email, she didn't even read it back. Just clicked and it was gone. And even through the blur of too much booze, she knew that she had crossed a boundary, that what she'd done couldn't be taken back.

Next morning, her tongue was stuck to the roof of her mouth, and her head was swollen. She blinked herself awake and rushed over to the computer. And there it was, lodged in the Sent box like an unexploded bomb. Opening it, she could scarcely recognise herself. It was a shock to read a rant like that when she was Sheen now, and had a job that half the girls in Montauk would give their eye teeth for. But the person who had written that email didn't sound like Sheen. The voice was angry, raw, accusatory, and she was suddenly afraid. In the click of a mouse, her New York self had slipped away.

Downstairs in the pub, Cat has customers. Glasses are being stacked and the radio is on. Sheen looks up from the screen and out over the harbour where a fan of spring sunshine is unfolding from behind the clouds. On Lamb, she is discovering, the sunshine never lasts for long. She glances over towards Molly's shop and her breath catches. The man she met outside Lonergan's house is loading carrier bags into the back of a jeep. He pauses a moment. Then, as if he senses her watching him, he turns and looks straight up to where she's sitting. Her hand leaps to acknowledge him, but he doesn't react. She feels a twinge of disappointment. And then he climbs into the jeep and is gone.

There is a muffled ringtone somewhere far away, and it's a little while before she realises that her own cell is ringing at the bottom of her bag – it hasn't rung since she got here. But the number that flashes up is her sister Maura's. The hurt she felt when Maura barred her from attending Ma's funeral has hardened over but not yet healed. And because Maura has no idea that she has come here, she switches off the phone.

Boyle is heating up a can of beans in the embers of last night's fire when the Nokia rings. Dee dee dee dee dee

dee dee dee. Dee dee dee dee dee dee dee dee. Lonergan again? Let him haul his arse over here and do his own dirty work. But it's not Lonergan, it's the Dutchman.

'I've just seen her, over at Cat's,' he says, 'and she's looking pretty relaxed to me.'

'Of course she's relaxed. She's on holiday.'

'You've been avoiding his calls.'

'Ah fuck away off and play with your carpentry set.'

'Get rid of her, Boyle, or I'll do it myself.'

Boyle pictures the Dutchman with Jennifer – long, lovely Jennifer – and his heart frosts over. He sees them tangled together on the slate floor of the house at Reen, her white throat, the long pale hair. And then he sees them on the high cliff path just a day or two later, the wind scrambling that hair and jumbling their raised voices. He should not have left Jennifer to the Dutchman. This time, it will be different.

He's been inside her house twice now. He likes to lie on her bed. He likes the silk gown she keeps on the back of the door. He thinks he smells her in the silk – a sweet vanilla smell. But that sweet vanilla's not the whole of it. That email in her Sent box has told him more than she could ever dream he'd know. And he thinks she might be making excuses for herself. Because the way she tells things in that email, she's coming out smelling sweeter than that silk gown of hers. And, surely to God, she couldn't have been that thick, could she? A girl like her, brought up to trouble? With a da who gives prison leather as a present?

Mind you, he's learning things about Lonergan, too. And maybe they wouldn't be all over him – Murphy and Molly, and half the country if the newspapers are right – if they knew what he smelt of. Lonergan is a fake and Boyle can't stand fakes. Years ago, when there was still a commune on Lamb, Boyle was the one to draw up the manifesto.

We do not manipulate
We are what we say we are
No liars
No cheats
No fakes

Right then, he decides that this is the day he'll introduce himself properly. Offer his assistance. Do the neighbourly thing. Make a bit of a fuss like his mother used to do whenever someone new moved into the park. She'd bring out the Royal Albert – country rose with a fine gold rim. Lay out the sugar, the milk, a plate of Mikados. Prepare a plate of sandwiches: salmon paste and egg and onion. Crusts off, cut in quarters, covered in a damp cloth. She'd send him on ahead to ring the bell and there she'd stand, the tray held out in front of her. He wonders what he can bring with him to break the ice. He thinks about all the rubbish that Murphy didn't bother his fat arse removing when he rented out the place – the plastic flowerpots, the coal bags and the scrag ends of bleached blue rope – and he decides to offer to help her clear it up. After he's worked some Palmolive into his armpits, he digs out his best shirt, hoists a shovel on his shoulder and sets off. Standing outside her house, he sees her shadow flit across the frosted-glass panel in the door. The curtains in the back bedroom are drawn. He hopes she's not hiding from him. That would be a bad way to start. Already, he has half a mind to lean on the bell and see how much she likes it, but he holds his fire. He wets his finger, gives the bell a girly little buzz.

She opens the door, but just a crack. He can see right away she has no clue how to behave. You can't be hugging your front door to your chest on an island, woman.

'Yes?' she says, like he's a gippo come to lay the tarmac.

Does she not remember him from the other day? He could easily be made small by the sharp look of her, but then he remembers the manifesto.

We are what we appear to be.

So he pulls himself up straight and sticks his chest out.

'Would you want a hand clearing out around the place?' he says, asks, tries.

She says she's only just moved in and there's not much need for clearing out.

Sure I know that, woman, he feels like saying to the first bit. And, you must have low standards, woman, he feels like saying to the second. She's not even bothering to crack a smile. He should have brought a cup of sugar with him to sweeten her up.

'So I guess the answer's no,' she says. 'But thanks anyway.'

And then he remembers the Céilí – just blurts it out, and asks her if she's going.

'Sure,' she says. 'I'll be there.' And she starts closing the door.

'Boyle,' he blurts out.

She looks puzzled, and then she smiles. 'Oh,' she says, 'I thought –'

'I know,' he says. His stupid fucken name.

And before he knows it, she has the door shut on him. He doesn't know why he brought the shovel. He can't decide what to do with it now so he just leans on it. He waits a moment to see if she is going to open up again, but she doesn't.

What if he just let swing with it? Would she come out then?

Back at the schoolhouse, he tries to cheer himself up by rummaging through the paintings he did of Jennifer. He has her by the Marriage Stones, up on the cliff at Reen, out by the one remaining wall of the castle, down by the cove where the three flat islands of Slea break the sound. And even though she's gone now, she's also still here.

When the new one heads out for her run, she has a string bag on her back. Sandwiches? Tea? Book? Her top is that horrible colour again: an unnatural DayGlo pink. She heads up the hill and he watches her start to climb, then slow down, then stop. She's bent double, her head hung between her knees, beaten by the south hill. When she starts up again, it's easy to keep track of her.

She turns off towards the west, the road that leads

down to the sandy strand at Reen. He can't believe his luck. She's taking to the sea. Jennifer was a skinny-dipper, a long pale streak through the green water, her blonde hair swept out after her. He wonders will this one strip off too? And will she wade right in or stand in the shallows, shivering? He thinks of her little bare feet, the night she arrived, her cold bare feet tiptoeing across the tiles. He imagines those feet clambering across the barnacled rocks, or sunk into the soft sand of rockpools where there are cockles and mussels and the crabs are waiting to snap.

She has eleven minutes on him, but by the time he gets to the top of the cliff, she's still fully dressed. He crouches down in the grass, then spreads himself flat so he won't be seen. Are you swimming or what? He waits a while, but she's still just sitting there, looking out to sea. He climbs down the skittery path to the strand. When he dislodges a few pebbles that go stuttering down the hill, she jumps.

'Uh,' she goes, with her hand to her chest. 'It's just . . .' she says. 'It's you again.'

You're right, he thinks, it's me again. You're here, what, a couple of days? And you're treating me like shite already? It's me again, too bloody right it is.

'I guess I react like I'm still in New York.'

He starts to say, 'It's just, like . . .' then thinks, why the just and why the like? 'I spotted you from the road,' he says then. 'You mind yourself in that water.'

'Oh, I'm not planning to swim,' she says, as if that's not what the sea is for at all.

'There's currents, that's all,' he says. 'Rip tides.'

She heaves a sigh and gives him both thumbs up. 'Got it.'

And he doesn't know if the sigh is about him or the currents, or if she's just the type of female that sighs a lot. But it better not be about him. It better not. They haven't even got to know each other yet. And who's been talking to her about him, anyway? Molly, Murphy, Cat?

'I used to lead a commune here,' he says. 'You might have heard tell of it.'

'I didn't think communes had leaders,' she says.

'Well, this one did. And well run it was, too.'

'Good for you.' And then she turns away, not even the slightest bit scared of him.

There she is, on a lonely beach with Vincent Boyle who hasn't had a woman in years (apart from Jenka twice a month, more or less). Is there not the slightest bit of bother on her? And what if he was Lonergan? Would she be scared then?

She turns back again, but it's only to dismiss him. 'Well, thanks for that, Boyle.'

But he doesn't go away. Instead, he takes baby steps down the steep, shingly path towards her. When he gets to the sand, she can't be more than ten feet away. The thing he says next just comes out because he's mad at her. He blurts it out without really meaning to.

'How come you know Lonergan?'

As soon as he says it, he knows he's played his hand too soon. She looks like her face might slide right off the end of her chin. She looks worn, tired. He's beginning to think she might be nearer forty than he'd realised. And though he shouldn't have let on he knows about her, he can't help feeling satisfied by her reaction as she backs away from him towards the sea. He's not the eejit with the shovel now. He's the man with information. 'Take care you don't step into the sea.'

But she just keeps on going, and he can see from the expression on her face that she is trying to figure out how come he knows about her being here for Lonergan. Thanks be to fuck those photos were on the windowsill.

'Remember I came with the shovel?' he says.

She doesn't say anything.

'Of course you do. Sure it was only this morning. When I came up to the house, yeah? Well, that wasn't the first time I was up at your place. I came looking for you the other day, too. To see if I could help out, like, with anything. You had those photos laid –'

'I don't need your help.'

Now he hears the Northern in her voice, and there's a hard wee edge to it. You don't need my help, love? That's what you think.

'Don't you be coming nosing around my place.' And she mutters something else under her breath. It sounds like *fucken weirdo*, but surely not because that might ruin everything. 'Just go now,' she says.

Up close, her mouth looks thinner, meaner than he'd realised. Her eyes are hard. But her colours are good. He tries to memorise them, to match her up to things he knows well. Her face is the colour of the patch of exposed plaster in the schoolhouse where the teacher's desk used to be. And those freckles are like the lichen that speckles the stone to the right of the schoolhouse door. Her eyes are pebble grey, but with a reddish rim. She's not been crying, has she? What's there to be crying about? What's she keeping from him? He steps in close to get a better look.

She turns and snaps at him. 'Fuck off,' she says. 'And don't annoy my head.'

Back at the schoolhouse, he feels as if his face has been slapped. He reaches for the padded envelope from Lonergan and tips the little metal slug on to his palm. He lets it roll – forward and back again. She's blown it now. He's giving her the bullet. He imagines dropping it into her tea caddy, working it into a bar of soap. He can't get her expression out of his head, the mean little puss on her when she told him to fuck off.

But then he thinks of what it might be like to paint her – the plaster tint of her skin, the uncertain eyes. It's early days yet for the bullet. He rolls it back into Lonergan's envelope and reaches instead for the yellowed wad of newsprint. Opening it out, he discovers a big moon face that takes up almost half a page. An artificial face, made up of strips and stripes of this and that. There are two sharp eyes, a Roman nose, a fleshy, pouting mouth. Boyle has studied faces all his life, but he's never seen one like that. He thinks they call them e-fits now. Computer-generated. This is the old-fashioned type, jigsawed together from random facial features.

He sticks it up on the wall, on top of Dev, between JFK and the Pope before last. And he can see, right enough, how a mug like that might be enough to scare the shit out of her, with her delicate bones and her fear of the dark. The face is hard, yet fleshy. Dark, yet pale. It's time she realised how much she needs a friend.

She should not have angered him, she knows that now, but she couldn't help herself. This time she had been determined to try to read what was written on his arm. When he was right up next to her, she was able to see that it was an email address: bgl@nrp.ie.

A moment later, she realised whose address that was.

And right away she knows that she's been read. The shock is like a blow to the head, and her thoughts are reeling off again. She has not been careful enough.

She watches him walk back up the stretch of sand on to the shingle and through the rough tufts of seagrass until he has moved out of sight. She should not have made an enemy. For a moment, she considers shouting something after him, offering an olive branch, but the shock has frozen her into silence. And she can't help thinking there must have been a better way to do this.

After she sent the email to Lonergan she waited. One month, then another. Nothing. She read everything she could about the O'Neills until she almost felt she knew them. Gemma, the daughter with the sallow complexion and the crooked teeth. Séan and Colm, the sons who couldn't meet the camera's eye. The emphysemic husband who attended every press conference with his oxygen machine in tow.

In interviews and articles, the daughter always used the exact same words: 'We need to bury her. Then we'll rest.' Her tone was inexpressive, as if she no longer expected a result. But it never failed to break Róisín's heart. For months now, she had felt this visceral urge to see where her own mother had been buried. How much worse must it be never to have had a body to bury at all.

The first time she realised that her email was not going to get an answer was when Lonergan made a statement.

Jacinta O'Neill had had a history of depression, he said. Her marriage was in trouble. Her disappearance was sad, of course, a terrible tragedy for her family. But it had nothing whatsoever to do with him.

At that point, she'd seriously considered contacting the family directly. Several times, she'd gone as far as lifting up the phone. But the shame was just too great. And in the glimmer of this new idea that she could help Jacinta's family – a benevolent unseen presence engineering a kind of closure – there was a glimpse of something else. If she could only confront Lonergan, then maybe she could free herself. If she could look him in the eye and force him to admit that none of this had been her fault, that she could not have prevented any of it. That this half-life she's been forced to lead is down to him. Then, maybe, she could be whole again.

Back at the house, she gathers up all the images she has of him and shoves them into a plastic bag she slides under the sofa. She feels like she is losing her footing, so she tries desperately to summon up Sheen. Her hands are shaking when she touches the delicate blue glass of the perfume bottle belonging to the imaginary mother, but it no longer seems to do the trick. She pulls on the pale suede boots that cost the earth, clips the diamanté clasp into her hair, drapes the silk scarf around her neck – a dappled greenish-blue. Dressed up as Sheen, she feels calmer. She opens iTunes on the computer and scrolls through the music. There is nothing from Róisín's past in there. No Bowie, no punk. Everything on there is smooth and safe, like Sheen. MOR, retro crooner, American songbook. She finds a Sinatra track. *It happened in Monterey.* She sits at the window and watches the clouds surge slowly but surely towards her. *A long time ago.* She inhales the last traces of an old perfume from the scarf. *In old Mexico.* And feels her panic ease.

But it's not old Mexico, it's old Belfast, and the things she can't escape are too ugly to put in a song. She doesn't know what to do with herself now, all dressed up as Sheen. Somewhere out at sea, the clouds have burst. The day has darkened and she remembers that she hasn't even eaten yet. Eat something, she thinks, why not? She uses a little of Renzo's oil and vinegar on some sliced tomato, nibbles at some bread, but the hole in her stomach won't be filled by food. All the while, her mind's eye lingers on the crude inked letters on the inside of the weirdo's arm: bgl@npr.ie.

Later, she goes to put a bag of rubbish into the bin outside. She gathers some brown plastic pots, relics from some long-dead bedding plants, and stacks them by the bin. When she turns she sees it, written on a large square of pale pink manilla paper pinned neatly to the back door, a single word. She looks around, but there's no one there. She takes the paper down and flips it over, but the back is blank. The writing is as careful as the pinning. Large letters made in marker pen, each one the length of her thumb and separated by a perfect equidistant space. Some superstition prevents her from crunching the paper in her fist and flinging it away. Instead, she brings it into the house and places it on the kitchen table.

WHY?

Belfast

7

Belfast was tight and hard and grey. It scowled under Cave Hill and caught its rain and most days black billows replaced the sky. For all the greyness there was colour too, screaming out from tattered flags and from the yellow shipyard cranes. As for the way things were, her ma always said there'd be worse to come yet. And there was. Much worse. Róisín. Even her name was a diminutive. Roe-sheen. A little rose, a flower of a thing, a wee dote. Roe-sheen. Róisín. Eager and dutiful and dull. The dullness didn't seem to matter until Dolores arrived. But just by being there, Dolores made everyone else fade. She'd come after mid-term break, from one of those new estates in Craigavon. Burned out of the house, people said. Da on the run, they said. Involved? Maybe.

Dolores wore an Afghan coat over her school uniform, and earrings that swung as far as her chin. In class, she sat in disdainful absence, her face all sharps and flats. There were whispers of a married man somewhere up the Antrim

Road. The first time Dolores spoke to Róisín was in the dinner queue, over the cake and custard.

'Are you on for a bit of craic?' she said. 'Somewhere new, where you don't get the same saddos every week?' She looked over Róisín's shoulder, chewing luxuriously, seeming not to care what the answer was. 'Well? Are you into dancin' and that?' she said then.

'Aye, I suppose.'

'Say nothing or they'll all want to come. We'll pick you up outside Markey's Bar. Rebecca Street. Thursday night. Half past seven.'

And so Róisín felt chosen, as indeed she had been.

Thursday evening, she waited on the corner of Rebecca Street outside the ruined hulk of Markey's Bar. The corrugated iron only went halfway up, and the charred beams inside looked like black velvet. She watched the rain hover in the street light, putter into pavement cracks. A trickle ran down her fringe and on to her nose. She skimmed a finger under her eyes to save her mascara, and waited.

Rebecca Street died when the last of the school kids carried their wrapped singles home from the chipper. Ever since Markey's Bar went up in smoke, the parade of shops across the way was braced with grilles and shutters, like mouths full of metal. Róisín turned aside and brushed a haze of raindrops off her sleeve as a clatter of hoods passed by, their Doc Marten boots scraping over broken glass. She was just wondering if Dolores would turn up at all when a black taxi appeared – a dirty number plate and a bockety door.

Dolores was sitting in front with the driver, her black

hair backcombed off her forehead, her eyes done up. She stuck her head out of the window and smiled. 'Well, hop in then,' she said.

The driver and Dolores didn't make conversation with her at all, just talked in low voices like they'd known one another all their lives. Róisín tried to join in, wedging herself forward on the seat. She asked Dolores what the place was like, decent music and that? But Dolores just said it was progressive stuff and turned away. The driver's eyes, greenish and sharp, flicked up at Róisín now and then. Eventually, he slid the glass hatch shut.

They drove over to the north of the city and, before she knew it, Róisín had lost all track of where they were. No burnt-out buses up this way, no barricades either. Not even that many bombsites. There were front gardens and, here and there, a swing park. It was, she thought, an odd kind of a place. They stopped on a side road within sight of a plastic sign with flashing palm trees. As Róisín got out of the taxi, she noticed the driver slip Dolores something she put in her spangly bag. Maybe it was change, but she didn't think so.

'By the way,' she said, 'I'm Dolly when I'm out. You can be Rosie, that'll do rightly.'

Róisín thought Dolly was a stupid name. 'I didn't realise we'd be going so far from home,' she said, 'just for a disco. We must be nearly in Larne.'

'Well, you're here now, aren't you,' Dolores said, playing with one of her eyelashes.

Róisín glanced around to see if she could spot the taxi, but its lights were already disappearing round the corner and back on to the main road. 'Where are we anyway? There were loads of Union Jacks all the way down that road back there.'

'A wee flag's not going to hurt you, Rosie. Just don't let on you've got a Taig name, that's all.'

The Copacabana Disco Club was a great big shed of a place with a thin row of Christmas tree lights strung up over the door, even though it was already March. There was a queue of girls with pinky-bluey legs and anoraks worn over their skimpy frocks who shuffled slowly towards the man checking bags on the door. Inside, white lights whirled around the walls, making mist of the smoke in the air. There were no palm trees.

Dolores bought them both a vodka and Britvic. It smelt OK, but she'd never really drunk spirits before and wasn't sure how strong it was. She kept thinking she shouldn't be here, what with it being a school night and having lied through her teeth to Ma. Dolores had a glittery top on, and red wet-look hot pants. She'd drawn thick black lines under her eyes and then there were those lashes. Róisín was wearing hot pants, too, but hers were white and since she didn't have curves like Dolores did, she suspected that they looked more like gym shorts.

Once she'd knocked back her drink, Dolores put the spangly bag down on the floor and started to shimmy to the music, her fingers making circles in the smoky air, her body more snaky than it needed to be.

She threw her head back a lot, like she was laughing at something Róisín had just said. Except Róisín wasn't saying anything at all, with the music so loud. As for the music, she was surprised that Dolores liked it. She didn't think it was what you would call progressive at all.

Looking round, it struck her that there were an awful lot of men at this disco; a whole line of grown-up-looking men with crew cuts standing at the bar. More filled out, most of them, than the fellas that hung around the chipper on Rebecca Street. Well turned out, too. They were peering out at the dance floor over their pints as if waiting for their moment. The throwing the head back and the pretend laughing appeared to work because loads of men seemed to want to dance with Dolores. A fella would ask her to dance and, when she nodded, his mate would slip in opposite Róisín. It was like everyone was there just to worship Dolores.

Róisín began to get sick of this game. 'How are we getting home?' she said.

Dolores was still jiggling around, even though the latest fella had slunk off back to his pint. 'Lonergan'll be back when we're ready.'

'Is Lonergan the taxi man?'

'Taxi man? Aye, I suppose he is.'

There were a lot more syrupy drinks, the men paying now. Róisín couldn't hear what anyone was saying so she just smiled, which was easy because she felt all syrupy herself. Then somebody else came and danced with Dolores. She nodded to stay on at the end of that dance, and at the end of the one after that, and soon they were wrapped round each other. Róisín was dancing with his mate and, because she didn't want to get split up from Dolores, she just kept nodding too and then she kind of leant against him because it was easier to keep her balance that way. There was a bump in his jeans when they slow-danced and he nuzzled a bit at her hair. She felt quite proud of causing the bump, even though she didn't fancy him back.

It was only when the lights went up at the end that she sneaked a proper look at him. He looked as though they hadn't got the colour mix right when it came to his skin. He was blueish with a rash of red on his chin, and his lips were puffed out like little pincushions. He had the look of someone who was always cold, like the cold had stuck to him. He asked Róisín was she doing her Highers. She'd no idea what he was talking about, but she said aye anyway to get him off the subject of school. His sister was, he said. Highers, he said. Dead clever. All his vowels had the juice squeezed out of them.

'Are you Scotch, then?' she asked.

'Aye.'

His name was Ian. She didn't know too many Ians.

He asked did she mind if he put his arm around her. She just shrugged because it seemed a bit rude to say no since he'd asked, but really all she wanted was to get home. She hoped to God Ma had taken her sleeping tablets and wasn't waiting up for her.

Next thing, Dolores was tapping him on the shoulder. She was all breathy and her lipstick was smudged. 'I'm just borrowing Rosie a wee tick.'

Róisín tried to ask her when Lonergan was showing up. At first, she pretended not to hear and then she said, 'Brian? He's deadly. God knows where he's got to.

Probably drinking his head off in some club. He said he'd meet us later on.'

'What do you mean, later on? Dolores?'

Dolores spun around at her, and for a moment Róisín thought she might hit her. 'Dolly, you thick Arab. The name's Dolly.' She spoke right into her ear and the heat from her breath felt prickly. 'Me and that fella, we nearly done it in the car park.' She was all flushed and slurred, but there was a glitter in her eye that was the soberest thing Róisín had ever seen. 'Och, come on, Rosie. My one's best mates with your one. You said you'd be on for the craic. Sure you're late now, anyway. There's somewhere we can go, the four of us. Sure you may as well be hung for a sheep as a lamb.'

She got a good look at Dolores's fella, standing over near the door with his jacket on already. She couldn't think what Dolores saw in him. He looked a bit old. He looked a bit drunk too, but maybe that was just from being with Dolores. His eyes were thirsty when he looked at her. Like he wanted to drink her in with his pint. The last thing she wanted was to go anywhere, but she hadn't a clue where she was and no idea how to get home.

It was freezing cold outside, and nothing looked familiar. She had no idea what time it was, but it must have been late because there was scarcely a car on the streets. Ma would go nuts if she knew. At least, the old Ma would. Most of the houses were in darkness, but for the occasional glimmer in a downstairs window. There was street after street of back-to-back houses – similar to the ones at home, but a bit better-off looking. Then they passed a street with a gable mural of King Billy mounted on his white charger and brandishing his sword, where even the kerbstones were painted red, white and blue. She was afraid suddenly, and the shivering was only half from the cold. Ian began to rub her arm like it was some magic lamp, round and round in small circles like he was polishing it. He took off his denim jacket and draped it round her shoulders but, even though she appreciated the gesture, it didn't make much difference because the fabric was thin and the cold bitter.

The house Dolores stopped at was at the end of a row where most of the others seemed to be boarded up. Róisín began to wonder if they were in the right place at all. She wondered, too, how Dolores could get this dump of a street mixed up with the nice ones they'd been down earlier, but it must have been the right one because Dolores opened the door with a key she took from her spangly bag.

It was dead quiet in the house. There was a fire smoking in the grate and a music centre over by the far wall. One of the fellas went and had a look for the music collection, but there was only one record and that was the Bay City Rollers. Dolores said her sister used to listen to it, years ago. Nobody admitted they wanted that on, even with them being Scotch and that, until Dolores said, 'Sure throw it on anyway.'

Ian asked was there nobody else coming to the party. Dolores said they were a bit on the early side, but that it was her sister's house and Glenda would be back home soon, and that things would liven up after that. 'Anyway, isn't it nice to have the place to ourselves for a wee while after the disco? Sure yiz wouldn't say no to a wee court, would yiz?'

Róisín began to wonder about this Glenda one, what kind she was to be living in a place like this. She didn't realise that Dolores had a sister, much less one called Glenda. She wondered where Lonergan fitted in, whether he was Glenda's boyfriend maybe. Dolores took some candles out of one of the kitchen cupboards and dripped the wax on to saucers, placing one in each corner of the room.

The music sounded like it was coming from inside a tin can. *Bye-bye Bay-by, Bay-by goodbye*. A white bulb hung over the sofa with a plastic shade around it, shaped like petals. The sofa was stained, a mustard velveteen, and there wasn't even a carpet on the floor. Róisín felt ashamed of the place, for Dolores's sake. To be taking visitors to a kip like this. She wished they could get rid of the white light bulb because it was doing her head in. Then, as though she'd read her mind, Dolores turned it off. It was even worse with the light off. With the candles flickering, it looked like there'd been a power cut.

Róisín hated it all, the Bay City Rollers and the candles and her tummy rumbling and her head beginning to ache after all that vodka and Britvic. Dolores was generous with the beer. There was plenty of that: someone had left a pile in the corner – Tennent's and Bass and Smithwick's. Ian took a can in each hand and said cheers.

Róisín was getting really worried now about when the car was turning up. She began to work out in her head how long it would take to walk home, until she remembered that she'd probably have to walk through Tigers Bay to get there, and there was no way she was doing that.

By now, Dolores and her man were wrapped round each other. Dolores was making little moans that you could hear in the space between tracks on the album and her fella had his head buried somewhere between her boobs. Róisín caught Dolores's eye, even though she was trying not to, and the glitter was still there as she looked out over his head. She took him upstairs then, and Róisín wondered where that left her and the lift home.

It was a funny place to live. There was no sign of a life at all. No photos, no posters on the walls, no magazines, food, nothing. Just the candles, and the beer, and the Bay City Rollers. Dolores shouted down from upstairs that Glenda would be back soon with her man. 'She won't be too pleased if she finds you pair using up her fire on her. Yiz better come upstairs and I'll sort her out later on.'

Róisín didn't want to go upstairs in case it gave him ideas, but Ian seemed to guess what she was thinking and said not to worry. There was a strip light in the bedroom that hopped into life when he flicked the switch. It rained down a vinegary chip-shop light. The room was small, with two divans and wallpaper with little brown-and-orange flowers on it. There was a jam jar with coins in it, a bottle of Old Spice and a few other odds and ends strewn over the surface of a dressing table with a triple mirror. She sat on the end of a bed because there was nowhere else. He sat on the end of the other one.

They stayed there a while, not saying much, Roísín still wearing his jacket, till he asked did she mind if he switched the light off. She said she did, kind of, because she didn't want her bones jumped. He said not to worry about that too. It was just nicer to wait in the dark, he said. Because after all they both had to wait. Her for her lift, and him? For his mate, maybe.

The place smelt gassy. Damp, perhaps. Or something dead under the floorboards. A street light shone in, not quite like a moon.

'I'll be killed for being out this late midweek,' she told him.

'Aye, it's late all right.'

'So what brings you to Belfast then?'

'Just a wee bit of construction work,' he said. 'Don't mind it too much. It's not that different from home.'

'Same crap weather?'

'Same crap everything.'

She felt queasy from all the vodka and orange, and cold, even with the jacket on. He told her he was from Livingston, and she said, 'I presume,' and he said, 'Very funny,' even though he must have heard that a hundred times. He kissed her neck then, little soft kisses, and she pictured the lips like little pincushions and how it was them that was making this feeling she had. She relaxed then and let him just kiss her because it was easier than trying to figure out everything else.

She thought she heard the door banging downstairs. How would Dolores explain to Glenda about them drinking the beer and using up the fire and all being upstairs?

She pulled back from him and listened. He seemed to hear it, too, but then he just seemed to decide to ignore it and go back to kissing her. His lips were soft, and soon she was kissing him too and telling herself the sound must have come from some other house. She was lying down now, and so was he, and their legs were getting tangled up and she could feel the bump again, where it nestled in at her thigh. She started to feel she would like to touch it and they were kissing deeper now and wider. There was a hum in her head that blocked out everything else. The kissing made her someone who wasn't in Belfast any more, some place much warmer and brighter and greener. Like she was in that shampoo ad with the long grass and the sunshine.

Suddenly he stopped, and so did she. Her hearing was fuzzy, as if from underwater, but she felt his sharp intake of breath as if it was her own, felt his hands tighten as he held her at arm's length and listened. She sensed the danger, long before she'd had a chance to think it, when it was just a quivering of something in the air outside the room. Not quite a sound, not quite. And then, from just the other side of the wall, a thud, a gasp, a dull thump like a fist in a pillow. By now, he knew. He scrambled off the bed. 'No, no,' he was murmuring. 'Fucking no.'

He'd reached the window now, was pulling at the latch but he couldn't open it. And then he was desperately casting around for something to smash it with. Outside the door, men's voices. Dolores's too, high-pitched and over-excited. He was jabbing at the window, now, using his elbow. She flung herself against the door, to try to give him time. And then he found something that looked like it might be heavy enough to break the window. He was battering away with it when the men came crashing through the door and sent her flying.

It didn't sound like much, like a dart puncturing a board. But it got him. His body slumped back over the windowsill and fell heavily to the floor. She was kicking out now, kicking and kicking and kicking until the room, the house and even Belfast itself got lost inside her scream. One of the men had her by the hair, was dragging her out through the bedroom door. He flung her against the wall on the landing, just next to the banisters, as though she was a sack of rubbish they needed rid of. The wall rocked as her body hit it, and she thought of those houses on the telly, the ones in *Coronation Street* that wobble every time someone runs down the stairs.

She crouched there with her thumbs jammed into her eardrums, fingers pressed hard into her eyeballs, chin in her knees. And in the moment that she let herself peep out, she saw them go. Through the banisters, a pair of runners, dirty white with two blue streaks on the side, then a pair of desert boots. She heard them thud down the stairs and the scrape of something metal along the wall. It was then that she saw Dolores standing with the zip undone on her skirt and no tights on and a man who looked like Lonergan with his tongue in her mouth. Róisín shut her eyes tight again to get back to that lovely green field she'd been in before with the floaty music. But Lonergan wouldn't let her stay there. He brought her back into the bedroom, and when he'd made her see, when he'd smeared her with the soldier's blood, he flung her back out on the landing.

Someone half lifted, half dragged her down the stairs. She was clammy and cold and there was still the sound of someone who might be her, screaming. Next thing, she was in the back of a car and Dolores had her face too close to hers. Her lipstick was all smudged and her mascara made her look like a panda.

'Don't you dare boke your guts up in here,' Dolores said. It was only when someone gave her a newspaper to sit on that Róisín realised she must have wet herself. She couldn't understand how it had come to this.

'Are they both dead?' she heard herself say, but nobody answered. She could tell Dolores and the man were talking about her, could hear bits and pieces of it, even though it felt they were talking on the surface and she was down with the *Titanic*. Dolores saying she'd shut her up, not to worry, when he asked why the fuck she'd picked a spa like that.

When they got to Rebecca Street, Lonergan opened the back door and held her tight by the shoulders. She found it hard to hold her head straight but he rapped her cheek sharply and shoved her chin up to make her look at him. That was when she realised he was worried, scared even.

'See you?' he said, and his eyes – so green and sharp – taking in every scrap of her face. 'You done good.'

Maybe she pulled away from him or maybe her head dropped. Whatever the reason, he slapped her again. 'One word to anyone and I'll do you.' He let go of her then, and his voice was softer now. 'You done all right.'

Car door, engine and they were gone and there was no one there at all any more, not even her. Rebecca Street was silent, but somewhere in the distance the women were out clanking at the bin lids. There was probably a raid on in the flats. She leant against the wall and let the rain wash her face. The street began to take shape around her: the dark husk of Markey's Bar, a line of milk bottles, a Stewart's bag some wee glue-sniffer must have left. She noted these things in separate snapshots, went from one to the other, then tried them in a different sequence. Whatever she did, the things she could see just didn't block out the images inside her head. They all jangled around together in there, the normal things with the terrible ones, till she wished she had the nerve to scream. She held herself together, her arms crossed tight, hands clutching and pumping at the fleshy bits above her elbows until she realised she was still wearing a dead soldier's jacket. She shuddered, pulled it off, then flung it as far away from her as she could. It lay in a crumpled heap under the lamp post, gathering silvery droplets of rain while, way over to the west, the beam of a helicopter jerked across rooftops.

8

The hallway of her house was dark, with just a thin line of light visible from under Ma's bedroom door at the top of the stairs. Ma called down, her voice thick with sleep. 'That you, Róisín?'

When Róisín found her voice, it was a tiny far-off peep.

'Thangod.' Ma said it like she always did. 'At least you're safe. We'll hear in the morning.'

In the bathroom, she tried not to make too much noise for fear of waking Maura. She dribbled a little water into the hand basin, smeared a face-cloth with soap and began to wash. She scrubbed at the place on her forehead where Lonergan had blooded her. Around her breasts, between her legs, down her thighs and up over her buttocks. And all the while she avoided the mirror for fear of catching sight of herself. Not that washing would change it. Not that all the washing in the world could wash away a murder. She was doing that one for O level. She wrapped a towel round her breasts, another round her legs. Pulled the cord for the bathroom heater overhead and watched the two bars glow dark red, then fizz orange with a tang of burnt dust.

She sat on the edge of the bath, the towel tucked under her feet, then closed her eyes and rocked herself, smoothing her hands along her thighs to push back the thoughts and the sobs. She could feel the extent of herself, wrapped like this, small but complete. Not ruined. Not wrecked. Still here.

Then she was struck by a terrible thought. Ian might not be dead at all. He might still be there, moaning in agony, inching his way across the carpet. Calling for her. Cursing her for being a lying, deceiving, murdering bitch. She plunged her head into her hands, pressed down hard on her temples to block out the thought of him. What if he could be saved? She remembered there was a confidential number, but not what it was. She could find out, though. Wasn't it written up on all the billboards round the place? She could sneak out down to the roundabout and ring the number from the phone box there, if it wasn't smashed up. Maybe they would find him. Maybe someone would get there in time.

But she didn't even know where the house was. She knew nothing except for the Copacabana Disco Club, the black taxi, Dolores. She couldn't tell them any of that. She couldn't tell them about Lonergan either. What if she was the one to get the blame for it all? What then? Besides, there was no way either of them had survived. No way.

She made herself look in the mirror. Her face was stained with black tracks, like she'd been crying ink, not tears. And on her cheek, four bright-red fingermarks from Lonergan's hand. She looked mental, her hair all frizzed up, her eyes wild. She made herself squint right into the mirror. Keep on staring at the light till you can't see the pictures in your head any more. Don't look away. She stayed there for ages, just letting the light blind her. When her eyes were burnt out, she crept into the bedroom she shared with Maura and got into bed without turning on the lamp.

The next morning was a school day and, when Róisín awoke, Belfast was still there. The radio made morning sounds, and then the news came on. Soldiers had shot dead a joyrider on the Andersonstown Road. Two aeroplanes had collided somewhere far away and the Queen was in Australia. There was no mention of the night before. Nothing. They mentioned the rioting and the roadblocks, but not a word of Ian.

Ma bustled around, clinking jars of marmalade and jam from the cupboard on to the oilcloth where the sun made a little puddle next to the butter dish. Maura, her history book propped up against the toast rack, eyed her suspiciously.

'You look like death warmed up,' she said. 'Where were you last night?'

Róisín shook her head. She didn't have a name for it. Besides, she was afraid that if she opened her mouth to talk, let alone eat, she might be sick.

'Out gallivanting on a Thursday night?' Maura said. 'I suppose you were with that Majella one. Had you no work to do?'

Ma sometimes went all spacey when the doctor changed her pills, and that's how she was now. She was sitting at the other end of the table with her arms crossed, looking right past Róisín into the hallway beyond. When Róisín went out there to get her bag ready for school she could hear Ma and Maura, but mainly Maura, talking in rapid, low voices that stopped again once she came back into the room. She felt dizzy, and thought she might be sick. They watched as she gathered her things and slung her bag over her shoulder. It felt so heavy, and the distance between home and school, or home and anywhere, seemed so, so long. Ma got up slowly, like her sciatica might be troubling her again. She stepped forward and put her hand on Róisín's shoulder, so gently it made her want to cry.

'Will you tell us what's wrong, love?'

Róisín didn't look up. Even at the best of times, she avoided looking too closely at Ma for fear of picking up the sadness that clung to her face like a second skin. When she leant forward and kissed Róisín on the cheek, Ma smelt of Yardley English Lavender and Strepsils – for Róisín that had become the smell of sadness now. That was something that could be understood. Last night was not.

'I want you here at home tonight,' said Ma. And that was it.

At school, the girls took turns to ask her about her date, trying to guess which of the skinny fellas outside the chipper it might have been.

'Go on, spill the beans,' Majella said, her eyes like moons. 'Was it Brendan Farrell? Did you get off with him? Your ma was up to high doh when you weren't at the Bosco. You probably got murdered, did you? Did you get murdered?'

In class, she stared into the book on her desk. Her head was as gloopy as a raw egg and there was no way of fighting through the membrane that seemed to have grown up overnight inside her. She knew that the world was still there, as concrete and plastic as ever, but she just couldn't seem to reach it any more. As the lines on the page stretched and twisted before her, she sat pulling out hairs from the crown of her head, one by one, like bad thoughts. She gnawed at the knuckle of her index finger until there was a red welt on the side. She didn't eat. Not even the liquorice torpedos that Majella placed on her desk after lunch. Five brightly coloured sweets, squat as bullets, resting in the groove designed for pens.

Most of the time, Róisín managed to avoid Maura. They met at breakfast, but that was easy because Maura was always focused on the day ahead and barely noticed her. In the evenings, Maura studied late at the library in the training college even though Ma worried about her getting caught up in a hijacking or something like that. Three nights in a row, Róisín played dead when Maura opened the bedroom door, her blankets pulled up to her cheeks, her head burrowed into the pillow. She loved being in bed because it was the only place she didn't have to act normal. On the fourth night, Maura marched in and switched on the light.

'What's up?' Maura sounded pissed off, like she often did. She pulled back the covers but still Róisín lay there, even though she knew it would make Maura mad. She could feel the cold air settle on her legs, and then as Maura sat on the side of the bed, her body tipped a little.

With her instinct for the weak spot, Maura was rattling open Róisín's private drawer, the place where she kept her cash book and the card she got from Vincie Flynn last Valentine's, the closest things she'd had to secrets up until now. Now that she was beaten, Róisín lifted herself up on one elbow and rubbed her eyes. She heard Maura shove the drawer shut again. When she had gathered the sheets up around her, Maura was peering at her, arms crossed.

'What's wrong with you?'

'I'm just trying to get some sleep.'

'I said, what's up?'

'For God's sake, what's wrong with wanting a wee bit of peace.' She pulled the sheet up over her face, but she could still see the light through it and the outline of Maura, stubborn as a blot. Róisín didn't say anything else, and they must have stayed like that, Róisín still as a mummy and Maura just there, not moving a muscle, like she knew she'd win in the end. Sure enough, Róisín was the first to give in. She lowered the sheet, inch by inch.

'That's better,' Maura said, in that Miss Primmy voice of hers, the one she was practising at the teacher training college. She never knew when it was best not to push home your advantage.

'What do you want?' Róisín said. 'Now that you've woken me up.'

'Ma's worried sick you've gone and got yourself pregnant or you're on drugs.'

'Drugs? Where would I get drugs?'

'You're not hanging round with those fellas from the chipper, are you?'

For the tiniest tick of a second, she thought of telling Maura everything. Landing it all in her capable lap and asking her if she had any bright ideas. I've just killed a man, Maura, that's all. Happens all the time in Belfast, doesn't it? Not to worry. Never mind. Now, settle down and do your homework.'

Instead, she expressed a thought that she hadn't even realised she'd had yet. 'I'm leaving school. Sure what's the point anyway? There's no jobs in Belfast. And I hate this place. You can't even have a pane of glass in this city without it getting broke.'

She pulled up the sheet again and waited for Maura to soak up what she'd said.

'What's that to do with anything? You can't leave school without a single O level.' This was happening more and more often, Maura deciding to act like the parent now that Ma had gone all quiet.

'Why not?' Róisín said, from under the sheet.

'I can't tell Ma that. It'd kill her.'

'Tell her I'm pregnant then. Tell her whatever you like. Make something up.'

Maura pushed her on the shoulder. 'My God, but you can be one evil wee cow!'

Maura moved slowly towards the door, like each step was a separate thought. When she was gone, Róisín felt her mouth twist down and her face crumple and then the tears flooded back again. She waited and waited for Maura to return. So long that she must have fallen asleep. When she woke up in the middle of the night, she forgot that David Bowie was just a poster. He had a halo on him from the street light outside and for a moment she thought she was in heaven.

She was on her own when they stopped her, the two men who followed her home from school a couple of days later, their hands shoved deep in the pockets of their bomber jackets.

'You're not yourself,' said the one with the ghost of a tache, falling into step alongside her.

If she'd had the energy, she might have taken to her heels, but she felt flat, ancient, worn out. Instead, she kept her head down and hoped they'd go away. But nothing just disappeared, not in Belfast. Every time you looked, there was more.

'Word is, you're cracking up,' said the tache.

'What's it to you?' she said, still walking.

The other man, fat slob, was in front of her now, blocking her way. 'Take a look at yourself. You're in bits. You're a fucken mess, you are.'

Róisín stopped dead, made herself look straight at him. 'Not as much of a mess as that fella, though. Nothing like him. Haven't had my brains blown out. Not yet, anyway.'

Fat slob steadied himself, legs apart, stepping from foot

to foot like a boxer. 'Catch a grip,' he said, like he was catching anything. 'Stop acting like a fucken headcase.'

The other one told her she'd done all right, just like Lonergan did. He went to pat her on the back, but she shrank away from him.

'It wasn't me,' she said. 'I didn't know nothing.'

They didn't mention Dolores, which made it worse, like Dolores hadn't been there at all. And, at school too, Dolores had seemed more absent than ever, whiter and blacker, sharper and more shadowy.

She didn't know what to do about the tears that threatened to spill out on to her cheeks. She wouldn't give them the satisfaction, so she tilted her head to keep them back.

Eventually, the tache spoke. He put on the kind of voice you use for toddlers. 'I know it's a shock, like, the first time. But you've got to pull yourself together. Lonergan won't take any crap.'

The voice made her mad and the mention of Lonergan even madder. She spat at them. 'That's what I think of him.'

Next thing, they were wrestling her into the doorway of a boarded-up shop. The fat man was twisting her arm, making it hurt.

'See you?' he said, his voice hard now. 'You better wise up. Do you not know who Brian Lonergan is? He could screw you into the ground like that.' He made to stub out a cigarette with the toe of his boot.

'Look at the cut of ye,' said the tache, looking away from her like he couldn't stand the sight of her, like she was a lump of shite.

It crossed her mind that it was because she'd kissed a soldier. Maybe for them that was worse than killing one.

'Word's getting round about you bursting into tears at school, like you're mental.'

She told them to fuck off, even though she'd never said that to anyone before and she hated the way it made her mouth feel ugly.

'Oh, we'll not do that,' the fat man said, and she noticed the pale blubber around his waist as he reached up to scratch his ear.

Her head felt fuzzy now, and when she glanced up they were still standing over her. From the look on their faces, she could see that she was a problem, a fingerprint, a trace. Outside the doorway, people were still passing, like nothing was going on at all. She'd stepped over the line and left the normal world behind. Out there – those boys with their schoolbags, those women with their shopping, that oul' fella taking a drag of his fag – they were the normal people who worried about getting caught up in bomb scares, and whether the roads might be blocked off. She was on the other side now.

That night, there were helicopters in her head. She crept down to the kitchen and drank tea till her tongue was tinny with it. There was gunfire from somewhere over near the Falls, and out back, past Ma's peony beds and the broken-down shed where Da used to hammer things, the women were at the bin lids. She could hear them clashing against the ground like blunt cymbals. She put the radio on low and let the streams of fake misery shower around her. Song after song about hearts being broken, being torn between lovers, and nothing at all about the breaking and tearing and screaming inside her own head.

Once, when she was younger, she'd had her tonsils out. Da brought a flask of vanilla ice cream up to the hospital and, for a while, the sweetness had cooled her throat before the burning began again. If she could only talk to Da about it. Every time she thought of Da, it made her want to cry. She'd watched him shrink down to a string vest and a bag of bones, the expression in his eyes flatten out. In the end, he'd hardly had a word to throw to the cat. The words bubbled on his lips, but they rarely made it out of his mouth.

The sweet creamy music smoothed out the metallic sounds beyond the house until Belfast broke through and a newsflash told of an off-duty policeman shot in the Short Strand. She tried to work out a hierarchy of badness in her head. To kill someone you didn't even know just because of his uniform, was that the worst kind of killing? Did the hate in it make it burn fiercer than the other kind, where you didn't worry who you killed with your too-short warning? And what about when you let yourself be a sap for the killers when if you'd a titter of wit you'd have guessed what was coming?

The statements released to the papers always said the people killed were legitimate targets. She pictured them lined up in an identification parade. Shop girls and soldiers and barmen and taxi drivers. And Ian, who'd thought she was lovely. Once you're dead you're legitimate. Even though she'd promised herself she wouldn't let the thoughts come, they battered at her head through the music, the stupid, mushy music. How could Ian be legitimate when he spoke soft and had pincushion lips? When he had no gun on him and put his denim jacket round a girl's shoulders?

Even though she wasn't a smoker, not really, Róisín kept a packet of Black Cats in her bottom drawer for days when she wanted to be someone else. She leant on the back door that was never locked, even these days, and stepped out into the garden. It was only a patch of a thing, with flat white stepping stones through the wet grass to Da's shed. There was the frame of their old swing, the seat long gone, its struts colonised by Ma's creepers and climbers. These were thorny or bare for most of the year, cultivated for their brief yell in July. One windy autumn, Da had dug a bed in front of the kitchen window and Ma had planted bright durable things that kept returning each year, like plastic to a beach.

Róisín tried hard to smoke. Each time, it was an effort to get anything out of it, the smoke too bitter, too thick. She liked the idea of poisoning herself, though, sucking the evil into her until she became the same colour as everything else in this bloody place. It was a penance to do it. Smoking did nothing for her but add to the hollowness in her stomach and coat her gums with bitterness, but she kept on trying because Majella said you just had to persevere.

In the distance, a helicopter. It was somewhere over Lenadoon, she thought, its searchlight trembling then steadying, as though the thing itself was being led by the beam. It was raining mistily now, and the helicopter was getting closer. The noise of its rotors began to drill into her head. Then the beam was in her eyes, and the garden was gone. There was nothing but noise and white light and a strange mechanical hurricane. She was lime-lit, the star of the show. She almost laughed and she almost cried. Instead, what she did was scream. She threw back her head and screamed for everything that had happened. But even though she could feel the rasp of it at the back of her throat, her scream was nothing. The helicopter screamed louder still. The thing was whirring and blowing above her, whisking up the grass around her, whipping at her hair. It was getting so close that she thought it might shear the roofs off the houses. She felt she'd either be sucked up into it or crushed right down into the earth. Then she remembered that it didn't fly itself. There were eyes behind the beam. Laughing, maybe. Enjoying the hunt. She looked down at herself to see what they could see. Her nightie shone out around her like a parachute just landed. She had to hold tight to keep it from billowing up around her neck. Her heart like a tom-tom, she rolled away from the beam. It jerked for a second, then found her again, pinned against the shed. She turned her back, daring them to shoot her.

She could feel someone dragging on her dressing gown and then there was Maura, shouting and yelling at the helicopter, tottering around like she was doing everything in slow motion, her mouth all out of shape. She looked like one of the angry wee women you'd see at the barricades. Róisín felt a moment's respect for her, and forgot to be something small and white and fearful.

9

At school, Dolores was wearing a new ring on her finger. It flashed as she turned it over and back under the classroom's neon strips. She had a new friend, too. Teresa was a mousey wee one from the Markets, and Dolores used her like a barricade. It was as though she had never even spoken to Róisín. As though Róisín hadn't been the one she had chosen to come to the Copacabana Disco Club. And even though she had to hide behind a sap like Teresa, Dolores still walked with a swagger in her three-inch platforms. Teresa relayed messages to her, kept her sweet by telling her what she wanted to hear. Then, one day, Teresa was off sick. It was break time, and Róisín spotted Dolores mooching about on her own over near the cindertrack that overlooked the railway line. She got right up behind her before Dolores even realised there was anyone there.

When Róisín tapped her on the shoulder, she jumped. 'Eff off, you,' she said, and turned away.

Róisín wondered what she was looking at. There were hardly ever any trains.

'Dolly?' That got her attention.

'Don't you dare call me that.'

Róisín could tell she was rattled, even though she jutted her chin forward like a wee tough.

'You didn't mind at the Copacabana club. It was Dolly this, Dolly that.'

'I said shut your face or you'll have it shut for you.'

'You knew what was going to happen to those fellas. You tricked me into taking Ian there.'

'Who's Ian? Fucksake.'

'I didn't know what you were going to do to them fellas. I'd never have come.' She could feel her breath start to catch, and she hoped she wasn't going to cry. She wanted more than anything to hold it together until Dolores wasn't there.

'You knew fine rightly. Shoulda done anyway. And they weren't fellas.' Dolores looked around her to make sure she couldn't be heard. 'They were legitimate targets.'

That phrase again. Dolores was closer now, right up against her. She smelt of sweat and mints and something musky, left to go off. There was a big red blotch on her neck, next to a mole with a black hair wisping from it. 'They got what was coming to them.'

Dolores made to move away, but Róisín stayed with her, close by her ear. 'Did he give you the love bite?'

Dolores was walking faster now, heading towards the dinner hall and its meat-pie smell.

'Was it him? Do you remember what he felt like, Dolly?

I heard you – all them grunting and chugging noises you were making. Like the bloody Enterprise. I know. I was there.'

For a split second, Dolores hesitated. Then she rounded on Róisín, pinched hard at the soft flesh on the back of her upper arm. 'You're gonna end up in a tin of dog food if you don't wise up.' But her voice sounded different now, like the confidence had choked and died at the back of her throat.

'Do you see him, Dolly, when you try to go to sleep?'

Just for a moment, Dolores turned full face. Róisín hadn't noticed before how much she'd changed since the night with the soldiers. She looked like she'd hardly slept since. Her eyes were bloodshot, her skin pimply under the thick make-up.

'I bet you'll always see him.'

Róisín came across the same two words on every newspaper billboard that she passed while walking home from school.

Honeytrap Photofit.

At the corner of Frangipani Street, she grabbed the folded paper from the paperboy and shoved it into her schoolbag. She walked on with her head down and the hood up on her school gabardine, even though it was only drizzling. She hadn't looked in a mirror since the night it happened. The last image she had of herself was of wild hair and fright. She didn't dare see the darkness in her own face that she could see in Dolores. She didn't want to see a hardness in her own mouth that hadn't been there before.

Her hands shook as she brushed a strand of hair away from her eyes. Maura would recognise her face in one of the photofits, she was sure of that. Maura would have to listen to it all, then. It would be up to Maura to figure out what to do.

She hurried along Acacia Street. Past the home bakery with the pineapple creams and the baps, past Anderson's pub with its brown-and-green Grecian-urn tiles, past the burned-out TV repair shop, and the Wimpy bar with the giant plastic tomatoes on the tables, and Pat O'Boyle, Turf Accountant. Deep in her gut, there was panic. Now that she was in the paper, they'd be watching out for her. In Belfast, there were eyes everywhere. Snipers and touts, security cameras and Special Branch. Inside the traffic lights, listening at the doors, taking down the colour of your three-piece suite.

The sky was like potato water – it would be raining again by the time she got home. She clutched hard to the newspaper, still folded under her arm. She wondered how many policemen they'd send. She thought of Ma's nerves and hoped they weren't there already, a forest of RUC men in the front room sipping tea from the cups with the goldy rims. A wee chat? Or come the heavy right away?

That night, Ma clattered at the pans and clicked at the gas. Three pots, boiling furiously. When eventually the meal was ready, she began slicing a lump of purplish gammon, served up with cabbage and some floury spuds. 'We'll put Maura's aside for her.'

When she turned around to serve the food, her eyes rested on Róisín's stomach. 'You know you'll always be my wee girl.' She snapped a tea towel into two sharp folds, then sat down opposite and took Róisín's hand.

Róisín drew her school cardigan around her. 'I'm not pregnant, Ma.'

'Thangod.'

'And I'm not on drugs either, in case you're wondering about that. I'm just a bit tired, that's all.'

'Only a few weeks now till the exams, love. Just keep your nose to the grindstone and get a few good nights' sleep and, please God, you'll be right as rain.'

She knew then that Maura hadn't said anything about her leaving school. She was glad of that. Glad, too, Ma hadn't brought Da into it. It made her heart crinkle the way Ma's eyes wavered, then dropped to her shoes, whenever his name was mentioned. By now, Róisín was desperate to get a chance to see what was in the paper. She brought a mug of hot milk up to her room, then let a thick skin form on its surface as she pulled the newspaper out of her bag, where it had rested all evening like an incendiary.

She didn't know how they made up these photofit pictures. Did they have a catalogue of noses and mouths and chins, a selection box of eyes? She supposed they must do. The face looked strange and smooth, like something from the silent movies. Its features were like points on a globe. They were all in the right places, but there was nothing real about them. That mouth had never tasted anything. It hadn't lied or sucked or kissed. There was a nose you might have said was Roman, a helmet of black hair and, dominating it all, those expressionless eyes, cinder-black and neutral, gazing stupidly out of the page. But, even though it was just a shell of a face, Róisín knew that she was looking at Dolores.

Police are now convinced that just one woman was involved in the double murder last Thursday night, when two off-duty soldiers were lured to their deaths in North Belfast. Police are concerned at this revival of a tactic thought to have been abandoned by terrorists, and the atrocity has been strongly condemned by politicians across the divide. Witnesses have been able to provide an accurate description of the suspect, said to be of medium height and build and of Mediterranean colouring. The woman was seen talking to the soldiers in the car park of the Copacabana Disco Club in Altnamurry Road. Corporal Ian McNair was dancing with a number of girls at the disco itself but is now believed to have left the premises with the suspect whose likeness has been issued. Staff Sergeant James Gordon is thought also to have left in the company of this woman. The house where the killings took place is said by locals to have lain vacant for several years.

Astonished, she read the article again. And again. No one had remembered her. No one. Not the doorman, nor the barman, nor the other men she had danced with. Her hands shook, relief pricked at her eyes. It was all there in black and white, so that was how it would be from now on. One suspect. One face.

She felt the crown of her head and the little tufts of

regrowth that had started to sprout back where she'd been pulling out her hair even before all of this had started. She decided then and there that it was fair, this version of events. None of this was down to her. They had had her tanked up on vodka and Britvic. She'd wanted to go home from the start, but they wouldn't let her.

She went over to the window. There was nobody in the street outside. Just the blueish glimmer from Mrs McKeever's TV set across the way, and the weighed-down trees behind a screen of rain. By the time she'd drawn the curtains, the story of that night was already bedding itself down. She hadn't actually been in that house at all. Not really. So it was right that she hadn't been remembered.

If she'd been unlucky, if her face had been in the paper alongside Dolores's, there's no way that would have been the truth of it. There's no way a photofit could show who hated and who was the sap. As far as Belfast would have been able to tell, she'd have hated just as much as Dolores did. But she'd been lucky, and didn't she deserve a bit of luck after all that had happened? No one would ever wrestle that stroke of luck from her. Not guilty. Never even there.

She opened her bedside cabinet and had a packet of Maltesers to celebrate, dunking them in the warm milk and sucking at the softened chocolate. But then she thought of Lonergan, of the two men who had followed her home from school, of Dolores and her curranty eyes, and she was afraid all over again.

Next day, Dolores was gone.

'Down South,' Teresa said, barely breathing the words.

No one mentioned the photofit. No one said, 'Do you not think that was awful like Dolores?' Majella said she was probably off to join the da on the run, but Róisín didn't think she meant anything in particular by that. She pictured Dolores in Dundalk, in a wee job. A shop, maybe, or a factory. Sulking and spitting, getting fatter.

10

That afternoon, a car stopped alongside her as she rounded the corner into Claymore Avenue. The passenger window was wound down, and there was the fat man. Before she knew it, a lad in a Celtic shirt had got out of the back seat and was drawing her by the sleeve. She wanted to scream, but she couldn't. She went like a lamb. There were four of them this time. They put her in the back seat between the Celtic shirt and a man in a brown suit who kept his head turned away from her. Someone had BO. They'd driven a couple of streets in the opposite direction from home before anyone spoke.

The fat man said that she was shaping up great now. Word was she'd really got her head together. He smiled at her, but she couldn't bring herself to smile back. She needed a wee and squeezed her knees together, made herself even smaller so that she wouldn't knock against the men on either side of her. The man in the brown suit seemed to be shrinking away from her, like he didn't want her to see his face. The Celtic shirt sat with his legs wide open, his hands clasped at his trouser zip. She was trying to see out of the window, to work out where they were going, but the car was all steamed up. The brown suit sparked up a fag, which made things worse, and she wondered how the driver could see out to drive. Then he leant forward and tapped the driver on the shoulder and the car came to a stop.

She knew that she needed to concentrate very hard to work out what was going on. She'd already figured out that the brown suit was in charge and it frightened her that he didn't seem to want her to see his face. She had an inkling that she was better off while the car was moving, when they had something else to concentrate on and not just her.

The fat man in the passenger seat swung around to face her, his arm slung over the back of the seat. He said something about her not being actually, like, a volunteer yet. But then the Celtic shirt said that girls came in wild useful. The fat man nodded. He said the type of girl who doesn't draw attention to herself, who blends into the background, she's worth a whole truckload of flash fellas.

Even though her head was all messed up, she copped on soon enough that they wanted her because she was lucky. And because she felt lucky she was suddenly brave. 'No offence, like, but I don't really want to get involved.'

She didn't look at anyone when she said it, but she thought she heard a snigger, from the driver, maybe, or the brown suit. Celtic told her she was with friends here. People knew how she felt about the other thing. Not pretty, the other thing. 'Course it wasn't – we're not doing it because we're a load of psychos.'

The driver didn't say anything and neither did the brown suit.

But wouldn't her da have been proud of her, all the same, said the fat man. His wee girl, doing her bit for Ireland. Wouldn't it make his suffering worthwhile?

She wanted to snap back at him, to shut him up about her da, but she didn't dare. She shook her head and let her hair fall over her face so they couldn't see the tears. She heard the creak of the seat as the brown suit turned towards her, the mumble of the others among themselves. Out of the corner of her eye she could see him stub out his fag in an old Mild Virginia tin he pulled from an inside pocket.

'Sit up,' he said.

She shrugged herself away from him, turned her shoulders in on herself.

Celtic said she'd better do what he said.

'Sit up,' the brown suit said again.

She turned to face him, wiping her eyes with the back of her hand. He had tired skin and his eyes were watery blue. They scanned over her face with little interest, like she was just the latest episode in an exhausting day.

'You're not as green as you're cabbage looking, love. It might have dawned on you by now that we tell and you do.' He slapped the back of the seat in front of him and the driver turned the key in the ignition and set off slowly. 'Anyway,' he said, 'Lonergan will be on to you. He wants a word.'

The elation she'd felt when she saw the photofit was gone now, like the steam from a kettle. They dropped her off just a couple of streets from home. She gave them time to drive off before letting her body fall back against the wall of Cullen's Fancy Goods.

She tried to recall exactly what the man had said about her da and making him proud. She hadn't really known Da long enough to know what he'd hoped for her. She hated to think that Da might have been proud of her when she was so ashamed. And what did she know about Da anyway? No angel. Lovely singer. Gas man.

Things had started to go wrong for Da when Róisín was only wee. She'd been staying up in Antrim with her Auntie May: a fortnight feeding chickens, running wild through wet green fields. When she got back to Belfast, though, Da had been lifted, the settee was fucked and there were holes in the floor where the soldiers who'd come for him had prised up the boards. Later, Ma said that if it had been the winter you might have seen it coming, but summer nights don't feel like they can have any bad in them.

For days and days, their house was like Belfast Central. Politicians came and drank tea from the flowery cups Ma kept in the best china cabinet. A priest said the rosary. Men with funny accents took flash photos of Ma's flower-bed, the one with the big fat peonies. Everybody had a view on things. The grown-ups said there'd maybe be a White Paper or a Green Paper. The Boys would go ape. The whole city would go up in smoke. But when you boiled it all down, there was only one thing that mattered: Da was gone, interned, locked up for God knows how long. Meanwhile, strangers had taken over the good room. Ma said it was a wake without a corpse.

A couple of weeks later, they had their first holiday in years with money raised for the internees' families. They took the train all the way across the border to a great aqua-blue wonderland called Butlins. All week, while Maura swam and ate mounds of beans on toast with other hearty girls, Róisín thought about Da in his camp while they were in theirs. She asked Ma whether Da was called for breakfast through little horns on poles in Long Kesh. Ma said she doubted it. She said they did have chalets though, kind of. Except they were all thrown in together and there was no pool with mermaids at the bottom, no underwater king with a pitchfork.

Maura sang her Feis song in the Top Talents with her hands clasped together and a hairband on. She didn't win, but Ma said she was robbed. The girl who won was from Dublin. Ma said her smile was pure plastic, but to Róisín she looked happy as Larry. She looked like she'd never had a care in the world, tapping away with her feet and singing 'Yankee Doodle Dandy' at the same time, shaking a top hat and twirling a baton like an Orangeman. You could tell her da wasn't in an internment camp.

When Da finally got out, he just sat in front of the telly all day in his vest. Even Róisín could tell he wasn't really watching it. He didn't last long after that. Mrs McKeever said he died of a broken heart, but Ma said the cancer got the better of him because of all the bad thoughts and the lack of sleep and the noise he'd suffered in that place. All that, she said, was what rotted away his insides.

Da was never done for anything. Ma always said that was because he never done nothing. Even now, they mentioned his name a lot in the papers. Ma said it was because he'd died. He was a martyr for Ireland, because he never done nothing and yet they locked him up anyway and then he died. Sometimes, though, Róisín wondered. If he never done nothing, then why did he seem to know so many people who did?

She thought that again now as she considered the men in the car. Why did they all think so much of Da for dying if he never done nothing? It's not like he'd ever had a job. It's not like he'd written letters for people or filled in forms or given them advice. She just let the thought come to the surface, but she didn't take it any further. She didn't want to fiddle around with it in case it went up in her face.

Back home, Ma was rattling a pan on the hob, frying up something for the tea. The hall smelt of hot fat and air freshener. Róisín went straight up to her room to make sure the wallet was still where she kept it. It was a man's wallet really, but she didn't mind. Ma brought it back, one time she'd been to visit Da, and the leather had smelt like new school shoes. The harp on the front looked like it had been coloured in with felt tips. She was upset that it was a bit squiggly around the edges until Ma explained that he was shaky these days, that he'd done his best.

'He made it for you, Róisín,' she said. 'With his own hands. Look, turn it over.'

On the back there was an inky rose, with the words 'Róisín Dubh' in Celtic script beneath it. That's what she was for him: his little dark rose, his lovely girl, his cáilín deas. Maura pretended she didn't care, but she did. Maura cared about everything that Róisín got and she didn't. But then, because she was the older one, Maura got all the new things, and maybe Da knew that when he made Róisín the wallet.

She had a book in her bedside cabinet, hardback, with the words 'Cash Book' stamped in red. Inside were columns of Christmases and birthdays, First Holy Communion, 11 plus: milestones marked by money. These columns seemed to keep things in control even when things weren't. They seemed to cool her head, so she totted up the numbers, all the pennies and the pounds, and, as she thought, there was enough.

The easiest thing would be to go over to England. It was cheap enough to get the ferry, but she didn't like the English much. She hadn't met any in real life, but the people on the telly were all teeth, and they sounded way too pleased with themselves. As for the politicians who came to visit the aftermath of Belfast disasters, they understood shite. In England, too, the bombs would follow her, and maybe even Celtic or the fat man, if Lonergan could be arsed to send them after her. And even if he couldn't, people would wonder about her, whether she really was who she said she was or whether she had a wee job on the side, blowing up pubs. No, she wouldn't go there. Even so, she imagined standing at the back of a big hall where she knew nobody and nobody knew her. And, there on a stage in the distance, David Bowie like a long white streak, singing about planets where no one had ever heard of Lenadoon or Ballymurphy or Andersonstown. She imagined looking out at the world through David Bowie's eyes. One pupil swollen with possibilities and new worlds, the other narrowed and alert, keeping Belfast at bay. Maybe England wouldn't be so bad if you approached it like that.

Most of the rest of the world was boarded up, barricaded off by strange languages or great distances. In Scotland, every voice would accuse her in Ian's accent. As for the States, that wasn't somewhere you just went. If you went to the States you were gone for good, like Auntie May in Boston whose only trace came once a year at Christmas – a curly signature and a pair of green notes ironed nice and flat. Róisín felt the walls of her bedroom close in on her, her chest tighten. In the greying light even her oldest friends – her frayed old teddy, her Aladdin Sane poster – seemed to leer at her. It was Tuesday already. What could anyone do about anything by Saturday?

All the family documents were kept in an old breadbin in the concrete-shelved cubbyhole her mother called the larder. That evening, when everyone was in bed, she took out the passport with the green cover and the harp on the front that her mother had arranged for the parish trip to Lourdes with the spastics and the dribbling old people with the bockety legs and slipped it in the bag she'd already packed with her best jeans, a pair of runners, a couple of handfuls of knickers and bras and socks. She didn't know where she was going, but she wasn't planting no bombs.

The next morning on the way to school, she saw a car like the one from the other day. It was sitting outside the bookie's on the corner of Cecilia Street with its engine running. She felt bad that Majella would be waiting for her, but she just couldn't pass that car. She hadn't mitched off school before. Even last term, she wouldn't have dreamed of mitching off, but everything had changed now. She crossed the road and took a bus in the opposite direction from the stream of boys and girls yelling and giggling and chewing and effing and blinding and singing and flirting and scuffling.

Inside the bus, the windows were all steamed up and you could hardly see for the smoke but, just to be safe, she slunk down in her seat until they'd passed the gasworks and the roundabout and she was sure she'd not run into anyone she knew. She noticed a woman with a tartan shopping bag clocking the tie and the blazer so she took them both off, first chance she got, and shoved them in her schoolbag. At Donegall Square, she saw a travel agent's with a red-and-white plastic sign. There were package tours advertised in the window, and on the back wall there was a great big picture of the Eiffel Tower and another one she thought might be the Colosseum. But those were places you didn't go. Even if you had the money to get a package holiday to somewhere like that, you only went for a week or a fortnight or whatever. At the end of it you still had to come back. Maybe the best she could hope for was to get down South. She bought two newspapers and found a milk bar to shelter in out of the rain. It was nice in there and, because the people who ran it were Italian, you could imagine that you'd managed to leave Belfast. Hot water gurgled and steam hissed and there were two revolving tanks, orange for juice and white for milk. Each of the papers had 'Irish' in the title so she hid the front covers, in case one of the other customers gave off to her for reading Free State papers.

Dolores's photofit had disappeared from the front pages, but the news was still the same when you boiled it all down. Killing and bombing and wrecking the place. But Róisín hadn't bought the papers for the news. It was the ads at the back she was interested in. Housekeepers and nannies and things like that. She didn't care how much they paid, she'd do anything to get away.

11

They set a hijacked bus alight on Frangipani Street and a crowd gathered, waiting for the fuel tank to explode. All over Belfast, buses were like burning bushes. From a distance it was beautiful, but you wouldn't want to get too close to the fire. By now, her conviction that she would somehow get away from Lonergan was weakening. As she turned into her own street, she almost expected them to be there already. She pictured the men from the car, all clustered round her front door. She never thought they would send just the one saddo. But there he was, just before teatime, the fella in the Celtic shirt, standing on her step with his boot in her door. He let out a hurricane of a sneeze.

'Hayfever?' she asked, like she cared.

He took her arm, said the lads would be waiting. But she shrugged him off and opened the car door herself. You can only take so much fright.

On the corner, McGrogan's was caving in on itself, its

carcass still hissing after last night's bomb. In the entry, bin lids were piled up ready for bashing when night fell. Celtic was jumpy enough for them both. His driving was shocking: stopping and starting, then bucking off like a runaway horse.

From what she could tell, they were heading up to the posh part of town, up Malone way, where people spoke with marbles in their mouths. She'd lived in Belfast all her life, but she'd never been south of the Falls. She didn't know anyone who lived round here. These people wore sheepskins and silk squares and gloves with gaps for your knuckles. The houses looked like they'd grown there along with the trees. Solid and red brick, with fancy bits of turret. There were even pubs that hadn't been done yet.

A great jaggedy red-brick building sailed past. It looked dead pleased with itself. I'm above all of this, it said. I'm on my way to New Worlds. I bet that's the university, she thought. This time, his sneeze went off like a tornado, twisting him in his seat, and the car went sheering towards the kerb. All around there was beeping and blaring and the squealing of brakes. When she asked him where he was taking her, he looked up at her in the rear-view mirror, and then it hit him.

'Shite!'

He started rummaging around in the glove compartment with his free hand, then tossed her something that looked a bit like a black tea cosy. 'Put that on you, quick.'

He was bashing the steering wheel: a dead, fisty sound. 'You tell anyone I forgot the blindfold, I'll fucken do you.'

It wasn't really a blindfold. It was more of a hood. At first, she wore it low over her eyebrows like a Smurf, but Celtic wasn't having that. 'Pull it right down. Over your mouth so it keeps your trap shut. Then get behind the seat.'

She gave him the fingers when he wasn't looking, but she did what he said. The hood made her panicky. It smelt of human, like Celtic had his hand over her face even though he was still behind the wheel, jerking and swerving his way down the road. She forced herself to breathe, and soon she found she could do it without thinking.

She wanted to say that his driving felt even worse in the dark, but she kept getting bits of fluff stuck to her lips. Anyway, sometimes it's best to say nothing. Instead, she watched the stars that floated in and out of the blackness in her eyes. She gave up counting the turns he made. He never cancelled the indicator, so it just kept on clicking, like a time bomb from the *Beano*.

When they came to a stop, he turned off the engine and it ticked and settled. The seat in front creaked and the car door went thunk. Next thing, he'd opened the rear door alongside her, and was rapping her on the shoulder. This time she let him take her arm. No choice, when she couldn't see. They took a few steps together, then he told her to just stay where she was. All she could hear was the sound of feet crunching – gravel, maybe broken glass.

'What now?' she said. Out loud, she said it. 'What happens now?'

She stood there swaying, the stars still dancing away behind her eyes. She stuck her toe out into the gravel to make sure the ground didn't fall away in front of her and then she listened hard. No sound at all.

She started to swing her arms around to see if they hit anything. Nothing. In the distance, she could hear a siren streeling away. She stood there, her arms stuck out in front of her like a zombie. She could feel the rain, blobs of it on her forearms. Her chin started to wobble no matter how she tried to stop it.

One of her knees was rocking back and forward, and the rain was pelting down now. She pulled her arms in, wrapped them around herself. But even though she couldn't see a thing, there was an eye in her head and it kept telling her that he was still there, that others were there too, watching her.

'Come and get me!' she shouted. Her knee was rocking away like crazy now. And, even though it was nearly May, it was freezing cold. 'Get! Me!' She yelled it out so hard, she lost her balance and toppled over.

The eye in her head was right, because they picked her up soon enough. Hands gripped her armpits. It was like flying. And then the air changed: no rain, no cold any more. Something pillowy under her head and the hood drawn slowly away. Voices then, and a sun through the eyelids she kept squeezed shut. Maybe they would make it look like the other side had done her: twisting knives, romper room, a turn for everyone. But there were cool hands on her forehead, a wee whisper in her ear, sweet perfume. Somebody's girl.

'Ssooooh-kay,' said the girl. 'Ssooooh-kay.'

When she forced her eyes open they were all looking

down at her like she was something fallen out of a space-ship. She remembered Lonergan from the night of the soldiers, though she'd tried not to. He sat apart from the other three, doodling on the front page of the *Irish News*. His two fag-stained fingers matched the hair he wore long and tucked behind his ears. He might have been a bookie in his big bright tie and his car coat. You could tell straight off he was the boss man round here.

Celtic cracked open a beer and gave it to him while the girl got up and did a tour of the room, emptying ashtrays into a bucket. Róisín caught her eye a moment, but the girl flicked hers away and shut the door behind her.

The boss turned to Celtic. 'Well, go on then. Fuck away off. You're done now.'

Celtic skulked out of the room like he'd been kicked, and she was surprised that she felt sorry to see him go. That left just Lonergan, and a man who looked like some-body's uncle. Lonergan didn't even touch the beer. Instead, he poured himself a cup of tea that looked stewed to death. For the first time, he looked up at Róisín. 'Sit yourself down there, love.'

She waited while he stirred his tea with the end of a biro. He kept his eyes on hers, and even though she was desperate to break the stare, she didn't want to let him win. Holding his gaze was like holding her breath. She pretended to be invisible, and hoped that would help her get through this.

'I need a wee Saturday girl,' he said. 'I'm a bit short without Dolores.'

He joined his hands under his chin. It put her in mind

of a film she'd seen: a Yank in a mafia suit, a wee man on his knees, kissing, begging. Except there's no way she was doing any begging or that. No way.

'It's not my fault about Dolores. She's nothing to do with me.'

'Aye, well, it's her fault she's in the paper. I'll give you that,' he said, half to himself, stirring the tea again, not looking at her yet. 'Showing off, flashing her tits . . . Twenty, thirty people remember her dancing with them soldiers. Some Spanish-looking disco goddess, apparently. Whereas you . . . Nobody remembers you at all. You have to say there's some skill in that there, Brendan.'

Uncle cocked his head like he was considering the matter.

'Anyway, Dolores is no use to us right now,' Lonergan said.

'She's a great wee worker.' Uncle's face was red, his eyes all swimmy. But Lonergan looked at him like he was a cowpat, and he shut up.

Róisín felt the anger fizzing in her ears. She was underwater now, swimming further and further out of reach. She had to strain to hear what he said next.

'We've a job for you, Róisín.'

'No way.' It was out before she knew it. She wanted to tell him to stuff it, but she didn't dare.

'Excuse me?' He spun around and took a step towards her, all in a single move. She knew he wanted her to jump, that it might be better for her if she did, but some pig iron in her wouldn't let her do that. She kept her chin up and her mouth clamped shut.

Behind him, she could just about catch a glimpse of Uncle. He was shaking his head, a warning shake, but she said her piece anyway.

'I'm not one of youse.'

He didn't really look that put out, so she pushed a bit harder. 'I never swore nothing in front of no flag.'

'No need for oaths and flags. This is just a wee one-off for a girl who can keep her head down. Normally I'd get Dolores to do it, but, like I said, she's out of action for a while.'

'Them fellas –' she started.

'Soldiers,' he said. 'Legitimate targets. They were fucken eejits actually, getting caught out that easy. Nobody likes all this. Except for the head-the-balls like Brendan here, of course.'

Uncle looked like he wasn't sure that was a compliment.

She said nothing. If she just let him blather on about what heroes they all were, if she just let him lecture her, then maybe he'd forget all about his wee job. He moved and she jumped and that seemed to please him. He was jabbing the air with a finger and she noticed his nails, all bitten down to the quick.

'We'll show you what to do, and afterwards if you want to get out we can arrange that. Right, Brendan?'

Uncle said nothing.

'Out where?' she said, without meaning to.

'Oh, there's lots of places. Right, Brendan?'

Uncle didn't look too sure.

'Brendan?'

'Aye. I suppose we could get her out, all right. If it came to it.'

'But first, there's that bit of work, Róisín.'

She felt her upper lip quivering, like it had lost the will to stay stiff. A clattering outside in the hall made her jump again. A clattering and a horrible wailing sound. Uncle moved quickly to open the door, and she glimpsed two men as they spilt along the hallway. They had a smaller figure with them, hooded and stumbling.

'Get that bitch the fuck out,' Lonergan shouted. 'I told you I didn't want her brought here. I told you to take her straight to Peggy's.'

Róisín saw that the woman had lost her shoes, and was being bundled along in stockinged feet. She'd been thinking that they didn't really do anything to women or girls. Now, she was beginning to realise she couldn't take anything for granted. The night with the soldiers flooded back: the dirt and the cheat of it, the grimy meanness of it. The noise and the hate and the desperation to hang on to whatever it is that makes you take one breath after another. Then, all quiet. Over. Gone for good.

Róisín must have screamed because Lonergan was on to her now. He slapped her hard. Her head jolted backwards and her cheek smarted. His face was so close to hers it was an angry blur.

'I've more on my plate than you. Do you hear me? You'll do as you're told.'

He left the room then and the door slammed behind him. When Lonergan was gone, Uncle sat next to her. He smelt faintly of chips.

'It's no great shakes,' he said. 'A kid could do it.'

Outside, the night had drawn in and for the first time she noticed the mesh on the windows.

'Davey and Reid's,' he said. 'Ladies' Fashions. Saturday, just before closing.'

She opened her mouth to say something, but the fight had gone out of her. He said there'd be a warning. No problem with that at all. The idea was to do five shops in a row. But he'd have to see.

'They'll search your bag at the gates into Royal Avenue and again on the way into the shop. You'll have it on you. You need to wear a pair of them oul' granny knickers. Your ma might have some hanging round the house. Long johns, you call them. All you do is stuff it in the gusset. You try something on in the changing room. Take the yoke out. Plant it where I tell you. And then you go. Like I said, it's a piece of piss.'

She loved Davey and Reid's. She loved the way the floors upstairs creaked. She loved the sparkly chandelier and the perfume counter with the posh Prod girls made up like air hostesses. Most of all, she loved the marble staircase and the enormous golden mirror on the landing, all covered with little fat angels and bundles of plump fruit.

'You heard what the boss said. There might be a wee ticket out, maybe, if you play along.'

She imagined herself on the deck of a ferry, sailing off into the sunset to where David Bowie was, standing there waiting for her. As for the job, she could always fuck it up, couldn't she? That would be easy. She'd just say yes, and get the ticket off them, and then she'd do it wrong. Once she'd decided that, she felt a bit better.

Uncle dropped her off at the end of her street. When she got home, Mrs McKeever was sitting with Ma at the kitchen table.

'Long time no see,' she said, peering out at Róisín over the top of her glasses. 'My Gawd, she's awful failed, Joan,' she declared at last. 'A wee ball of butter she was once. Are you not feeding her? Put on a drop of scald, there.'

Next thing she was out of her chair, taking Róisín's hand, stroking it, squeezing it, and Róisín was afraid she might burst out crying right there on the spot.

'I think it might be a broken heart. Am I right, Róisín? You tell me his name and your Auntie Mary'll sort him out. Don't you be wasting your time on fellas. Get your exams, for they're your ticket out.' She turned back to Ma. 'Is she working hard, Joan?'

Ma shrugged as she swirled the leaves round in the pot. Then Mrs McKeever sparked up a fag and Ma sparked up the telly and Róisín was forgotten. Ma sucked up news wherever she could get it. Round the shop, after Mass, *Scene Around Six*, *News at Ten*. Mrs McKeever was still talking, the red bow of her mouth stretching and pursing, but Ma turned up the volume till the blast of *News at Ten* filled the room.

'We'll be top of the bill tonight,' she said, settling herself in her chair.

After the bongs and the gongs and the clatter of typewriters that passed for music, there was Belfast. It was still raining, even on the telly, and the screen was full of flags: Union Jacks and Red Hands. A wee fat man read out a statement. Behind him stood a solid wall of men in shades, like the sunshine in Belfast would blind you.

'If them'uns kick off again, we'll be back to baked beans and primus stoves,' said Mrs McKeever.

'Sure they got nowhere with that nonsense last time. Damp squib.'

'Aye, maybe not. But what about the time before that? Make sure you get your candles in, Joan. Thick as champ but fingers on buttons in the power stations.'

And Róisín remembers another news bulletin, another wee fat man, and him reeling off the list of places where Da never had a job and never would have got one, even before he was interned. Shorts and the shipyards and Mackie's and the Sirocco down the road.

'Away in the head,' said Ma. 'Sure don't them'uns have the whole place sewn up anyway? Alls we ever get's the scrag end of everything. And people wonder why we need the Boys.'

'All very well,' said Mrs McKeever, 'till you've blood running in the gutters. Till there's young ones losing arms and legs. Till we're all as bad as each other.'

And Róisín was half listening to them and half watching the telly and it was all jangling around in her head. She realised, then, that none of it ever stops. Not the burning buses, not the men in shades.

She'd had enough of guns and hoods and everything good always blown up or burnt down or broke. She wanted out. She thought about what Lonergan had said.

She imagined somewhere it didn't rain so much, where things weren't always getting wrecked. Davey and Reid's was just a lump of bricks at the end of the day. She'd be sorry about the big gold mirror and the staircase, but it would be daft not to do one wee job, if that's all it took to get out. Liverpool, maybe, or even London. A bit of peace, and lovely things around her: silk see-through blouses and strawberry pavlovas and Italian high heels. But what if things went wrong? What if people got hurt? She couldn't bear the thought of that.

12

On Saturday morning, Uncle was waiting for her at the corner of Frangipani Street. He jerked his thumb towards the back seat and she sat in there behind him. He said he wanted her to have a trial run. 'You didn't think I'd start you off on the real thing, did you?'

She was so relieved she felt the tears prick at her eyes. 'Not real?'

'Ah no, I've just a wee dummy for you today. See how you get on. Stick that at your neck,' he said, and passed her back a brown-and-cream scarf. Silky, with big soppy-looking horses printed all over it. 'It's a sophisticated kind of a look you're after.'

As for the package, it was small, rectangular, solid. Much heavier than you'd think to look at it.

'Did you wear your ma's long johns like I told you to?'

She nodded.

'Well, just stuff it down there then.'

She slipped in behind the back seat. The package made a great big bulge, hanging down between her legs.

'Hold your head up when you walk in,' he said. 'Look like you own the place. You're headed for Ladies' Fashions. First floor. Dresses and that. Just ask to try something on. Go to the fitting room over near the windows. There's a wee shelf high up behind the door. That's where you'll leave your parcel. If it's still there when we come to find it, I'll know you've done good.'

He dropped her off at the City Hall, right in the centre of town. It was awkward getting out of the car, and even once she'd managed that, it took her a while to get the hang of the walk. She moved carefully, her thighs pressed tight against the thing that was hanging there half-born.

At the security gates into Royal Avenue, a woman with a boy's haircut felt her up and down and peered into the empty shopper. She smiled at the dote with the lovely hair and the angel face. 'Are you having a wee day out shopping, love?' she said.

Uncle had told her not to be making conversation with people, and to keep her head down, so she just nodded and moved on. The woman was nice, though. 'It's well for you,' she said.

And all the while, Róisín's heart was battering with the knowledge of how different she really was from what they thought. She stepped into the revolving doors of the shop, and her bags were checked again by a man with a bald pink head. Ma's old shopping bag with the faded red stripes looked all wrong beside the patent handbag next to it but the security man didn't say anything, just ran a black wand over it and nodded her on.

At the perfume counter, a girl with big white teeth sprayed something at her that smelt like the Parma Violets Maura liked to suck when she was doing her homework.

All across the ground floor, security men had spread themselves in among the shoppers, patrolling the aisles, turning their heads this way and that. Everything in the shop seemed hushed, padded, expensive. Even the music from the grand piano that nestled in under the huge winding staircase belonged somewhere else. The lady massaged the keys, making loose, lazy chords while Róisín's chest felt tight enough to burst. Maybe they knew all about her. Maybe they just hadn't published her picture because they wanted to catch her red-handed. They might even be following her right now, just waiting for her to put a step wrong. There must have been some-body who recognised her from the disco, the night of the soldiers. How could nobody have remembered her face? Was she that ordinary? She stopped at the bottom of the stairs, and almost turned back. But then she thought about the ticket out.

As she mounted the staircase, the old boards creaked beneath the deep pile carpet. It was difficult to climb, with the weight hanging between her thighs. She stopped a moment to gather herself, looking down into the shop below where people went about an entirely different life from hers. It was like a village where everything was tidy and beautiful: a lady with a blonde bun stood by a stand of jewellery that winked in the light of the chandeliers;

another with a neat brown perm tended a glass case packed tight with gloves. There were twin girls in velvet, an old woman with a hump and a tiny purple hat. Róisín had come here herself once at Christmas with Da, a special treat to visit Santa's Grotto. They'd stopped on the landing, right in front of the huge curlicued mirror with the golden angels perched on top, and looked down into the magnificent shop below. Róisín had twirled round and round in front of that mirror, making her skirt spin out until she was dizzy with laughter.

At the top of the stairs, she turned right into Ladies' Fashions. She stood by a rail of dresses while she tried to see where the fitting room might be. Now that she was here, she wanted it over and done with. But her body didn't seem to want to play along. She was dying for a wee, and her stupid hands just wouldn't stop shaking. She jumped sky-high when an assistant, an oldish woman with mauve hair, seemed to beam up out of nowhere. 'Can I help, madam? Or are you just having a wee browse?'

'My cousin's wedding,' Róisín blurted out. 'I'm looking for an outfit.' Her face was burning up because there was no way the pastel lady was swallowing that someone like Róisín Burns shopped in a place like this. But the lady just smiled and started flicking through the dresses, scraping the metal hangers against the rail.

'It's a bit on the mature side, that collection,' she said. 'The peach is lovely, though. What about this one, here? Fitted bodice, bias cut, jacket to match. Ideal for the wedding season coming up. Would you have a wee try on? You would? Yes? Right you be.'

The woman led her towards a row of white-and-gold-panelled doors. She gave her a scarf to use so that she didn't get foundation all over the fabric, and left her to it.

Róisín pulled off her jumper and skirt and slid the dress over her head. She glanced at herself in the mirror. She looked terrible. Pale and skinny, with blueish rings under her eyes. Just as she was about to fish the package out of her drawers, the mauve lady came back. She rapped at the fitting-room door, and when Róisín opened up, she was standing in the doorway, beaming. In her hands was a hat. Sky blue, with feathers from some purple bird. She crowned Róisín with it and stood back to admire her work.

'You just have a look at yourself, now, in that blue. You're a picture. Who is it you remind me of? *Dial M for Murder*. She killed him with the scissors. Went off and married a prince on the Continent.'

When the woman had left, Róisín tore off the clothes. She couldn't get them back on the hangers quick enough. Her hands were shaking so badly the fabric kept slipping off. She could hardly see for the blur in her eyes, but she stood up on the rickety gold-painted chair anyway, and shoved the package as far back as it would go on the shelf above the fitting-room door. And then she made her getaway, hoping to God she wouldn't be spotted again by the assistant.

'No good?' the woman called after her.

She glanced back, and the woman was smiling, her cheeks plumped up into tiny plums. 'Oh well, next time.'

But there wouldn't be a next time, because Róisín had

already decided there was no way she could do this for real.

She couldn't have been further than the City Hall when the flames began licking at the fitting-room door. Ten minutes later, the whole of Ladies' Fashions was engulfed. Róisín didn't go straight home. Instead, she went to Majella's house, where they tried on make-up and listened to Radio Luxembourg. The first she heard of the fire was from the newsboy calling the headline on the corner of Rebecca Street. By the time she got home, she was hysterical. She went straight to her room and buried her head under the pillow.

The next day, Celtic stood on her doorstep and muttered something about a new formula, about them not getting the mix right yet, about the timer, as though it could be all of these things at once. 'Trial and error,' he said, and then he sneezed. Pollen, he said. From the grass. He handed her a bus ticket. Dundalk, it said. Sure that was only over the border. What use was that?

One look at her face and he was in, quick as a flash. 'They've got you a wee job, too. Dog food factory.' He had this weird look on his face, and then she realised that she hadn't actually said anything yet.

'How did it just go off like that?' she said finally.

He looked at her like she was a headcase. 'See you, you're always talking through your arse. I suppose somebody else must have done it. Just like them soldiers. Because you didn't know what was going to happen then either.' He turned away, like he was talking to some invisible mate. 'My Gawd, but she's something else, so she is.' He paused and took a long look at her. 'What did you think you were planting? Tulips? Just take the bloody ticket and get out of this hole. You done your bit.'

'Dundalk?'

'Aye,' he said, offended now. 'Why? Not good enough for the likes of you?'

The mauve lady was in the paper, all wrapped in white linen like an Egyptian mummy. Celia was her name. They said she was lucky to have survived.

Ma got home later than usual. She struggled through the door with two string bags bulging with tins of soup, Heinz spaghetti and God knows what. She was huffing and puffing and, as she dumped her bags, one of the tins rolled right across the kitchen floor and under the table.

'It's bedlam out there, so it is. Roadblocks everywhere. City centre sealed off. The power could be cut off any time now.'

She'd just managed to boil up the kettle and flop into her armchair when the lights went out and the fridge stopped dead with a shudder. 'Well, that's just great,' she said. 'It's like the whole place is shutting down around us.' Her voice sounded different with the lights off: closer, louder, older.

Even though Róisín had stopped listening to what Ma was saying, her voice still filled the room until she turned in for the night. For a while it was quiet, but then there were other voices. The man who'd checked her bag, the mauve lady, the girl with the perfume that smelt of Parma Violets. Yelling, screeching voices.

She sat in the dark to empty her head, but the fire was

everywhere inside her. She was filled with screams. She clamped her hands over her ears to try to block out the racket. When that didn't work, she scrabbled around in the drawer at the end of the kitchen table for some matches. She fizzed one match off the other as she trailed round the room in search of the candles Ma had bought, then melted the bottom of one so that it would stand upright in a jar.

At first, gazing into the candle flame seemed to quieten her. This flame was kind, holy even. But soon her attention shifted to the wick. Bent double, it carried the flame on its back. Before she fully realised what she was doing, she had placed her finger next to it, in the centre of the flame. She bit into the fist of her other hand to force herself to keep her finger there until she could bear it no longer and the flesh began to smell. It was the least she could do: know what it felt like to burn.

13

There was no way Róisín was going to Dundalk. She
wasn't going to school that week either. Her hand was in
agony. Ma tried to make her go to the doctor, but she
couldn't think how to explain what had happened. It
started to feel like the world was ending. They said that
soon there might be no electricity and people would be
living on cold soup and cornflakes. She began to carry
Da's wallet with her everywhere. She wanted to be ready
so that if the chance came, she could take it. As it happened, the chance came crawling after her, all the way
down Bangalore Street. Uncle, in yet another car.

'Hop in,' he said.

She was scared, but she got in anyway. She was wrecked
from lack of sleep on account of the finger throbbing all
night long, never letting her forget Celia and her burns.

When she was settled in the back of the seat, Uncle
turned off the ignition. He spoke to her through the
rear-view mirror. She was getting used to that. She

couldn't see his mouth – just his eyes, and they were bloodshot. She was expecting an apology, but she didn't get one.

'Forget Dundalk. There's been a change of plan. We've had enough drama with Dolores.'

She wanted to ask what was up with Dolores, but she couldn't bring herself to mention the name, any more than she'd walk under a ladder. 'You'll get your ticket out. Not down South though, nor England either. We've too many fish to fry over there.' He was fumbling away under the passenger seat, and then he pulled out something black.

'You don't mind a wee hood, do you? I'll stop round the corner and you can put it on and get down behind the front seat.'

'If I'm not going to Dundalk, then –'

'You got lucky.'

She saw that he wasn't joking, though that didn't mean he was telling the truth.

A Saracen came alongside, while a little way ahead a reversing lorry was holding up the traffic.

'Fucken eejit,' said Uncle. He kept clicking his ring against the steering wheel in time to the indicator.

And then she remembered what Lonergan had said about Uncle being a head-the-ball. She was learning when to be scared and she was scared now. Of course she wouldn't be let out of Belfast just like that. A ticket out costs a load of money. Way more than a bullet. She went to open the door, but he'd thought of that already. It's not like they were in some deserted street, though. There were plenty of other cars around. If she banged on the window. If she yelled her head off.

The Saracen had pulled in ahead of them now. Two soldiers sat at the back with their rifles dipped out into Belfast. She thought she saw a hand waving at her from the darkness inside. Automatically, she waved back – a frantic, childish little wave, as if polishing a pane of glass. Uncle glanced up at the rear-view mirror, and his face changed.

'What the fuck are you waving at? Jesus, but you're some daft wee bitch.'

When the lorry moved off, so did the Saracen. And maybe no one had been waving at all. Uncle was jumpy now, and that made her jumpy too.

'You know the score, Róisín,' he said. 'Just take deep breaths. You'll be fine. We're not going that far.' He looked away, scratched his neck, then took a roll of brown packing tape out of the glove compartment. She tried to scramble away from him, but he grabbed her fist and held it tight. 'Believe you me, there's no other way. You've been lucky, so you have. You'll be all right where you're going. Just do what you're told.'

'Not so I can't breathe.'

He took both her wrists and started to bind them. 'Don't start playing up on me now. You'll breathe. We need to hurry up. Lonergan's in a shite fucken mood and you've got a lift to catch.'

He wasn't even trying to be nice, now. Just wanted the back of her. The longer she was in the car, the more some things made sense. The more there was to be scared of, too. He must have known it was a real bomb. He mustn't have cared if it went up in her face. And she was starting to understand that, while they could have her blown up by her own bomb, they couldn't just shoot her. They must be pissed off she was still alive and causing them all this hassle. And who exactly was Da, anyway? It would answer a lot if she knew that. She really wanted to ask Uncle. Who was my da really? How come everybody seems to remember him? But maybe whatever magic Da had had was gone now. She stayed still while he taped her wrists together and her mouth shut, and put the hood over her head. She allowed herself to go limp, let him put her in the boot of the car, and told herself that at least it would be quick.

When they opened the car boot again, there were two of them at least. It felt like they'd driven a couple of miles, but for all she knew they could have been going round in circles. She felt two hands at her shoulders, two more at her knees. The men carried her a short distance but once she was indoors they set her on her feet and told her to walk, that there would be stairs and to kick her foot out to find the first step. Very slowly she began to climb. Two feet, then one. Two feet, then one. It was hard for her to manage the narrow treads with her hands still tied. Once or twice she stumbled, which was when she realised there was still one man in front of her, another behind. From the smell of beer, the distant buzz of conversation, she decided there was a bar downstairs, or maybe a shebeen. But upstairs?

They pushed open a doorway and put her down gently enough on a rickety chair. Someone whipped off the hood and it took her a moment, wincing in the light, to realise that Uncle had already started sawing at the tape on her wrists with a penknife. The light was grey-bright and washed everything out until gradually the details of the room revealed themselves. A scattering of chairs and a cluster of old bar stools. Windows on two sides. And there in the corner was Lonergan, sitting at a table piled with newspapers and mugs, a rumpled blue sleeping bag laid out on the floor behind him. He leant back in his chair, then took a fag out of the packet and tapped the tip of it on the table. He didn't mess about.

'I'm sending you away,' he said. 'You're going to work for my brother in a place called Queens, which is in New York.' He seemed to be expecting a reaction, but when she didn't say anything he just kept on talking. 'I bet you like the sound of that.'

She was so shocked she didn't say anything at all, but Lonergan wasn't really waiting for an answer.

'Well, just let me tell you something. This won't be any holiday, not with Joe. You'll work for him. He reports back to me, so you'll do what he says and earn your keep. Look after his kids, wipe his arse, suck his dick, whatever. There's just one wee catch. Once you go, you're gone for good. You can't ever come back.'

Róisín was trying not to cry. Getting out, properly out, should have felt amazing – but for ever? She had never even tried to imagine that far ahead.

'What about Ma?' she asked, her voice very small.

'Don't worry about your ma. She'll listen to me,' said Uncle.

'Why would she listen to youse lot? She doesn't know you from Adam.'

'She knows us well enough,' said Lonergan.

'Your da was a great friend to me,' said Uncle.

Da again.

'Aye,' said Lonergan. 'If it was up to me, you'd be dog food.'

Uncle drove her to the car park behind Stewarts supermarket and she was taken straight into another car. Two fellas in the front, Róisín in the back, and that was the end of that. Uncle stuck his head in the window before they drove off. 'You watch yourself with Joe now. As for your ma, she knows all about this, so don't worry on that score. Leave it six months or so till you get in touch with family. Let things die down a bit.'

And then he was gone, not even shaking her hand or wishing her luck, and she still hadn't had an answer to any of her questions. She hadn't had the nerve to ask them in case the answers hurt too much.

14

Half an hour out of the city there was a roadblock. The car was stationary for ages and she thought about making a run for it. In the end, though, she decided it wasn't worth the risk. And where would she run to anyway? She'd overheard them talking about the boot of the car and whether that was the place for her.

'Makes no odds,' the skinny one said, 'she's not coming back.'

'Serious? That wee girl?'

'No, you daft fucker, not like that.'

She'd only been down South twice before. They gave her a running commentary once they got south of Newry. Who lived where, and what they'd got away with. Your man with the Hiace van and the underground tanks full of smuggled red diesel. Your man who was the bane of the lives of all the excisemen. The huge gates some hood had nicked from a church and put up in front of his bungalow. The safe house Sean Fry stayed at, the whole of last year. The skinny fella sounded breathless when he mentioned Sean Fry, like Sean Fry was some sort of god that even a gom like her would have heard of. There was a map of those fields that only they could read.

The driver asked if they were headed for Jonesboro. He mumbled it, like it was bad luck to say it out loud.

'What kind of a question is that?' said the skinny fella. 'Sure isn't she sitting up there in the back like a wee princess. VIP, this one.'

The driver took his eyes off the road, looked at her for a long time in the rear-view mirror and sniffed. 'A wee bit further down the road then?'

'She's going all the way. Peggy's place.'

'Dublin? Are you sure?' He took another look at Róisín.

'Aye, I'm sure. You know whose daughter she is?'

'Serious?'

Róisín noticed their mood had lifted, now that they were south of the border. Once they'd passed Dundalk, there was less talk of names and places. There was less talk altogether.

The man in the passenger seat kept farting, then winding down the window. If the driver noticed, he said nothing. Neither of them seemed to think to turn on the car radio. Just beyond Drogheda they seemed to leave the North behind. The land broadened and the houses looked better off, with hedges and gardens with shrubs and flowers.

She didn't know much about New York. There was Kojak and skyscrapers and real leather jackets. She thought of Aladdin Sane, too, though she didn't think he'd anything to do with New York. She felt like Aladdin Sane, with his two different eyes. One of her eyes saw Telly Savalas. He was licking a lollipop, cruising in among the yellow cabs and the big shiny Chevvies. The other one saw Ma, stirring the tea in the pot and crying like she did when Da died. She felt all mixed up, excited and scared, and she decided to try not to think about it any more.

She began to study the backs of the men's heads instead. The accents weren't local. Derry, in the case of the driver, or Donegal. The man in the passenger seat was Southern, but she couldn't tell where exactly he was from. She wondered whether this was a regular job for them, like being a breadman, driving people that Lonergan wanted out. Everyone knew about the nutting squad and how there was a house somewhere down here where terrible things happened with pliers and black bin bags and bodies dumped on border roads.

They seemed nice enough, though she'd learnt that you couldn't tell a person's actions from the look on their face. She'd searched her own face, night after night, for traces of what she'd done, but her eyes looked as clear blue as ever. She glanced at the driver's hands clamped on to the steering wheel and wondered why they looked so ordinary. Why did none of the things he'd done show up on the surface? Was there a terrible itch beneath the skin? A tic in the eye?

She examined her own hands laid out, palms down, on her skirt. They were pretty and little and she'd always liked them. It gave her some satisfaction to notice that they weren't perfect any more. The ring finger was all reddened round the nail, where she'd taken to pulling off little bits of skin along the rim of the cuticle. And there was the burn, scabbed over now, on the outside of her index finger. There was something in that, she thought.

The two men seemed wrapped up in themselves. Perhaps that's how it panned out. Maybe you ended up not being able to relate to anything, you were that busy busting a gut to keep a hold on yourself so you didn't think about all the things you'd done. The silence was beginning to get to her. Did they not have a football team they could talk about? Was there nothing they could say about *Crossroads* or *Coronation Street*?

'Do yiz ever get a look at the telly?' she asked.

The front-seat passenger shuffled round a bit. 'Aye,' he said. 'I don't mind a bit of telly.'

'What about yourself?' he asked the driver.

She realised then that he didn't even know the driver's name, that they might not even have met before. She didn't know why this should be frightening, but it was.

'Darts,' the driver said, 'I like a bit of darts.'

There wasn't much in the way of conversation for the rest of the journey. Then the rain started pelting down, and she was relaxed enough to nod off. When she came to, the car was being parked on a quiet street, and the rain had stopped.

The house was tall and red brick, with a scuffed front door that opened on to a wide hall scattered with unopened mail. A black butcher's bicycle was propped up against the wall. They led her past the staircase and down into a kitchen that smelt of damp and fried onions. Here, a thin-lipped woman with rows of hard pink curlers in her hair put the kettle on to boil. The men seemed to know this woman, but Róisín could see that she made them uncomfortable, nervous maybe. There were four or five chairs, but nobody sat down.

'How're you keeping, Peggy?' one of them asked.

She glared at him, but didn't reply. She jerked a thumb at Róisín. 'Is she on her own?' she asked. 'What happened to the other one?'

The driver said he didn't know, just did what he was told.

The woman turned to Róisín then. 'She's to go to Joe Lonergan, you say? Any reason why?'

'Fucked if I know,' said the driver as he headed for the door. 'I'll bring back the burgers and chips. Salt and vinegar?'

Róisín was starving, but nobody offered her anything to eat. The room they put her in was cold and smelt funny, but at least they didn't lock the door. She was dying for a wee, but nobody had told her where the toilet was. She sat at the end of the bed with her legs crossed, then moved to the door, trying to distinguish the lower pitch of the real-life voices downstairs from the TV chatter. Eventually, she made her move, guessing that the toilet must be at the end of the corridor.

She couldn't find the light switch. She felt her way past one door then another. There was a crack of light under the third, a tap, tap, tapping from inside as she hurried past. At the end of the corridor, the bathroom door was open, the lino cold underfoot. She was as quiet as could be, and didn't flush. Downstairs, the waves of canned laughter just kept on coming.

She had no idea how many other people were in the house. It was quite a big place, as far as she could tell. She was on the first floor, but there were another couple of floors above her. The banister wound its way up into darkness. She listened hard to try to work out what was going on down there, still trying to separate the voices inside the TV from those outside it. They sounded calm enough. Just the two men, she thought.

She wondered where the woman had gone, whether she even lived here at all. Their voices came and went. There was something about a match that was being played at the weekend, a goalie who was a heap of shit. She couldn't help wondering where she'd be when that match was played. Would she be in New York, in some bright brassy place with subways and skyscrapers? Or would they have got rid of her by then? Her chest tightened at the thought of Lonergan's brother. Uncle had told her to keep her head down and she'd be grand. He'd said she should do what she was told if she knew what was good for her. But she knew that Uncle didn't give a shit what happened to her. None of them did.

On the way back to her room, she passed the door that leaked light from underneath. Its old-fashioned wooden doorknob was moving a little, rattling uselessly. She edged closer. Whoever was on the other side of that door seemed to sense she was there. There was another noise. Muffled, but human-sounding. She remembered the panic of being beneath a hood, under tape, in the boot of a car. She didn't want to see someone who sounded like that. There was no room for any more bad things in her head. And as for the people downstairs, she couldn't afford to make them mad when she was just on the brink of getting out. She half hoped that someone would start to come upstairs and she'd have an excuse not to open that door. She knew it was madness, but she couldn't help herself.

She grasped the doorknob firmly and gave it a sharp twist. At first, the door didn't budge, and then she realised that something on the other side was blocking it. She pushed a little, was able to ease it open six inches, then a foot. She listened hard for any sound of alarm from downstairs, but nobody seemed to be paying any attention to what was happening up here. And so she pushed a little more until she had enough room to be able to slip inside.

Just beside the door, there was a woman lying like a caterpillar on the floor. Closer to Ma in age than to Róisín. Permed hair. Tweed teacher skirt. American tan tights. The woman was bound – hand, mouth and foot – the same kind of tape that Uncle had used on Róisín.

There was a sour spicy smell in the room. The odour quickly became unbearable and Róisín jammed the hem of her cardigan into her face so as not to have to breathe it in. The woman's eyes didn't seem to react to that at all. They barely even flickered. No hope, or even pride. Once Róisín had put a name to that look, she knew that she didn't want anything at all to do with this woman. She didn't want to know her name, or why she was here, or why she had so little reason for hope. She didn't want to have to guess what might happen next.

She felt a flash of fellowship, then pity. But she would not be untying this woman. They would not leap together through that first-floor window and off to freedom on the butcher's bike in the hall. Róisín knew that. And maybe the woman knew that too because she didn't seem to be asking for anything at all. She just seemed to want to be seen, for her presence there to be noted.

But then Róisín noticed the woman's stockinged feet, curled together like two small birds. She thought of Ma with her feet up on the pouffe, watching TV. That was when she remembered that none of this was normal. Just like what had happened to Ian wasn't normal either. The woman suddenly began to flip back and forth on the floor like a fish. Downstairs, a door opened and the television blared. Footsteps clapped across the hall. Terrified they'd come upstairs and find her there, Róisín gestured to the woman to be still. When she was sure the door down- stairs had closed again, she got to her knees. She was so close now that she could hear the harsh exhalations of the woman's breath through her nostrils. Her skin had the texture of shop-bought cake, spongy and over-yellow. Her eyes were yellowish too, and her mascara had leaked into the sharp lines beneath her eyes. It was obvious that the woman wanted Róisín to remove the tape from her mouth, but Róisín was afraid. She didn't know if it would stick down again, or what she'd do if the woman screamed.

Next, the woman was gesturing with her eyes towards her own chest. She started to move again, rocking back and forth on the floor. Desperate to keep her quiet, Róisín came closer still to try to shush her up. The closer Róisín's hand hovered towards her chest, the more vigorously the woman nodded. Warm, warmer, hot. She seemed suddenly so eager and hopeful that Róisín felt a wave of pity that made her eyes water. She saw that the woman was wearing something round her neck. A small silver locket, and etched across the front was a name.

'Jacinta? Is that you?'

The woman looked like she might cry. She was trying to say something. She made three hooting syllables, and then another two. She had her eyes fixed on Róisín's and when she could see she wasn't getting through she tried again. 'Uh UH uh uh UH.'

I want to go home? Jacinta's my name? Without pulling back the tape there was no way of knowing.

Róisín tried to distract her with another question. 'Are you from Belfast, Jacinta?' Even as she was asking the question, she remembered the small stockinged feet of the woman she'd seen being bustled through the hallway at Lonergan's place. Of course she was from Belfast.

But that was weeks ago. Two, three? And all at once Róisín was more scared than she'd been since she last saw Lonergan. She could hardly think for fright, and the words just tumbled out of her. 'You'll be back home in no time,' Róisín said. 'I'm going back to Belfast myself in the morning. Don't you worry yourself. You'll be grand. Sure look at me. They had me tied up in a room down the corridor for near on a week.'

From the woman's eyes, she was choosing to believe

that this was true. And sometimes it was better to be kind than to tell the truth, when the truth was too terrible to tell. A young fella shot on a bedroom floor, a woman burned in Ladies' Fashions, and now this Jacinta woman. What was kindness these days? Where had it gone? She didn't even know any more. And then she thought of herself, because it was the only thing she could still be sure of.

'I have to go now,' she said. 'They're OK if you just do what they say.'

She tiptoed back to her own room and lay down on the bed and tried to work out if there was anything at all she could do. She thought through the possibility of climbing out of the bedroom window. And going where? Of sneaking down the stairs. And doing what? Of going back to Jacinta and stripping off the tape from her mouth and her wrists and her ankles. And then what? She imagined herself returning to Jacinta's room and doing the right thing – untying her, setting her free. Like a fairy tale where Róisín, little rose, was a saint or a superhero or a warrior princess. Even though she knew that none of this would happen, she told herself that Jacinta would be all right. They wouldn't dare do anything really bad to someone who looked like somebody's mother.

But there was no way she could sleep. The nylon sheets were horrible, cold and slippery, and there was only a cellular blanket for warmth. She couldn't stop shivering, even though she was dressed warm enough for outside. She couldn't stop thinking about the woman. She wondered what she could have done to end up on the floor of

Peggy's house in Dublin. She just looked like one of the women from the post office, or a secretary maybe at the school. She didn't look legitimate at all.

Róisín lay in the dark, trying to remember when she'd last eaten, trying not to speculate about Jacinta and the parcel tape and whether Uncle had been the one to tie her up. She tried to say a prayer for the woman, but she knew her prayers would cut no ice because she didn't really believe in them. They never worked anyway.

She must have slept because when she woke up she was half inside a dream, though it was still dark and the road outside still quiet. The dream had been quite a nice one. Not the usual kind – no blood, no fire, nothing like that. But there was something wrong all the same. She was being watched, she was sure of it. Maybe it was the way the moon had moved in the night – if moons move, for they seem to – but there was definitely something there. A car's headlights flashed across the window and then she saw it. The face was drained to dregs and framed by a mop of greyish hair. She thought of the woman in the other room, and bit her finger hard to stop herself from screaming. Maybe it was one of the old biddies from Davey and Reid's come back to get her. Maybe it was time for the ghosts. Once she realised what it was, she went over to the tallboy and touched it. Mrs McKeever used to do the same weird thing: put her wig to bed at night on a white Styrofoam head that she kept at the window to scare off burglars. Returning to sit on the edge of the cold clammy nylon bed, she let out all the laughs she might never get a chance for, once she got to New York.

Then she remembered Jacinta on the floor in the room just down the corridor, and there was no more laughter after that. For hours more, it seemed, she lay there listening for footsteps on the stairs.

Next morning, they had breakfast at the kitchen table. Peggy and the two men sat opposite her like an interview committee, but nobody said anything. It was rashers and a thin sausage, and a green passport with a gold harp on her bread plate. Flicking through, it was her passport. At least, it looked the same, but there was a visa in it now. Da's wallet was underneath, but by the flat, saggy shape of it she could already tell that they'd taken her money. She looked up at the man who'd been the driver, but he didn't meet her eye. By the side of her chair, the bag she had packed. Years ago, it seemed now, before Davey and Reid's. And then she realised that the only person who could have given them these things was Ma. She knew better than to say anything, but her heart went blank.

Peggy scraped back her chair, scooped some thick porridge into a bowl from a pot on the stove and disappeared upstairs with it. Later, when she came back downstairs again, she was carrying a Dunnes Stores plastic bag, one of the thick green ones, its handles tied in a knot. In the other hand was the porridge plate, its contents congealed and untouched. The men looked up, munching quietly, then looked away.

Nobody had explained about the airport and what you did when you got there. One of the men stood nearby as she queued up at the check-in desk beneath a fat green shamrock, but he acted as if he didn't know her at all. He was still in sight when she showed her ticket at Departures, but when she took a last look back he was gone. Róisín had been so busy being terrified of everything else that she'd forgotten to worry about the plane. She'd never been on a plane before, or even thought much about them. The odd time, she might have noticed one roar far above Belfast, but that was it.

She'd never have thought they could be so big. The plane to New York was like a great white whale with a patch peeled off its belly to let the passengers inside. It didn't look like it had much chance of staying up there in mid-air.

The woman at the check-in desk had asked her if she'd flown before. 'Grand, so you'll be wanting a window seat. The view over Ireland is only gorgeous. The forty shades of green.'

So there she was in her window seat, next to two American tourists in green Crimplene trousers and Aran sweaters. They looked just like the dolls on sale in the airport shop. The woman even had a little green ribbon in her ginger ponytail. Róisín tried not to look out of the window at what she was leaving behind. She tried not to think of the sky, either. How high it was, and how little support there was for a thing as big as a whale. Her thoughts kept rushing everywhere they shouldn't. *Bye-bye Bay-by, Bay-by goodbye*, and a hat as blue as the bluest sky and Ma's tears dripping into the dishwater as she bent over the kitchen sink. A woman in American tan tights, with her mouth taped shut and her eyes half-dead already.

She planted her feet to the floor of the plane, but even though she could hear the man beside her ask her if she was OK, she couldn't stop the shaking. She couldn't both answer him and hold herself together, not at the same time. He put his hand on her shoulder and maybe that was what did it, because after that she was an earthquake and a flood and any other natural disaster you would care to mention. They called for a stewardess, and there was a glass of water and a discussion as to whether Róisín would be able to fly.

The thought that they might not let her out of the country was even more terrifying than the prospect of the plane not being able to stay above the clouds long enough to get them to New York. She accepted the water and gulped it down. She let the woman take her hand in hers. She concentrated on the three little diamonds on the ring band and let the warmth of that hand comfort her. She listened to the woman's voice murmur, 'Breathe two three four. Out two three four. Breathe two three four. Out two three four.'

She didn't want the woman ever to let go, and the man felt big and solid next to her, whatever about the green Crimplene. She hardly noticed take-off once she'd swallowed the two white pills the woman emptied on to her palm from a little round box.

'Goooood girl . . . goooood girl . . . goooood girl . . .'

Once they were airborne, Róisín was too drowsy for celebrations or regrets.

15

Joe Lonergan was a big, lumbering man who looked at least ten years older than his brother. There was a weird gleam off his bald scalp, like Brylcreem had been swiped on, then rubbed in hard. He didn't shake hands or offer to carry her case. She walked five steps behind him and watched his feet, clad in big white runners, leading the way to his car. She wondered if she should have scarpered as soon as she got through Immigration, but what could she have done without a penny to her name? She'd watched enough TV to know that New York was a jungle.

In the car park, they walked past row after row of Chevvies and Dodges and outlandishly huge vehicles she'd never seen before, not even on TV. Joe Lonergan's car had blacked-out windows, and it was only when he opened the door that she realised there was someone inside there already. The woman was scrawny, with dry ruddy patches on either side of her nose. She didn't utter a word, just let out a sigh and looked away.

'Say nothing.' Joe dug his key into the ignition. 'He won't ask for anything more after this.'

'She'd better not be another wee bonus, Joe. She'd better not.'

They started off in total silence, then Joe twirled the radio knob until he reached a song about a blue bayou. Róisín had no idea what a bayou was, but it sounded better than what was outside the window. The height of the road and the size and speed of the cars on it was astonishing. She couldn't believe how many advertising hoardings flashed by, how many diners and motels and service stations. The woman flicked down the lipstick mirror and started examining her spots. Róisín could tell she was examining her too. Her recent experience of car journeys had taught her that anything was better than silence. 'Are you from New York yourself?' she asked.

The woman flung her arms out in an alarmingly sudden manner. 'Jesus. I mean, fuck this, Joe.'

Joe said nothing.

'She's going to live with us, you say. Is she going to ask questions all day long, too?'

They didn't bother telling her where they came from, not that it mattered anyway.

Róisín didn't dare fall asleep in the car. Her ears felt spacey and she didn't start to feel right again until something made her sneeze and suddenly, magically, they cleared. Nothing else felt any clearer, though, and she had to press her lips together hard to stop herself from breaking down.

Was it two nights since she'd gone off with Uncle, or

three? She didn't even know what time it was. Didn't know if the clocks went forward or back once you crossed the Atlantic. She tried to see the clock on the dashboard, but Joe's shoulder was in the way.

Outside, New York didn't look as shiny as she'd thought it would. It was kind of scrubby-looking, and the weather dull and grey. She thought they might still be on the outskirts, though she couldn't really tell. The car whipped along the highway, past blocks of flats that went on and on like a Lego world with all the colour wiped away.

She couldn't work out whether it was the music or the smell of petrol, but something was doing her head in. She started to feel sick, then panicky: like someone had put a hood on her again, or taken out the parcel tape. When the fuck was she going to stop being driven along in the back of a car by people she didn't know? She wound down the window to get some air. The woman glared at her in the mirror, but neither of them told her to close it.

The Lonergans lived over a pub called the Claddagh Ring. The street name was Steinway, which, as far as Róisín knew, was a piano. They gave her a camp bed and some sheets to make it up with, and a prop-up alarm clock in a leatherette case. Although it was still light and the clock said ten past four, Róisín lay down and fell fast asleep.

When she woke up, it was night. In her dream she'd been back in Belfast, crouched down behind the garden shed, trying to dodge a searchlight. Then she realised she wasn't outside at all, or even in Belfast, because the cars sounded completely different and there was a kind of heatwave echo in the air. She tried to roll over, but the bed was too narrow and the metal side bar cut into her hip, and by then she was well and truly awake.

Outside, neon light blared from a shop sign: 'Astoria Bargain Center'. She already knew about Americans not being able to spell, but she'd always thought the Astoria was a cinema. She couldn't sleep anyway, so she got up for a look. A metal zigzag ran all the way up the front of the house opposite. And caged-in metal boxes were stuck on to the windows, too. She'd seen those on the telly, but it was funny seeing them for real. It was weird that they didn't hide things like that inside the houses instead of sticking them on the front. It was like you just stuck everything out on display, no matter what. Now that she was properly awake in the middle of the night, she wondered if this was jet lag. She still had Da's wallet on her, stuck in under her bra strap. She had to peel it off her skin, and the ink had transferred itself to her like a tattoo. She sat awake for ages, just listening to the city roar and fade like a rough and dirty tide. It was terrifying and exciting and unbelievable.

The Lonergans put her to work the following day. She collected the glasses, emptied the ashtrays, washed and scrubbed and swept. Even though a sign on the door said 'No Work Clothes, No Boots and No Nonsense', most of the customers in the front bar came straight from the site up the road after work. They weren't young – white hair and whiskey cheeks. Their eyes were puddle-sad. There was a bit of banter now and then, but only between themselves. There was no fighting and no singing. These men approached their pints and whiskey chasers with grave faces, like drinking was a kind of ordeal. Because the telly was on, it took over the place and the men just stood there, separate from one another, and drank it in with the booze.

She'd thought there were kids. Hadn't Brian said something about kids? She asked Mrs Lonergan, which was what everyone called her, even though she had no ring on her finger.

'They're with their Auntie Rita out in Brooklyn,' she said. 'Them kids is nothing to do with you.'

'Sorry. I was only asking.'

'Well, don't bother your head.'

There was baseball on the telly. Róisín hadn't a clue what the point of the game was, but she didn't really care enough to ask anybody so she just stood there behind the bar, twisting a cloth inside a glass. The game was nearly over when Joe Lonergan arrived with a bundle of newspapers under his arm and plonked them down at the end of the bar. He seemed friendly enough, even called her by her name.

'How's about you, Róisín?' he said. 'Make sure you shift these papers for me now, won't you?' Then he rapped his knuckles on the bar in a fairly good-tempered way and disappeared into the lounge.

As she went round the tables collecting glasses, she could see through the two portholes in the door that he was sitting down in there at a table with five or six others while Mrs Lonergan shuttled back and forth with trays of whiskey and the ham sandwiches Róisín had prepared earlier. After a while, they pulled little white curtains over the windows, and she took it the lounge bar was shut for the night.

Róisín glanced at the news sheets Lonergan had laid on the bar counter. The front page was dominated by a row of black berets and dark glasses. There were balaclavas, too, firing off guns. The sight of those pictures made her realise what it was she'd been trying not to think about. Jacinta. The thought of that name etched into a silver locket gave her stomach a queasy little twist. She turned the berets and balaclavas away from her, facing out into the bar room where they could plague someone else. Then, because they were still bugging her, even upside down, she covered them up with a bar towel. When Mrs Lonergan came in to cash up for the night, the other men were still in the lounge next door. Her eyes were strangely glazed and she hardly seemed to see Róisín, just told her she was done for the night.

It took Róisín ages to get to sleep. She kept thinking about Jacinta and how maybe they could both have got away. She imagined all kinds of better outcomes. Sneaking downstairs in the middle of the night. Flagging down a car. Reaching a police station, a hospital, a newspaper office. Telling it all to a roomful of cameras and flashing lights. Which would have been fine, had it not been for Ian and the mauve lady and all the rest of it. No, this was the way it had to be. Instead, she imagined Jacinta back in the middle of a busy Belfast day: toasting triangles of white soda bread, frying sausages, hauling her washing down to the launderette past the Saracen at the end of the street.

Then, in the deepest velvet corner of the night, Róisín realised that something wasn't right. She pulled the sheet back from over her head. She listened harder. Someone was out there. A slide of feet. A pause. Another slide. The steps were slower than any normal steps, more careful, too. After a creak, they stopped. That's what alarmed her: whoever was out there was trying not to make any noise.

She assessed things quickly. No lock on the door. A window two floors up. There was always the fire escape. The footsteps moved from the wood on to the mat just outside her door. The sound was muffled now, so she could no longer make out exactly where it was coming from. She strained hard to hear better. She was about to launch herself in the direction of the fire escape when she heard a voice from the other side of the landing.

'Joe? Have you locked up yet? Joe? Come on to bed, would you? I'm up in four hours' time.'

He didn't say a word, but Róisín could hear his feet swivel on to the wood again as he walked back across the landing.

She wedged a broom under the handle of the door like they do in the movies. Her brain hopped back and forward – leave, stay, leave, stay – although there was really only one option. She thought she heard someone moving around on the landing sometime around three, but she couldn't be sure. She'd already decided to take what she needed from the till, though she'd never stolen anything before. She was too afraid to go outside in the dark though, so she sat and waited, watching the pale green arms of the alarm clock inch their way towards five. When the first hint of light reached the dirty corner of sky beyond the Astoria Bargain Center, she made her move. Silent and slow, down the stairs. But when she entered the bar there was someone in there already.

Mrs Lonergan looked as if she'd been crying. She didn't say anything at first – as if it was no surprise to see Róisín there at the crack of dawn, with her bag in her hand and her coat on. She just kept working away with a cloth on the tiles behind the bar, rubbing and rubbing away in cross little circles. Then, all of a sudden, she flung the cloth to the floor. For a moment, she hesitated, and then her eye seemed to catch the little cluster of collection boxes behind the bar. She grabbed a tin can labelled *Relief of Irish Prisoners Overseas* in thick black marker pen. She ripped off the lid and upended it on to the counter. As the coins went skittering off along the bar, she stretched her arms wide to contain them. Then, cupping her hands, she shuffled them on to a battered old Guinness tray. Róisín watched her bitten nails go to work, picking through the coins, building them into stacks. When she'd bagged them up, she plonked the little packages down in front of Róisín.

'And now you can piss off,' she said.

Róisín didn't bother to act shocked or upset. There was no point pretending she hadn't been about to leave anyway.

'Here,' said Mrs Lonergan, holding out a worn canvas shopper with a bitten apple on the front.

Róisín dropped in the little bundles, one by one, then opened the door of the pub on to the blare of the street.

Although it wasn't even six yet, the air was like a soft smack with a warm damp face-cloth. She might be free, but that was just the start of it. She walked in the semi-dark past piss-and-beer doorways and garbage-strewn alleyways until she found a café open, a place full of men tired out from night work.

She opened one of the little paper bank bags, spilling the coins on to her lap and dividing them on to the chair beside her, like she'd seen the old men at home do with the collection money after Mass. When she'd worked her way through the whole lot, it came to twenty-six dollars and forty-three cents. It looked like a fortune, but she doubted Mrs Lonergan was the type to be giving away fortunes. As soon as the sun appeared, she left. She didn't care where she went, so long as it wasn't anywhere near Steinway Street.

Now that the sun was up, people seemed to appear from nowhere. She was amazed at their number and variety. All the different skin colours, the way-out clothes and hairstyles. Most people never even noticed her looking at them, they were that tied up in their own concerns. Now that she was here, she wanted to experience it all. She knew that this couldn't be all there was to New York. She'd never even seen the Empire State Building, for God's sake. And where was Brooklyn Bridge?

But then reality hit. She had to find a job, or else she'd starve. The only work she'd ever had was at The Claddagh Ring, and she'd hardly been there five minutes. She couldn't think what she could do apart from washing dishes maybe, or standing at the counter of a shop. She wondered how you got a job. Did you just ask around, in shops and that? Was there a newspaper you needed to read? She walked for hours down busy streets with lots of businesses and not a single 'help wanted' notice, and then she came out onto a big wide road called Astoria Boulevard, which sounded nicer than it was.

It felt like a good omen when she came across a place that was showing a re-run of one of her favourite films. They called it a movie theater, but it was really just a cinema. She spent the rest of the afternoon in a galaxy far, far away, and travelled beyond the dark times. Being free should have been terrifying, but it wasn't because the Force was with her. While she was in that cinema, it was the best feeling in the world. She was in New York and had got away from the Lonergans. They could never touch her now. As for the future, that had no meaning at all.

Lamb Island

16

Róisín is pacing back and forth across the tiled floor of the bungalow, while out on the headland a yacht is startling the sky. It is Good Friday, and she has become like Ma, bent over a transistor in her Belfast kitchen, listening out for disaster. The radio is crackling out a morning news programme. Lonergan's spokeswoman sounds young. Her accent is Southern, maybe even Cork. The presenter is excitable, with a fine line in outrage.

'So he has nothing whatsoever to say to the O'Neills?'

'Look, John, I don't know who put those people up to this, but it strikes me as very convenient timing. Their mother went missing before I was born, right? Now, that's awful and I'm very sorry for their trouble. But it has nothing whatsoever to do with the New Republic Party or Deputy Lonergan. Nothing.'

'I understand there's a sizeable crowd expected at that demonstration outside your party headquarters today.

And they say they won't be going away until a statement is made.'

'Deputy Lonergan has already said all he's going to say about this matter. Who benefits? Just ask yourself that. Not the O'Neill family, that's for sure. The same tired old parties, that's who. We are the party of progress, John. The party –'

'But Deputy Lonergan must be concerned, surely. Or is he off fishing for the holidays?'

'You can be as flippant as you like, but this Easter Deputy Lonergan will be doing what he always does. Working hard for those who don't seem to matter to this government. He'll also be on the canvass in Dublin East on behalf of our excellent candidate about the things that do matter. Equality, dignity, respect.'

'No peace for the wicked.'

'That's obviously not the phrase that I'd have used, John. But certainly, Deputy Lonergan is a busy man.'

The thought that she might have come here for no reason is devastating. She pictures Lonergan in a grey office with a filing cabinet and a dead plant. It will be harder to get to him in the city. She imagines him surrounded by the kind of men who drove her as a back-seat passenger all those years ago. Men like Uncle and Celtic. Older now, better dressed, but fiercer than ever when it comes to fighting off a threat. But if need be, she will go there after him. She is not giving up now. She fantasises about the moment when she finally gets to him, as if desire is enough to make it happen. He is at the empty desk she has imagined for him. And for the first time, she is the one in control and her demands are the only ones that matter. She fingers the phone in her pocket. Runs her thumb along its cracked surface. All the waiting has worn her out. For a moment, she is tempted to ring into that radio show herself, to get it over with once and for all, to do this live on air.

Opening the drawer in the hallstand to retrieve her keys, she comes across the folded sheet of pink manilla paper:

WHY?

She can't think why she kept it. The word seems to taunt her now, so she flings the paper into the grate and lights a match. She watches it flare then fall to dust, all but a ragged corner of singed pink. Every day, she times her jog down to Molly's to coincide with the arrival of the first ferry. It always feels like possibility is opening up again – just as when the last ferry leaves at dusk it feels as though the trap is set. And every day she encounters Boyle. Since the incident on the beach, he barely makes eye contact. She thinks of the email address scrawled on his arm and her throat tightens. The very sight of him sets her nerves on edge, and so she takes a different route today. Heading off in the opposite direction from the old school, she moves along the blank back of the island, where there is nothing but the high cliff road and the endless sea. Ahead, a narrow path flattens the bracken, and steps cut out of the rock lead down to a narrow beach. This is where Boyle approached her, and there is someone on the beach today, too. A woman is undressing furtively. She is holding a towel out from her waist with one hand while she makes complicated adjustments to her underwear with the other. Then, after all those efforts to conceal, she drops the towel and steps, naked as a blue cheese, into the water. She swims barely fifteen strokes, before getting to her feet and striding back out again. On the shore, she sluices herself from a large plastic water bottle. It's only then that Róisín realises that it's Molly from the shop. Afraid of being seen, she hurries on.

Murphy's boys have given the benches at the North Harbour a fresh coat of blue. The flower barrels outside the pub are bristling with newly planted marigolds, and the prayer flags strung up to the crooked tree look freshly, laundered. A pontoon has been floated into place to accommodate the visiting boats. As for the Portakabin at the head of the pier, it has become a craft shop again, open Easter Sunday, 12–4.

She arrives outside Molly's, where extra sailings are advertised on the door in A4 laminate, just as the ferry is pulling in at the pier below. A light mist of rain is falling as she waits there at a distance, jogging on the spot, affecting stretches she doesn't need as she scrutinises the disembarking passengers. The usual hikers, a couple of women pulling tartan-patterned shopping trolleys behind them as they struggle up the hill, but still no Lonergan.

Boyle is stretched out on the mattress, trying to keep his feet clear of a new leak that has sprung overnight. He has eaten nothing but tuna and cold custard for the past three days, and acid burns the back of his throat. He closes his eyes and conjures up a toasted special, the cheese dripping out between the crusts, the ham salty and soft. She has put the heart across him with her hard little mouth and he hasn't got the strength to face the world again just yet. He still has five briquettes left for the fire, but he has used up all the spelling books, and the last three copies of *The First Communion Catechism*. Above JFK, a large damp stain is taking on the shape of South America as the moisture trails down the corner of the room. The rain is splattering the surface of the half-filled buckets, and the Nokia that has been ringing off and on for hours has his nerves ripped ragged. The electronic buzz is right inside his head now. Dee dee dee dee dee dee dee dee. Dee dee dee dee dee dee dee dee. Octave after mean little octave. He clamps an old coffee jar down on top of it, like he's trapping an insect. But on it goes. Dee dee dee dee dee dee dee dee. Dee dee dee dee dee dee dee dee. On and on and on, until the jar is rattling with it and the phone is hopping like an angry wasp. Finally he tips it out and flips the cover.

'Jesus.'

But it isn't the Dutchman this time, it's Lonergan.

'Didn't I say I'd phone when I had news? Well, there isn't any.' Even as he says it, he knows it won't hold water.

'I had Theo on,' says Lonergan. 'She's been at my bloody house.'

'Well, she hasn't gone away, you know.' And he's pleased with that one, coming to him just like that. He hasn't lost it yet. 'Jesus, those O'Neills are something else, though, aren't they? No shutting them up.'

'Get rid of her, Boyle.'

'Ah come on now, Lonergan. She's your biggest fan. A great big fucken file she has on you. I didn't realise the two of you went way back.'

It's so silent on the other end of the phone that Lonergan might almost have buggered off. Boyle holds it away from his head, and listens to the room instead. That's the thing with Lonergan. You wouldn't know. He could be anywhere. Boyle wonders about that metal door. A boot would be enough. But there's silence. No voice and no boot. He tries talking into the phone again. 'Maybe she's a reporter, come to do a TV special. That'd be a good one. The rise and rise of Brian Lonergan.'

That does it. 'I should have put Theo on it from the start.' Lonergan sounds as if he's talking to himself. 'I gave you a bag of tricks, Boyle. Use them. I haven't time for all this shite.'

'The subtle ways take longer.'

'Just you do what I said.'

'Well, that's just it. What was it you said exactly? You were a bit on the vague side. And while you're on, who's your one in that photofit? She'd frighten the balls off a bull.'

'Why do we still have a problem here?'

'*We* don't have a problem, Lonergan. *You* do.'

He cuts the call, then goes out back to fill the coffee jar with water. He holds the phone with his fingertips, and then he drops it in. Now that he's got rid of

Lonergan, he feels euphoric. Breathing deep, all peace and relaxation, he lies back on the one good pillow and loosens out his ponytail. Come to think of it, he doesn't just feel good. He feels like a fucken knight in shining armour. But then he remembers her lack of gratitude, the mean little puss on her when she told him to fuck off. He's sticking his neck out for her here. Time she realised she owed him some respect.

At the pub, the blinds are down. 'CLOSED'. She'd forgotten about the Good Friday holiday, the one dry day. But the door is ajar, and she pushes at it gently. There are no punters inside, and the duty barman is just a school kid – pale and spotty, in a Man U shirt. She asks for a cappuccino. The kid flashes a look at Cat's shiny new machine.

'Only minerals today,' he says.

She asks for a code for half an hour's internet access, and he says he thinks the server might be down again. Her mood sinks, and then he says he'll check and it's working, yes, it is. By the time she is upstairs and sitting at the computer, her hands are trembling. She clicks on her inbox, but once again it's full of items from another planet – superannuation plans and manicures.

'If you want to know what a woman's life is like,' Ma used to say, 'take a look at her nails. When things start to fall apart, the nails are always the first to go.' Róisín looks down at her hands. Her pearly polish is chipped and the nails themselves uneven.

She gets a hangnail between her teeth and pulls. She imagines the reaction of Luella in the nail salon round the corner from the gallery.

'Uh huh? You did what to that nail?'

Luella would make it whole again instantly – just a dropper and a tiny ball of glue.

She has a sudden pang of homesickness for the comforting veneer of New York, for all the people who expect nothing from her but pleasantness and ease. The yoga girls will be having sushi tomorrow, and there is jazz in the park. Marcie writes to say that if she's had enough of rain, there's this yoga place in Guatemala. Somewhere deep in the rainforest where they fix you macrobiotic food after your Mayan sauna. On Lamb, all of these things seem unreal. Róisín finds that she cannot keep these two worlds in her mind at once. Her resolve is faltering. She deletes the emails and switches off New York.

In the latest pictures of Lonergan, he is on a podium. Photographed from below, he has transformed into an orator. Someone high and mighty, worthy of respect. It is an election rally, up in Dublin. He is surrounded by the faithful, their faces flooded with his light. And then she discovers a YouTube clip of the same event.

'They want to make us play old roles. Stay in your place. Shut up and do what you're told. They talk about truth, but all they want to do is tie us to the past.'

She wonders where he learnt the hand gestures. Open, offering palm. Double karate chop.

'Tell the truth, they say. Oh, we've all heard that before. But whose truth? That's what I'd like to know.

The people who buy apartment blocks and shopping centres and hotel complexes in places they can't even find on the map? You know who they are, right? We all know who they are. Well, let me tell you something, friends. Those people don't like me very much. They don't like me at all.'

And as she listens to them cheer, the red line beneath the video clip inches left to right across the screen. It takes thirty seconds or more for the applause to subside. She hadn't realised how convincing he was, how deft at managing the truth.

'So I'm an enemy of democracy, am I? An enemy of free speech? Well, look around you, friends, because it isn't hard to find the real enemies of Ireland.'

The great roar of the crowd gathers like a tide and then breaks over her.

'And they say that *I* have something to answer for?'

She knows exactly what he has to answer for. But maybe she's the only one who thinks that matters any more. Maybe she has come at this too late. The thought that most people would rather Jacinta was forgotten weighs heavily on her.

She is suddenly desperate to get outside, to breathe clean air. She remembers, at school, an old nun declaring that your mind could be polluted through the television screen, that you had to look away and stop your ears, or else be lost before you knew it. Satanic incantations hidden in the scream of heavy metal, spells muttered back to front in the scratched grooves of an LP. How they used to laugh.

At the door of the pub, the wind catches her hair and lashes it around her face. She gives herself up to it, swallowing down air in greedy mouthfuls. She forces herself to focus on the patched-up fishing vessels, the stacks of lobster pots, the coils of rope and tangled twists of net. Sheen. Róisín. Róisín. Sheen. She needs someone to remind her who she is. When she had Tom, she only had to look at him to remember she was someone else now. And because Tom never doubted Sheen, neither did she. He used to say he loved the way she wasn't interested in the past. He found her enigmatic. But his disillusionment, when it came, was total. 'Who are you, anyway? Is there anything real in there at all?'

She'd tried so hard. Those early years when she was working two, three jobs at once: waiting tables, changing diapers, pushing a trolley packed with files around the registry of an insurance company on Lexington. Learning, and using what she'd learnt. Step by step, becoming Sheen. And it had worked, it had. She became better than anyone could have hoped she'd be. She even became someone who could love and be loved back. She finds herself gazing through the glassy water of the inner harbour, where tiny fish glide and flick among the gently rounded stones. She imagines the water closing over her, the sunlight gleaming distantly above, as she finds her natural habitat among the camouflage of sea creatures clinging to iridescent rocks.

She switches her phone back on and jabs in Maura's number. The ringtone purrs and she tries not to think about the belt of dread that's tightening round her. She must sound offhand, normal. She mustn't be hysterical at all. She makes her voice bright, but she hasn't been using it enough these days, and it lies like a slug at the back of her throat. It's hard to affect the kind of daffodilly brightness she is aiming for. But she is only halfway through her happy Easters when Maura interrupts. And she is quite hysterical enough for both of them.

'For all I know the bastards might be back again tonight. The police said, go ahead. Replace the lot. If you don't it looks as if you're scared of them. Well, I am scared, Róisín. Jesus Christ, I thought all that was over.'

Was there a message that she missed?

'What happened, Maura?'

'My windows. That's what happened.'

The dread that's in her heart has risen to her throat now, and she hardly dares to breathe.

'They smashed the lot last night. So I'm kind of preoccupied right now. Where are you, anyway? I rang the apartment three times this morning.'

'I'm back.'

'Back where?'

'I've come home.'

There is a beat of silence, and then the anger comes. 'You'd better not be in Belfast.'

'I'm not.'

'Where are you then?' When there's no response, Maura's voice softens. 'I know you're in bits, Róisín. What with Tom, and you not being able to say goodbye to Ma.'

'You didn't exactly give me the chance.'

'Jesus Christ, you know the score. You got yourself

mixed up in things. It was ugly and horrible and you wanted out. And they didn't like that. They really didn't. But then Ma stepped in. She stuck her neck out for you. Our wee Róisín. She pulled a favour. And because of who your da was, they let you go.'

She tries to interrupt, to say that it had nothing to do with Ma, but Maura isn't stopping. 'So, great. You're out. You get away. But then you have to stay away. You know? You have to bloody play their game.'

Maura's voice is obscured now by the pounding of the sea in Róisín's ears. She doesn't even try to answer that – just ends the call and switches off the phone. And as she stands there, looking out at nothing, she picks at the crumbling surface of the sea wall. Crammed with grit and broken shells, it is bonded from things peculiar to itself. She understands so little. Breathing in the slightly acrid smell of brine and rot, all she can think about is Ma.

She got the news while she was having lunch with Lauren in a pop-up restaurant half a block away called Retro Sicilian – faux rustic with gingham wallpaper and comically oversized Chianti-bottle candles. The tables were crammed so close together that when her cell rang, she'd decided to go outside to take the call. When she didn't return, Lauren came out after her and found her bawling into the November rain. They must have taken a cab back to the gallery. She can't remember now. That day was blotted out by a new reality: Ma was gone. When she'd married Tom, she'd allowed herself the fantasy that some day things might change. A grandchild would be born, perhaps, and Ma would make the trip over and there would be some way of merging then with now. But that was gone now.

Right away, she knew that going home for the funeral was still impossible. And because she couldn't admit the situation to friends, she felt glassed off from their kindness. Deep down she was no one they would recognise.

The grief Sheen felt for Ma was raw and unrelenting. In a late-night phone call, she raised with Maura the subject of returning for the funeral. She could fly in and out in a day – there was no need for anyone to know. But Maura was adamant. 'Don't kid yourself. They'd know in five minutes. And anyway, you know yourself there's no controlling who turns up at funerals. You can't rely on them to have the decency to stay away.'

And that was that. When she thought of Lauren, with her family of sisters who rang each other twice a day, her plump smiling mother who made baked goods containing cinnamon for every conceivable occasion, Sheen knew that she would have to pretend. As for Tom, he was puzzled, then bewildered, then alarmed. 'I mean, who lives like this?' he said. 'Who doesn't go to their own mother's funeral?'

And she could see him processing her evasions, big and small: their wedding in Kennebunkport for which only Maura had travelled over; the lack of photos from before, the times she'd fobbed him off when he'd suggested visiting the farm where she grew up, its fields of cantering horses, its homestead like a Third Avenue bar.

The week of Ma's funeral, Tom was at one of his regular offsites somewhere upstate. Sheen was on her own in the apartment, and all the time she was supposed to be in Belfast, she stayed there with the blinds closed watching twenty-four-hour news with the volume down. As she worked her way through the pasta and the long-life milk, she was reminded of a documentary she'd seen once about a family in Brooklyn who, waiting for Armageddon, had stockpiled three years' worth of beans and rice, bullets and bottled water. She imagined them, still sitting there with their gas masks on, as she hid from the truth behind her own apartment door.

Walking away from the pub, she tries not to think about Maura and her windows and what any of this might mean. She gulps down sea air, moving briskly towards the pier, and attempts to distract herself by focusing instead on the boats tied up alongside. One, two fishing boats, a motor cruiser, then the ferry. In the inner harbour, halyards clink on masts, and the water is like a thick block of glass on a bed of shell-strewn sand. The boats are smaller here, and she makes herself recite their names. *Fandango*, *Summer Sunset*, *Aisling*, *Silver Swallow*, *Boru*. Once, and again, and again.

And then she sees him, right at the end of the pier, unloading something from a boat. This time, Theo greets her like an old friend, waving his hand high in the air. He drops what he's been doing and starts to walk along the pier towards her. It feels corny, and she can't think what to do with her face. When they meet halfway along the pier, he stops, says hi. And when they walk back towards his boat, he introduces it as if it's a small child. 'This is *Marianna*,' he says.

She doesn't know what you say to a boat. It's nothing special – whiteish, serviceable, with streaks of orange where the rust from weathered fittings has bled down on to the fibreglass. The stern is packed tight with strands of wood. Long and slim, like a druid's staffs, still sprouting tender tufts of green. She remembers then about the chairs that nobody buys. All of a sudden, he seems to run out of conversation. She fills the silence with the boy in the pub and the cappuccino he couldn't make.

'I'll make you coffee,' he says. 'In fact, I'm just on my way to stock up the workshop. I'll bet you haven't even been out that way yet, have you? So, why don't you come and have coffee with me instead?'

She hasn't done this for years, since before Tom. Habit makes her hesitate, though the last thing she wants right now is to be alone.

'Come and see the workshop. Then, when you want to leave, I'll drop you home.'

He touches her arm, cradles her elbow in his palm, and gently leads her away.

His blue pick-up truck is parked at the head of the pier. She gets in next to him as the engine wheezes into life. On the steep climb up from the sea, she wonders once or twice if the truck will make it at all. Up on the ridge, his mobile phone rings. He pulls into the verge to take the call, says he'll only be a minute.

'I told you he was useless,' she hears him say as he steps down from the truck, just before he slams the door shut.

'Yes,' he says, his voice muffled now. 'Don't worry. I'm already on to it.' And then he's out of earshot. Watching the cast of him, the decisive way he pulls stalks of long grass out of the verge as he talks into the phone, she has the thought that he is exactly the person she could do with right now.

17

Boyle watches them driving up from the harbour. He gives himself a whack. Wake the fuck up, Boyle. Wake up, you gobshite. Are you going to let it happen all over again? When you should have seen it coming last time?

When he first came to Lamb, the commune was in its heyday. Benders and love beads – Nuclear? Nein danke – the end of the world. The twins from Dublin with their long flowery dresses and tiny little tits. The girl from Galway who made cardboard pyramids to mark the ley lines, sitting naked by the Marriage Stones on rainy, full-moon nights. Your one from Bremerhaven who caught a goat and kept it in a field and put a crown of daisies on its head. Hours they spent on the beach out at Reen. They stayed there most of that first summer, corralled against the world, only sleeping in the schoolhouse when the weather got too bad to be outside. They thought it was gas craic to call a commune 'School', when school was what they'd just escaped. Right from the start, Boyle wanted rules, but the others were dead against writing stuff down. Who do you think you are, Boyle? Karl Fucken Marx?

He has never found out how Theo heard about the commune. He just showed up one day with a dirty yellow rucksack and never left. Names aren't easy to retrieve after all this time, so when he tries to picture the people who were there then, he has to think in labels. Redhead, lentils, nose ring, aggressive prick, no bra, psycho, big blue beads.

The first couple of summers were mental, but the winters were hard. Once the weather turned, most girls wanted showers, duvets, chocolate and before long they were heading back to wherever it was they'd come from. There were always some diehards, of course, and their numbers were swelled by a new batch that arrived each June once the exams were over. Until one year there were no new arrivals at all. In the end, even the twins with the tiny little tits went back up to Dublin. And then there were just the two of them: Boyle and the Dutchman. Until, one day, the Dutchman announced that he was off too. I'm all right, Jack. Buys himself a shack of a place over at Goat Point with some money he'd been left by an uncle back in Rotterdam. Starts making bockety chairs out of wet strands of hazel, and suddenly he's a craftsman. Turns out there's a whole rake of eejits over on the mainland prepared to risk their arses on the Dutchman's chairs. He buys an old rust bucket, gets in with Lonergan. Next thing, there's fellas from Rotterdam hanging round the place, and the boat is off at all hours of the night, phut-phutting out to sea and back again. And Lonergan up to his neck in it all.

But right from when he arrived on Lamb, one of the girls from School reckoned Theo had a dark secret. 'You can tell if you stand near him,' she said. 'You get an awful scald off his aura.'

Nobody else had a problem with Theo, at least not to start with. He was good with women. They lapped him up. Even Boyle was taken in at first. However, one summer night out at Reen, it all began to look quite different. There was a crowd of them there, and everyone was drunk or high, and playing Truth or Dare. On these occasions, the Dutchman usually stayed on the fringe of things – as if he was above it all, as if he merited a bit of distance from the rest of them. He hadn't slept with any of the girls at this stage, but that only made them want him even more. Boyle couldn't understand what they saw in him, but he already had two or three of them tucked in around him that night, their peaky little faces turned up at his. Unusually, it was warm enough to sit outside in the moonlight. Oddly, it wasn't raining.

They had lit a small spitting fire from blocks someone had bought from a man in Skibbereen. There were no trees to cut, even then, on Lamb. That felt like cheating to Boyle, but nobody else seemed to care. When the game began, the first one up for Truth or Dare was the Dutchman, who didn't seem to understand the rules. Something bad you got away with? Nobody ever told the real truth. The stories had grown ever more outlandish as the summer went on. But the Dutchman told his story with such attention to detail that it felt different from the story-telling games they'd played before. And all the time he had this smirk on his face, as if he was enjoying the fact that no one could tell whether he was being serious or not. Even then, when he couldn't have been more than twenty-two, he was a superior little shit. He stood up, so that his face was no longer lit by the fire and all there was to focus on was his voice.

He had been in love once, he said, and then he wasn't. The girl wouldn't get the message. She couldn't take no for an answer. And very soon she started to become a pain in the ass. Standing outside in the rain, gazing up at his window. Sending him letters. Phoning at midnight. Threatening to cut her wrists. It got to the point that he couldn't take it any more. It was December, just before Christmas. And this was the Netherlands, remember? It was cold. Really cold. He seemed proud of that cold. Proud that he understood cold they couldn't even imagine.

Then, one day, this girl followed him home from the university. There were lots of people around and he guessed that she was going to cause a scene. So he said, 'Let's go down to the lake and talk there.' That's where they went. He told her that he was going away, that he wasn't worth waiting for, that she should move on. But she wouldn't listen.

Boyle remembers the firelight flickering in the faces of the girls, all chanting at him. Truth or Dare. Truth or Dare. And the expression of scorn in his voice. For her, for them, for everyone maybe.

'I told her that if you want the truth, you can have it,' he said. 'You mightn't want it, though. *She* didn't.'

Because that's what he'd tried to tell this girl, he said. Back there, at that lake. He'd tried to tell her the truth. That he didn't love her, that she had never turned him on, that there were other girls.

'But she just kept going. "Love me, love me, love me." On and on and on and on.'

When he'd turned to leave, she came after him. And then, somehow, she tripped.

'I swear to God it wasn't anything to do with me,' he said, and the girls on either side of him threw their heads back and laughed, their mouths open like little calling birds.

'But over she went. Crack, on to the ice. After that, she didn't move again. One moment she was shouting at me. And the next moment she was completely still. I knew she would die if she stayed out there. It was minus, I don't know, eight, ten? I stood there awhile and watched her. You could never tell when that girl was acting. Believe me. But this time she wasn't acting. Not this time. I could have saved her, of course. But, then again, so could anyone. And if I saved her, she would only have loved me even more. She would have thought I was her hero. And so I didn't. I realised how easy it would be, just to walk away. And that's what I did. I walked away. And I felt freeeeee.'

He raised his arms and made them into wings. And he flapped those wings at the silly star-struck girls crowded woozily around the campfire. Boyle has never forgotten the insult in that. The Dutchman sat back down again, his Truth delivered, and the little bird-like hippies on either side of him laughed and laughed and laughed. But they were not as drunk as they seemed, nor as high. They were not as silly either. Next morning, they were down at the pier with their backpacks on, waiting for the first ferry out.

Boyle sometimes sees that woman himself, even now. In his dream, her face turns blue just as the light of dusk begins to cast an eerie light on the iced lake. He imagines her limbs turning into sticks, the skin becoming a taut casing for her frozen blood. He imagines the frost settling on her eyebrows and on the tips of her eyelashes.

As the pick-up plunges down the rough track out to Theo's studio, the cargo of wood rattles against the metal bed of the truck. Theo doesn't say much, just reaches out his hand for Róisín's. His skin is soft, uncalloused. She's surprised to find such hands in someone who makes chairs. She glances at him, but his eyes are still on the road. Overhead, herons *ack ack ack*, sweeping up from the strand.

'Here we are,' he says.

At first, she doesn't see the building – more barn than house – just a rough concrete structure set into an incline beneath screeds of black, fissured rock that are relieved here and there by clumps of sea pinks. When they get out of the truck, he stands there a moment, looking out to sea.

'Right out there in the distance. You see? Off on the

horizon? That's the inshore lane. Supertankers, cargo ships, even tall ships now and then. Sometimes there's a line of them way out on the horizon. I only have to look at that to know I'd rather be on Lamb. Who wants to be out there, travelling the straight lines?' And then he turns to her. 'I know what you're thinking. That it was a bit of a drive, just for coffee.'

'I hope it's good,' she smiles, not that she cares.

'Of course. Good coffee – it's the Dutch way.' He nods towards the small thicket of hazel wands on the back of the truck. 'Come, let me show you the workshop.'

The door to the house is just a sheet of metal to which a handle has been fitted. She associates metal doors with shebeens in West Belfast, with a certain kind of New York nightclub. There's an edginess to a metal door. He opens it just wide enough for her to squeeze through. Inside, she can hear the scurrying of paws, a low growl, an outbreak of hoarse, frenzied barking. She recoils, and then she sees that he is watching her.

He smirks at her. 'Who's afraid of the big bad wolf?'

He enters the house ahead of her, and she can hear him grappling with the dog, the faint ching of a lead being applied to a collar, the sound of a door being closed.

'OK,' he calls. 'All clear.'

The dog is growling, clawing at the wood of the closed door, but she tries not to show her fear. The main room is much brighter than seemed possible from the outside. There are two large Veluxes in the steeply pitched roof, and a battery of windows is set high into the bare white walls. There are no pictures or photos. No books, no sofa, no comfortable chairs. There seems scarcely anything personal about the space at all. The few items of furniture are angular, metallic, surprisingly modish for somewhere so remote. There is an industrial-style lamp and the only seating is a long low bench covered in a kind of sackcloth, a thick linen weave. The whole effect reminds her of a New York loft.

He catches her hand. 'Stop,' he says.

And even though it strikes her that he's a bit too ready with his orders, she acquiesces. Stands, waits, listens.

'Do you get that smell? Now, breathe it in. Burnt sugar, right? Hazelnut praline.'

As they walk through the main room into the studio proper, the praline smell grows stronger. She has a brief pungent flashback to New York and 31 Flavors – one for every day of the month. Butterscotch Ribbon and Vanilla Burnt Almond, and she is at Astoria Park pool with Tom one sunny day they both bunked off work.

In the Dutchman's workshop, there is an assortment of machines, a rack of carpentry tools – blunt, scuffed, sharp, scarred. He lifts a wand of hazel from a stack propped up in the corner. He switches on a machine, and when he drills out a plug of moist white bark, the hazel steams.

'Ice cream, right?'

He is pleased with her reaction and she has to admit that the aroma is astonishing. What really interests her, though, is the ascetic self-control of his living quarters. Everything measured and in its place. She is struggling to pay attention to the machinery, but Theo seems keen to show her what he does. He selects another wand of hazel, takes her hand and trails her fingers along the silver-green bark.

'See how fresh it is, so full of life?'

He peels off a long thin strip of bark. 'You see? Not like wood at all.'

The pith is cool and moist. More flesh than wood.

'Have I earned my coffee yet?' she asks. Something about the wood and the instruments that strip it down and gouge it out makes her uneasy.

'You really want coffee?' he asks.

She shrugs.

He brings her into the galley kitchen. She is trying not to look too inquisitive, but she notes the rolls of twine wrapped around sticks nailed horizontally on to the shelves, the cartons of small steel hardware items, the rolls of plastic sheeting. There are charts, fenders, unidentifiable bits of metal and plastic. It all looks very industrial for the studio of someone making something so organic. And there are so few half-finished pieces around, so little chaos or mess. In fact, it's so unlike any of the artists' studios she's visited with Lauren that she can't help asking him whether he sells many chairs.

He turns and looks her in the eye. 'It's not just commerce, Sheen. When you stop making things, the demons come calling.'

He starts spooning coffee granules into two white mugs. She is surprised that he uses instant after the claims he made about his coffee, but he makes no apology for it and she decides to let it pass.

'Do you have demons, Sheen?'

She is taken aback. She has no idea what answer she is expected to give, and so she decides not to play the game. 'Demons? I don't believe in those.'

He takes her in his arms and she is glad that, even after all this time, her intuition about men hasn't deserted her.

His lovemaking is no more exotic than his coffee. It isn't tender enough to open up her pain at losing Tom. It isn't passionate enough to disarm her. It is functional, and a little distant. But it does what she hoped it might do. It holds back her fear, if only for a while. And she thinks that maybe it has made her a new friend. Very soon, she might need a friend on Lamb.

Later, she watches him drowsing there beside her, his legs spreadeagled, his cock a curl on his thigh. She is out of practice when it comes to this, but she feels less fragile now, less alone. She gets out of his bed and finds her clothes and sees that the light is fading. Suddenly, it seems important to get back to Reen, to the slow sweep of the lighthouse beam, because Lonergan is almost within reach.

18

Boyle feels like breaking up the place. He imagines them together, laughing about him. He imagines the names they are calling him. In his head, the Dutchman has his hands on her. She is taking off her shirt for him, and her small, dark nipples are as hard as nuts. He thinks of her neatness, her careful ways. He thinks of the ribbon on the suitcase, the careful bundle of pens. He hopes she turns out to be a useless ride, that that bastard of a Dutchman has to jack himself off.

Standing on the threshold of her living room, he wonders whether she has noticed any of his little messages yet. The heart she wears on her schoolgirl sleeve. His DNA on her dressing gown. And then he sees the ruins of his pink manilla message in the grate of her fireplace. So that's all he means to her? Bitch. Well, she'll notice him now. He takes out the yellowed sheet of newspaper with the ridiculous photofit and tapes it carefully to the glass of her framed school photograph.

The bullet he sinks into the slightly hardened sugar in the bowl next to the teabags in the top cupboard. Then he changes his mind. She doesn't look like the type of woman who takes sugar on her cereal, so he makes a claw of his fingers and digs it out again. In the bathroom, there are jars and bottles on the frosted-glass shelf above the basin. Potions, lotions, creams and dreams. He looks at himself in the mirror and sticks his tongue out. White today. Scummy. He flips the cap off a bottle of shampoo that smells like one of her funny teas. For a moment he toys with the idea of leaving the bullet out there, just next to the toothpaste. But then he imagines it being knocked over, the moment lost. He unscrews the lid of a jar of foundation instead. Very carefully he presses the bullet down into the swirl of flesh-coloured cream. Just below the surface, a little fright of steel.

The photo of the young girl looking back over her shoulder, he folds in two – no point in everything being seen at once – and slots it in behind the kitchen clock, wedging it in there, so it won't be dislodged. Then he sets to work. He unhooks the catch on one window, then another, and another and another, until the whole house is wide open to the south-westerly whipping up from the bay. The bedroom curtains billow and fall. The photos on the windowsill slide into the air where the wind catches them. The ash from the fireplace powders the room.

A gust of wind, a shattering, and on the floor a hundred tiny glinting chips of blue. He starts sweeping at the shards, and several lodge in the heel of his hand. As he pulls them out, they release tiny bulbs of blood. He cleans up the mess as best as he can, keeps a flitter of tiny pieces for himself. But he's mad with himself over that little blue bottle. He is always breaking things he only ever wanted to admire.

And then, just as suddenly as it came on him, the anger is sucked out. His mood shifts like a West Cork sky, from orange to grey. He is anxious now. Concerned. Her and the Dutchman. Fuckit anyway. She should have let him look after her. She should have let him in. And then he remembers the thing she doesn't realise she showed him: her fear of the dark. Today, like every day, she has left on the outside light. He flicks it off.

In both bedrooms, he unscrews the bulb from the centre light fitting. He takes her matches and pockets the two torches she keeps by the bed. When she can't stand the dark any more, when she realises she needs him, he'll be there.

Before he goes, he picks up a few bits and pieces he can give Lonergan to shut him up. A couple of photographs, a sheet or two from the file she keeps under the sofa. Interviews and speeches. Bullshit and lies. Blah blah blah. Because he could do with his two hundred. He could do with a hot dinner and a decent fuck and a new pair of shoes. He could do with his old job back, too. The Dutchman must be too busy to sort out Lonergan's house, because he's seen Hannie Fogarty heading up there instead. Hannie will have made up the beds by now. She'll have turned on the central heating to take the chill off the place. Boyle has seen her buying butter and milk in

Molly's, collecting briquettes from the ferry. He's seen her heading out in her old green banger, up towards the middle road.

Down at the pier, Boyle watches the evening ferry lurching home. He sits on the blue bench outside Molly's and waits for the passengers to disembark. They are indistinguishable from a distance, wrapped up in all-weather gear. As they move up the pier, he can make out a young couple, foreign-looking, struggling with heavy backpacks. Then a family group, the mother carrying a toddler on her hip. Two men in jeans and bomber jackets walk smartly up the road. Black jackets, blue jeans, trainers. They carry no baggage. They could be anybody, but Boyle has seen their type before. It means there's a consignment due in at Goat Point. Which means that Theo will be kept busy, and that Lonergan won't be long now.

On the drive back across the island, Theo seems preoccupied with the messages that beep constantly into his phone. Now and then, he lifts it from the well between the seats to check it. Halfway across the island, they meet another vehicle and he pulls into the side and takes the opportunity to send a text. In the half-light, Róisín can just about make out Murphy in the oncoming car. He sees her too and flips a finger from the steering wheel. A greeting or a warning, it could be either.

When they arrive back at Reen, and the car crunches through the gates towards the front door, she notices two things that don't fit. The outside light has been switched off, and every single window at the front of the house is open.

'What's the matter?' Theo sounds irritated. 'You were the one who wanted to come back. I was quite happy where I was.'

She half remembers another encounter from years ago, one that turned sour within an hour or two. Before she can find her voice to say that she's certain she switched on the outside light before she left, that she never leaves anything open, he remembers himself, retrieves his manners. 'Have you got your key, Sheen? Then let me walk you to the house. Come.'

Opening the door, she is met by a through draught. A wild dance of tangled newspaper, the flap of kitchen blinds. The lighthouse beam sweeps across the room and shows things scattered on the floor. Then Theo switches on the light. A substance like watered-down white paint has spattered the tiled floor. The cereal box she left on the table after breakfast has been knocked over. There is ash everywhere. One by one, she slams the windows shut. The draught eases, and things begin to settle, but she is impatient for him to go now so that she can check that everything that matters is still there.

From the direction of her bedroom, a faint flutter. And there on the floor, a small dark bundle twitching on the tiles.

She's never seen a bird so close up before. A sparrow, one wing in the air, the other, half trapped, licking uselessly against the tiles. She touches it with her finger. Feels the fierce thud of its heartbeat. She goes to try to lift it, but its wings seem far too delicate to hold.

Theo is beside her now, standing over her. 'If you lift it up and fling it through the window it might just fly. Otherwise . . .' He shrugs. 'Nature.'

His attitude to the bird annoys her, but she is upset by the mess too. He starts lifting a few items in a desultory fashion, but she tells him not to bother, that she will clear it up herself. He looks straight at her. 'Sure?'

He has his phone out again now, punching in a text.

'If you need a hand clearing this up, just call me, OK?'

He moves towards her and puts his hand on her breast, trailing a finger across her nipple. She almost tells him to fuck off, to keep his hands to himself, but then he dips his mouth to hers and kisses her, and the moment passes.

'See you soon, yeah?'

When she hears Theo's engine kick in, she rushes to check that the envelope is still where she left it, tucked away in its cold oven. That established, she feels a little better, but there is still the matter of the bird. She lies down on the cold tiles and puts her head right next to it.

'Let's try, bird,' she says. 'Let's give it a go.'

Making a cage of her fingers, she carries it lightly to the window. Its warmth revolts her, the insistent drum of its heart. She hates the fact that, so near death, it is still alive and fighting. That somehow it has made itself her unasked-for responsibility.

Standing at the open window, she flings back her hands as if casting a net, and the bird is through. But it doesn't fly, just drops wetly into the grass. She stands there, watching its struggle. There must be cats, she thinks. Foxes and rats. It's only a matter of time. It has landed right in the middle of the lighthouse beam, like a blip on a radar screen. She forces herself to join it there, lifts it again, throws it again, and still it fails to fly. Next to the pebbledash wall, a pile of stones the previous tenant must have cleared from the grass. She chooses the most substantial one and carries it to where the bird has fallen. She stands over the bird with the stone aimed at its head, but she still can't bring herself to drop it. She can't bear to have to kill another thing.

Inside the house, she works non-stop to clean away the mess the bird has made. She mops the floor, wipes the surfaces and gathers together the papers that have been scattered by the draught from the open windows. When that's all done, she drinks thirstily from the tap, then boils a pot of water for some tea. She knows that she should make herself eat something, so she slices a tomato into thick red circles, criss-crosses it with little strips of pepper from one of Renzo's jars, grates on some cheese. She uses the good Sicilian oil that Renzo insisted she take with her, sprinkles some of his balsamic vinegar. 20 star. Aged. She makes time stretch, waiting for the bird to die.

She washes everything carefully, puts all of it away. By the time she's finished, an hour has passed and the sky is darker. She tells herself the sparrow will be gone by now. And finally, she allows herself a glance out of the window. But there it is, still caught in the sweep of the beam, still twitching. This time when she goes outside she is resolute. She finds the rock again, and this time she drops it on its head. When it is done, she screws her eyes shut and takes herself to a world where the bird has recovered. Where she has mended its wing. Where she is the child with the pen filler who has nursed it back to health.

She tells herself that the window catches are weak, that one might easily blow open when met with a strong gust. But all of them? The papers the wind has snatched are insignificant. But the temporary respite she felt has gone. She decides to sleep in the smaller room tonight, the one the bird hasn't soiled. But when she flicks the switch for the overhead light, nothing happens. So far, she has kept control of her imagination, but now she feels it start to slip away from her. In her head, the house is darkening. Desperate for light, she searches the other bedroom for the torches she keeps on the bedside table. They're nowhere to be found. She pats her pockets for the one she always carries on her, and breathes again to find it there. Her hands are shaking, and she struggles to steady the beam, but it's obvious that the centre light bulb is missing. There was one last night, she's sure, but now it's gone. As simple and shocking as that is, the certainty that someone has been inside the house cannot be got around.

She stands completely still, listening for any sound of an intruder – a rustle in the bathroom, a footstep on the gravel outside. She clutches at the mobile in her jacket pocket. Reception inside the house is terrible, but she can't bring herself to venture outdoors. She tries every corner of the house for signal. It's only when she returns to the living room that she sees Dolores.

The photofit is a pantomime version of the image that,

these days, is always in her head. It is no more real than one of the Japanese kabuki masks that Lauren has hanging on her apartment walls. But, even so, it almost stops her heart. The walls around her start to sag and swell with the weight of her own breath. She can visualise Dolores right in front of her – hands on hips, teeth grinding on a bulb of over-chewed gum. Eyebrows plucked to felt-tip swipes, slicked-on mouth, dead coal eyes, a blank moon-face. She imagines Dolores whispering in her ear.

Think anybody's going to take your word against his about ancient history? No one cares about all that any more. There's people have businesses depending on the likes of you know who. Financial interests. Political plans. Policies and jobs. And real power for a change. And anyway, you were up to your neck in it all yourself. Since when did you become Mother Teresa? You knew what would happen to those soldiers, and you let it happen. And now that your conscience bothers you, you're trying to rewrite the past in your own favour. But whatever else you do, you'll not get Lonergan. And you know why, Róisín? Because you'll not be let. So, if you're on that wee island, just take a look around you. Make sure to take a really good look, because I'll be there with you. Even if you haven't seen me yet, I'm there.

Time and time again, Róisín has googled her, but Dolores has left no trace.

Dolores Farry.

Honeytrap Dolores.

Even the incident itself is hard to trace now, buried under all that came after it. But the mark Dolores left on Róisín has never faded.

Someone has been in here. Someone who knows. Would she recognise Dolores if she saw her again? A small dark figure on the deck of a ferry? A shadow behind the pinched curtains of the yellow house? She remembers the sense of reprieve she'd felt when the photofit was published. The possibility it allowed her to tell herself that she hadn't really been in the Copacabana club at all. But here she is again. Dolores, claiming her back.

Suddenly, there are so many things to be afraid of that her brain won't work. She jabs again and again at Murphy's number, until finally, magically, it connects. She can tell she's woken him, but she doesn't care.

'Somebody's been in here. Who else has keys?'

'If you'd feel happier with the locks changed –'

'They've been in the house.'

'They?'

And then she realises that she's said too much.

'Someone.'

'Grand, so. I'll sort that out for you in the morning. I'll have the lads over –'

'I mightn't be here in the morning,' she says. She's being melodramatic, but she doesn't care.

The pause before he speaks is Murphy distancing himself. She recognises that reaction. From other people. From way back. From before.

'I'll be over first thing.'

'And meanwhile I'm a sitting duck.'

'Don't worry, now, you'll be grand.'

She starts to tell him about the note on her door, about the open windows and the bird. She talks about anything but Lonergan. She mentions the weirdo from the school-house, about him turning up with a shovel on his shoulder, and how she'd felt threatened without knowing why. She doesn't talk about the only thing that really frightens her – that she might not get the chance to do what she's come here for. Instead, she concentrates on Boyle. She can tell that Murphy understands that fear.

'You should have mentioned that earlier, about Boyle hanging around,' he says. 'I don't like the sound of that myself.'

She senses that he's begun to weaken and so she moves to close the deal. 'Get over here right now then, and put a fucking deadlock on my door.'

Once she's put the phone down, she is galvanised. She rushes through the house, whipping shut the curtains. In the living room, she balances on an arm of the sofa and drapes a double sheet across the redundant curtain pole, blocking out the night.

Now that she can't be watched, she turns on every light. Whoever he is, he'll have left a trace, whether he meant to or not. In the bathroom, the bar of soap has scum on it. There are shit streaks on the loo. Her dressing gown isn't where it normally hangs and the sugar in the bowl has had a hot coffee spoon in it. None of those things is down to her. And then she sees a small shard of blue, stuck in the grouting of the living-room floor. When she realises what that means for Sheen's mother's perfume bottle, all the other things that she has half-noticed before become obvious to her: the strange smell from her dressing gown, the freshly smoked rollie outside the back door, the little mislaid items here and there. Everything else seems OK, but nothing is really OK now. Now, at the edges of her mind, Dolores has returned. She has crept back in, with her white moon-face, her kohl-black eyes.

While Roísín waits for Murphy to arrive, she stuffs everything she can find – sheets, clothes, the lot – into the washing machine. She rinses every bit of crockery and cutlery in the place, scrubs the toilet and the shower. She tips the contents of the food cupboard – teabags, cereal, even the sugar from the bowl – into the bin. And when she's finished and Murphy has arrived she stands there with her hands on her hips and watches as he screws on bolts to all the windows and doors.

'That'll do the trick,' he says.

'But it won't make a blind bit of difference when I'm out, will it? There'll always be an unbolted door then.'

'We'll get on to the locks in the morning. I'll send two fellas over to you. The main thing is you're secure tonight.'

When he's gone, she tears Dolores into tiny pieces, but she forces herself to look Lonergan in the eye.

19

After the Good Friday drought, the bar is full. Cat's big green Buddha is in his usual place at the end of the bar, his neck draped with spare rubber bands and a key chain from the last World Cup. Pete's on duty tonight – skinny little Pete, lifting pulled pints like they'd crack his wrists. Already, the place is filling up with lads in to watch the match on the flat-screen telly. When the door opens, the wind blows serviettes off the stack on the counter. Each time, Pete goes haring after them. Some people never learn.

Pete leaves Boyle standing there while everyone else is served. Even when he finally condescends to take Boyle's order, he doesn't say anything – just puts a half of lager on the bar and tips the money in the till. As soon as Pete has turned his back though, Boyle has his revenge. He pours in a depth charge from a naggin of whiskey he keeps in an inside pocket, and takes his customary seat at the door. He expects to hear that Lonergan's arrived, that Theo has been over with the boat to pick him up from Baltimore, but nobody here is talking about Lonergan.

She's made a complaint. He can tell that as soon as they head for him. She's been shooting her mouth off. Murphy settles his fat arse on to one stool and that eejit Moore is propped up like Humpty Dumpty on the other. They pull themselves in close to the table so he's pinned in on both sides.

'You're to back off, Boyle,' says Murphy. 'It's harassment. You were warned the last time about creeping round the place.'

As he's sick to death of telling them, the last time had nothing to do with him. Nothing. The neon strip light flickers, and Boyle watches the specks of dead fly caught beneath its plastic carapace come and go.

'We've the season about to start and all the houses full for the break and the last thing we want is trouble,' says Murphy.

'No trouble now,' says Moore.

No trouble? Of course there'll be trouble. It's Easter. Won't there be a ferryload of teenagers over on the ferry for the fete? Crate-loads of lager and vodka and what have you. Camping and pissing where they like and vomiting over the fuchsia.

Boyle concentrates on the crack in the mirror over the bar. He traces its jagged little journey through the gilded script that's as faded as he is himself. The crack swipes through the 'o' in Powers Whiskey, and he recalls the headbutt that caused it, one regatta years ago. But now he's lost their drift again.

'We'll be under the spotlight more than ever this year. From the media and that. What with Lonergan just arrived up on the middle road, and him all over the news.'

Lonergan here already? Payday. Thank fuck for that. He plays dumb with them, though, puts his face back into neutral.

'For God's sake, Boyle. That politician fella. Sure you know him years. The yellow house, up the middle road.'

How thick do they think he is?

'So we might have the newspapers over, what with Lonergan and all that Jacinta O'Neill business. Hacks down from Dublin, crawling all over the place. Looking for a story. You remember what that was like, Boyle? Not pleasant, once you get those fuckers involved.'

They're talking to him like he's a headcase. They keep mentioning his stupid fucken name too, like he's ever likely to forget it.

'And the Guards. We'll have them over too if the new lady complains that you're some kind of weirdo peeping Tom.'

And then little Pete turns up the volume on the telly so there's no more talk, while red plays blue on green.

Back at the schoolhouse, Boyle hunts down the last sheet of pink manilla. His hands have a shake in them as the marker squeaks out the letters, but he keeps his hand as straight as he can manage. His heart is pounding at the back of his throat.

HE'S HERE

On the way up to her house, he hops over the wall into O'Driscoll's field for a quick check in under the bushes. He has a look under the big clumps of escallonia, swipes a foot beneath the gorse. Later in the year, there's often a stash of booze to be found in O'Driscoll's field. Left there by teenagers too pissed to remember where they put it. But it's early days for that, and today he's out of luck.

He goes to her back door, pins up the bit of paper, then walks around to the front. He's about to settle himself in his favourite vantage point, just beyond the blackberry hedge where he can get a good view of the picture window that looks out to sea. He can't believe his eyes. She's rigged something over it. The window is white, like a big blank canvas. He kicks at the woody tangle of undergrowth. What the fuck has she done to his window? A sheet. She's tacked up a sheet. Fuckit anyway. He comes in closer, examines the material for rips or tears, some place she hasn't tacked it down well enough. But she's done it like a pro. Not a gap anywhere.

Two can play at that game. Why should he bother to let her know? So what if she gets the land of her life when she walks in the door of that Céilí, and there he is in front of her, Brian Lonergan, and the whole island there too, bowing and scraping and fawning all over him? With a Deputy this, and a Deputy that, and a Fuck Me Rigid while I get you your tea. He reaches up and rips the notice off the door.

He stands there and gazes at the sheet like it's the bloody shroud of Turin. And, sure enough, something happens. An image starts to develop. An image of her, forming in his head. It's the first time he's felt the urge like this since Jennifer. An itch in his painting hand, a rush in his head.

Back at the schoolhouse he scrabbles in among the paint-stained rags, the dripped-on boards, the jars and yoghurt pots half filled with leftover pigment. Ruined yellows, murky Virgin blues and filthy reds. Deep in a cupboard, he finds a clutch of brushes. One by one, he tests them on the back of his hand, and finds just two that will still do the job. He's short of paint, but what the fuck. The main thing is to get her down some way. Scribble her on paper first, and leave the rest to later. But how will he depict her?

The Little Rose of Reen. Our Lady of the Lighthouse Beam. Róisín of the Sorrows.

He dashes down a sketch, then scratches it out again. He holds the pen like a dart, pinched between finger and thumb. A bad workman blames his tools. Narrowing his eyes, he aims for People You Should Know. The pen hits Leonardo right between the eyebrows. Whack, it goes. Bullseye.

He rummages through a pile of cardboard boxes for the one marked 'Music'. Three recorders, a triangle, a xylophone with a missing key. He blows on a recorder and wonders why he's never got around to doing that before. It truly is a dismal bloody sound. A sound more miserable than fifteen days of rain.

Pip pip Peeep
Pip pip Peeepo

I'm a creep
I'm a weirdo

He climbs up the stepladder and sits there like a Hare Krishna, playing the same tune, over and over again.

Pip pip Peeep
Pip pip Peeepo

20

The following evening, just before eight, Murphy arrives to pick Róisín up for the Céilí. He has a new kettle for her, still in its cardboard box. He is all solicitousness – trying the new locks, testing each key, explaining that this is the best kit money can buy. She is too distracted to take him to task over it any more than she already has done.

There's an overpowering smell of something sweet and musky in the jeep, and when she realises that it's probably for her benefit that makes it more cloying still. Murphy talks all the way to the other end of the island. The drive only takes fifteen minutes or so, but the talking goes on and on. All about Boyle and how he came to be in the schoolhouse. Not that she cares about Boyle.

'The place was vacant for years and then a group of young lads started using it – lighting fires and smoking your wacky baccy. The rest of them got sense and went back to the real world. But Boyle never did.'

'So it's your property then?' she asks innocently.

'Well now, 't'would be the government's property, if you got all cut and dried about it. 'T'would be theirs if they wanted it. But sure they couldn't be bothered. It must be thirty years or more since there was any school there. And not a penny have they put into it since.'

'But you should have it and he shouldn't. That's what you're saying, right?'

He takes his eyes off the road for a second to look at her and then he nods. 'That'd be the long and short of it.'

'What about the government? Why don't they do something about him?'

'This isn't America, you know. Come a gale and we're cut off from the world. Where's the government and the rest of them then?'

'Police?'

'We don't really have much call for them out here.'

'You had that woman who went missing.'

'And they made a right balls of that. Took them two whole days to get their act together last time. By then, nobody could remember if they'd seen her on a ferry out of here that week or not. We don't bother with official-dom out here. Most times, we sort ourselves out.'

He changes the subject then, begins to fill her in on the musicians, on the rivalry between this one and that one. She feels her mind start to wander. She imagines Lonergan up in that office of his, leaning back in his swivel chair, laughing on the phone about her, expecting her to have gone already. To be too shit-scared to stay.

*

The rain starts up again as Boyle leaves for the Céilí. *Meet the Community*. Community's a word that means whatever people want it to mean. It didn't mean much in the commune, back in the days of School. They all fucked off when it suited them, and to hell with Community. As for the Community Centre that Murphy says he'll build, Boyle spits on the broken tarmac and rubs the gobbet into it with the ball of his foot. No way will Murphy be building anything that doesn't line his own pocket. If he ever gets his hands on the schoolhouse he'll have it knocked down, the site marked out for holiday homes.

It's a fair old climb up over the ridge to reach the parish hall. He can hear a pair of feet behind him. He turns and sees it's Molly doing battle with the hill – head jutting forward and arse stuck out on account of her gammy hips. He stops, to be sociable, to let her catch up.

'We've not had you down here for a long time, Boyle,' she says, and sounds friendly enough about it, too. He wonders to himself when it was that they all stopped calling him by his Christian name. Pity. He might feel different about the world if it called him Vincent.

'It's good to see you joining in,' she says. 'No man is an island.'

I couldn't have put it better myself, he thinks, though I know a woman who is. He's seen Molly naked, though she doesn't know it. He's seen her tits, the greyish fuzz of her muff. A little bony island, she makes. He looks into the blue spirals of her eyes. They make him seasick, but even so he forces out a pleasantry or two.

'It's nice to have a new one here,' he says.

'Now you're not to –'

'I know,' he says. 'You said.' She shuts up then, and anyway he knows what it was she wanted to say.

They walk up the road companionably enough, Boyle a little ahead. As they climb higher, anticipation puffs his chest.

'New shoes, Boyle?'

He looks down at the trainers he got from the Dutchman, that time he helped out on a piloting job into Shawnee Cove. Ten hours of work. And in return a pair of trainers, a bottle of Paddy and a sample of the merchandise. She misses nothing, Molly.

Inside the hall, a pair of long, fizzing neon strips drain the place of any hope of atmosphere. The musicians are ready for action, sitting on the stage beneath a crooked tricolour. The accordion gives a wheeze, and he dreads the awful music they're about to inflict.

Over at the side, Hannie has a trestle table set up and she's doling out minerals and tea like it's back in the fifties. Murphy is on the door, doing what he's good at, collecting money. As for the eejit he has working for him, the lad looks like an Elvis impersonator, his hair slicked back at the sides and a big black quiff to the front.

The new one is there, of course, like a little queen, with a clatter of locals around her. And then Lonergan arrives. When he enters the hall, Murphy's nieces from the mainland are up on the stage in their Irish dancing costumes – all ringlety wigs and flat feet. Boyle watches the new one's reaction. She clocks Lonergan straight off.

And how could she not? Hasn't she every possible angle on him all laid out on the kitchen table?

She's clutching at her skirt, her fingers working out and in and out and in. You can see, right there, the fright in her. He thinks back to the little cold feet that first night. Imagines her as a teenager alone in New York. A kid, that's all. Boyle is not a man without a heart. She needs protection. What she really needs is him.

As for Lonergan, he doesn't seem to know which one she is. He makes a tour of the room, shaking any hand that's held out to him. No family with him, this year, by the looks of it. No teenage sons slumped at the back of the hall, jabbing into their phones, no anorak-and-trainers wife. Odd, that, at Easter. But then, he's come on business this time. Boyle raises his hand to greet him, but Lonergan looks away. Ah yes, of course. He stifles the little rush of bile.

The musicians have moved on to a reel. The most you can say for a reel is that it's nearly always better than a jig. Boyle is glad of the naggin in his inside pocket. He takes a swig and winces at the too-bright lights. Murphy has her up dancing now. Boyle is curious to see how she moves, if she's free in herself or not. Not, it turns out. She dances like she's watching herself doing it. He wonders if that's how she'd be in the sack. Always arranging herself. Never able to let herself go. Would that be her? He feels himself stir. Thank fuck, he thinks. He thought it had died on him.

She's looping the loop with Murphy now, head down under an arch of arms and out the other side. She's lined up between some Shirley Temple Irish dancer kid and Pete. And Murphy has taken the mic now. He's telling them all the different names they call that dance in other countries – Strip the Willow, the Kentucky Reel. Are you serious, man? Honest to God, who gives a fuck?

She's lunging from arm to arm. Swinging her way down the row of dancers. And half of Lamb is out on that dance floor, clapping and yahooing. Eejits, all of them. And she is on her own in that room, apart from him. Only Boyle understands that expression on her face. Only he can read that look in her eyes. The new one is desperate. She's terrified.

As soon as he sees the Dutchman at the back of the hall, he knows what's coming next. When he sits down next to Boyle, the Dutchman doesn't even bother looking at him, just speaks straight ahead like he's addressing the wall.

'Well, Boyle, what do you think? Will I or won't I?'

He doesn't answer. The Dutchman will have her whatever he says.

'Well, you know what? I already have.'

When the knot of men surrounding Lonergan loosens, Róisín spots the back of his head, pinkly polished, with a little trim of greyish hair. He wears glasses these days. Steel-rimmed. Brown trousers and an open-necked shirt, a V-neck patterned jumper. He is not as tall as she remembers him, nor as physically formidable, but she can't control the panic, the sense of being much too close for

250

comfort. Is it noticeable to others? Does it show on her face? She scans the room. Most people are still dancing or talking or lining up at the tea bar. Most people aren't looking anywhere near her. Except for Boyle, that is. He has seen the photos, so he is watching her watching Lonergan. He is reading her, and she is not accustomed to being read.

She hates the scrutiny. It infuriates her, but she has no time for that. She needs to concentrate, and so she turns her back on him.

Lonergan is moving slowly through the room, pumping hands, slapping backs. She follows the back of his head, a pale pinkish blur. She imagines taking him on and ruining him, aiming at that head, smashing it to smithereens, but then she checks herself. What is she thinking?

She has rehearsed for this. She has prepared a litany of reassurances to get her through this first long-distance sighting. She is out of context here, and Lonergan won't recognise her. She has never suggested she would come here. This is the last place he will expect to find her. Those things had sounded robust enough in a New York apartment, on a transatlantic flight, in the B&B near Cork airport. But they have been blown to bits, now that Lonergan is only feet away from her and Dolores has been on her wall. He is standing with his back to her at the other end of the room, talking to a short-legged priest whose jumper is pulled tight across the drum of his belly. And even though the confrontation she has planned is a private one, even though she envisages a negotiation behind closed doors, she is tempted to approach him now in case she doesn't get another chance. A little red-haired girl runs up to Lonergan. He pulls something from his pocket and hands it to her and the girl claps her hands in delight. She clasps him round the knees, then runs off to show whatever it is to her mother.

Róisín watches all this, the figures simmering in the middle distance like a mirage. Then, as though something has alerted him to her – her eyes on him, perhaps – Lonergan turns around, a full 180-degree switch, and stares right back at her. He skirts the line of dancers and makes his way towards her. All of a sudden, she is quite incapable of movement, let alone speech. Lonergan is approaching now, his glasses glinting under the neon strip lights, his hands clenched at his sides. He glances at her, then through her. And then he passes by. In amazement, she watches him walk out of reach. And then he's through the door.

Her eyes are prickling, her skin cold with sweat. She can't imagine that none of this is obvious, or that her head is managing to stay still. He is playing with her, and she has lost the protection there might have been in half the island here as witnesses. She has no idea what she says to Molly when she sits beside her and asks her if she likes the music, but she manages something that passes muster well enough.

'Do you have parents still living?' Molly asks then, out of nowhere.

Róisín starts to tell her about Ma, until she feels the emotion welling up inside her.

'It must have been a terrible time to be living there,' Molly says then. She seems to have abandoned the enquiry about Ma and jumped into an entirely different conversation. Her face is grave, her tone confidential. And for all Róisín knows, Molly might be talking about Belfast in the darkest days or New York just after 9/11, because right now her thoughts are darting between the two. Molly places a hand on her forearm and the touch startles her. And perhaps she jumps, because Molly gives a little peep, and then she realises that the sound has nothing to do with her at all.

Molly is on her feet now, and heading over to a girl who is showing off a baby swaddled in a yellow blanket, a knitted hat on his head. Molly takes the baby into her arms, clucking and cooing at the little red face. Meanwhile, Róisín is in the upstairs room of a Belfast pub, and Lonergan is telling her she can never come home. But she is in New York, too, with Ma barely audible on the other end of the phone. Ma is talking about peonies, and how difficult she finds gardening these days. And perhaps Róisín should have picked up on that, perhaps she should. But even now she is convinced that there was no real warning that that would be the last time she would hear Ma's voice.

The rapprochement between them took place over many years. When Róisín first arrived in New York, Ma just didn't seem to want to know. Somehow, it was always Maura who answered the phone, while Ma was at the shops, or at the doctor's with a migraine. Maura seemed disgusted by her, and Róisín didn't dare to find out how much she knew. After she put down the phone, the air would seem heavier around her, like someone had slipped a hood back down over her head.

That first Christmas Eve, she pushed through the throngs of shoppers big-armed with brown paper bags of groceries, and stood in line at the post office until a booth came free. And this time she was in luck. Ma's voice sounded faint and cracked, like something played back on a tape recorder, but at least it was Ma. There was a delay on the line and their sentences hung there useless and limp until time caught up with them. Sometimes they both began to speak at once, and their words got jumbled. The whole thing just made Belfast seem even further away than ever. This was the first time they'd spoken since Róisín went, and yet there was no sign that Ma wondered much about that at all.

'I suppose you wouldn't be bothered with the turkey, over in America,' she said. 'We'll just have a wee chicken. No call for a turkey for just two people.'

Róisín kept wanting to change the subject. To talk about the things she wished that Ma could see, and maybe would see one day. The city muted by new snow, and all the Christmas windows: the champagne woman whose boyfriend wore a diamond-patterned golfing jersey, the girl with patent boots and garlands of tinsel in her hair, the sugar plum fairy.

'You'd love the windows, Ma. There's this shop called Lord and –'

'Aye, well, everything's still all boarded up over here, but they pushed the boat out with the City Hall this year.

It's like a wee palace. You never know, maybe things are looking up.'

She'd found it difficult to concentrate on what Ma was saying about Maura's new boyfriend, and whose nephew he was, because it was just so hard not to ask the obvious questions. Did nobody at school wonder what had happened to her? Was the head nun not on the phone? And Ma, who was always on about schoolwork and being good, how come she just took it all for granted? How come she just let her go, and wasn't bawling down the phone at her? What about the passport, Da's wallet? What had they told her that made any of this OK? And then, out of nowhere, she thought of poor, dead Ian and how he'd thought that she was lovely. It made the tears spring to her eyes. For a moment she just couldn't speak. She screwed her eyes shut, dug her fingernails into her arm.

'Did anyone come and visit you, after I'd gone?'

'A wee fella your da knew came to see me,' she said. 'A wee hood, actually.'

She made herself say it. 'Lonergan?'

'Aye. That's him. Well, that's the way of it. Your da's gone, Lorda mercy. And now there's Lonergan.'

She wanted to ask about Da, but she couldn't get the words out. She remembered him having visitors, people who came to the stuffy little parlour next to the kitchen. She wondered now if Lonergan had been one of those visitors. The doorbell would ring, and Ma's pink mules would clap along the lino as she rushed to answer it. Sometimes there would be a car outside, ticking over, until the front door slammed again and it drove off.

'There's things Lonergan wouldn't want known,' Ma said. 'Things your da covered up because it was the only way he could keep us all safe.'

Róisín didn't think safe was the right word, but she didn't say so.

'You won't be able to come back for a long time, love. So build a life for yourself. It'll be best for all of us if you're not in touch with home for the next wee while. You understand? Best we don't know much about you, or where you are.'

The air was punched from her lungs. It was such a shock to hear Ma talk like this that she couldn't even muster a reply. She sounded matter-of-fact about it, as if it was simply the obvious truth. For a moment, she sounded like she was going to say something more, to acknowledge something maybe, but whatever it was remained unsaid.

'As for Lonergan, it'll all come out about him one day, believe you me.'

But Róisín couldn't struggle past her own stupid tears. She didn't want to talk about Lonergan, or to know what Da had covered up for him. She just wanted none of this to have happened. She longed to be wee Róisín Burns again, to be stewing over her books at the kitchen table while Ma cooked the tea. But she had been set loose, and there was no going back.

She'd pushed open the heavy door of the booth, and wandered blindly through the post office until she was swept into the revolving door and out on to the street. Snow clipped at her cheeks, coming hard and icy now, while the tender surface of her heart was sealing itself like seared meat. She passed a bar with a green tinsel shamrock stuck on to the window and an automated Santa who danced arthritically on a patch of artificial grass. She crossed the street. There was no use being Róisín any more. All she really had now was Sheen.

Molly is back beside her, and pressing a glass into her hand. 'Wait till I tell you about that girl there with the baby. She was off in New York herself, a few years back. Some student travel thing, waitressing I think it was, down below the Trade Center itself. Wasn't she only after leaving the city to come home when those planes hit? It's an extraordinary thing, fate,' she says. 'Even now, it's hard to credit. You'd never have believed those towers could go over so quick.'

The remark catches Róisín off guard, and suddenly Molly is apologising and offering a crumpled tissue and something from the tea bar. And Róisín has no idea if she is crying because of Ma or because of what happened to those towers, or because she is frightened that she is so far out of her depth here that she might never be able to swim to land.

She sits there with Molly awhile, trying to screen out the music, mustering the energy she'll need to get herself home, in the almost dark, as far as the ridge where the lighthouse beam will guide her the rest of the way. Then Molly says she has to go. 'Will you be all right, lovey? I'll make sure Murphy brings you home. Or you can come with me now, if you like?'

Róisín says she's fine, that she'd like to listen to the

music. And as she sits there alone, the reminder of 9/11 makes her shudder. That was when she realised that she would always carry with her a kind of secret stain. Because, while Tom was thinking only of the victims, Róisín knew that somewhere someone would be congratulating himself – a job well done.

The crowd is thinning, now that the music has stopped. At the door, Murphy and two other men are decanting coins into bank bags and over by the stage two stolid girls in jeans are stacking chairs. She is suddenly paralysed by the prospect of the dark and what might be out there. Then, out of nowhere, there is Theo. He comes and sits next to her. For a long time, he says nothing, and neither does she. He feels secure, strong. He feels like everything she is not. Solid, safe. Eventually, he stretches his arm around her and she lets her face fall into the soft wool of his shoulder. He smells smoky and sweet. And for now, he will be enough to get her home.

Outside, it's still dry. Cold, though, and pitch black. Boyle can recognise most of the cars starting up now in the car park by sound alone. He can tell which one is which from a broken carburettor or a trailing exhaust pipe or a rattling door. His eyes get used to the dark soon enough. Gradually, the hedgerows separate themselves from the jagged line of sky above.

He has the key to her house in his pocket. He plays with it, rubbing the jagged edge with his thumb. Will she dare walk home in the dark? Has she her torch with her?

Will she get a lift home with Murphy? And then he remembers that Murphy will have to stay on to count the money. Suddenly, it's obvious what he should be doing. He should offer to walk her home himself. He turns back towards the hall. He's about to go in again when he sees them leaving. Fuck. Herself and the Dutchman. Fuckit anyway.

He hops over the low stone wall that follows the road all the way up to the ridge. She has a torch all right, and so does he. The lights bob up and down as they climb. What will happen when they reach the V in the road at the top of the ridge? The Dutchman to go left, the new one to go right. And then he hears a little yelp out of her. Like a mew or a cheep or a girly little gasp. He shimmies himself towards a gap in the hedge until he can see the two of them, standing there dead still in the centre of the road. Instead of two beams, there's only the one now. She's got the torch and she's shaking it and he's saying not to worry, isn't he right there beside her? Boyle feels like shouting out to her. Sure you only need him till you get to the ridge. After that you'll have the lighthouse beam. You don't need him after that.

Maybe this is the time to make his stand, to nip it in the bud before she goes the way of the last one. But he can't risk handing public victory to the Dutchman. He can't risk a quick kick in the balls before he's even got started. So instead, he stays hidden on his side of the hedge – an invisible man, a nobody, a spare prick.

Their voices rise and dip with the road. He tries to keep pace with them, but there's no path his side and he keeps coming up against ditches and low drystone walls that block his way. By the time they reach the top, he can see how this is going. They are walking closer together and all the time they are bearing right right right. Suddenly they've gone over the other side, and those last few steps are slow and heavy when he knows he's lost. Sure enough, as he crests the ridge, he can see them heading down the boreen towards the cove. They are clumped together now, moving awkwardly like a single lumbering creature.

He could yodel his lungs out, lob curses down the hill at them. He could howl at the moon, if there was one. But Boyle just stands on the crest of the ridge, chest thrust out, arms open wide.

As the beam of the lighthouse swings his way, he closes his eyes and lets it wash over him. Tonight, the sea spread out in front is vast and sighing. It's too silent a night for a hunt, so he turns off at the V in the road and starts to make his own way home. But then he stops. A heron takes off, rasping overhead. He is hungry for more of her. He has the light bulb and the fleck of red paint, the panties. He'll need more than that before he can start to make the kind of picture he used to paint of Jennifer. Back to the sea, arms by her side, head cast down. And there on an altar in front of her, the items he has taken from her house. Just a couple more things should do the trick. Her photograph, perhaps. Her vanilla-scented dressing gown.

As he reaches her door, it gives him a thrill to be so far ahead of them. When he goes to slip the key in, though, it doesn't fit. He examines the fob to make sure he's brought the right one with him. He examines the lock, flicks his finger in to check it hasn't slipped. He puts his eye close to it, and then he knows for sure. She's changed the fucken lock. The cheek of her. And he knows it's the Dutchman that's put her up to this, smarming all over her. Doing his sexy foreign thing. The Dutchman's shut him out again. It's game on now, with both of them.

21

The walk has soothed her. The sea was syrupy, almost too lazy for a tide, and its gentle ebb and flow restored her equilibrium. In the harbour, the white snouts of the few boats on moorings were pointing east, shining out against the dark sea like bleached beetles. But now the wind has started up again, and by the time Sheen and Theo are inside her house they are both profoundly cold. They cushion themselves against the chill of the tiled floor with rugs and duvets. They sit close up to the fire she has built loosely, with air as well as fuel. She pours him a glass of wine, and a token one for herself, and they sit silently facing the shift and crackle of the fire. They are careful of the small space they have warmed, and soon she has forgotten the unseasonal cold outside. When he reaches out to touch her, they are flooded by the lighthouse beam. By the time the blackness settles again, they are a flurry of mouths and limbs. Tonight, the beam is benevolent, washing them white and then black and then white again.

And when they lie together, loosely covered in a scratchy rug still studded with burrs from someone else's picnic, she is calm. His skin feels familiar, and for a moment she even allows herself to pretend that this is Tom. It's only when Theo speaks that she realises they have scarcely said a word. And then she sees that there is something in the palm of his hand. A small brownish feather.

'What happened to the bird?'

She'd forgotten about the bird. And right now, that's the last thing she wants to focus on.

But he won't drop the subject. 'Did you have to kill it in the end?'

She nods, shrugs, but he keeps on going.

'To kill that bird, you must have felt a distance.' He is sitting up now. 'Right?' He has pulled one of the cushions off the chair next to him and is using it to support his elbow. 'But then, you always feel that distance, don't you? I'm sure you do.'

She is beginning to be wary. 'There's always a distance between people. Isn't that what keeps us all sane?' She pulls away, then. Finds her shirt, pulls on her jeans.

'Not everyone has our talent for distance.' He is looking at her as though the words mean more than their face value. She isn't sure when they became our. The assumption irritates her. But she is too tired to work out what the subtext is, and now she wishes he would just go.

'When did you first realise you were different, Sheen?'

And now her irritation feels more like fear. He takes her arm, and she shrugs him off.

'I'm not different,' she says, attempting lightness, but she can see that he knows.

'Somewhere like Belfast . . .'

She has trained herself never to forget a single thing she has told another person. She has certainly not mentioned Belfast. There is a twist in her gut when she realises she should have nailed Lonergan at the Céilí when she had the chance.

And he is still talking. 'That must be just the place for someone different. To join a gang, get caught up in a terrorist organisation. And then the killing that comes naturally is just the logical thing to do.'

He has come up behind her now, and she feels his breath on her neck. He is too close, and she is struggling to decide whether she needs to defend or attack. She is thinking about the photofit, about the proprietorial way he stopped outside Lonergan's yellow house that day, about the dog straining at the leash. The mating done, they are like two creatures who haven't yet decided who is predator and who is prey. Her heart is battering, but she is desperate not to let him sense her fear. Covering herself with the old picnic blanket, she moves away from him again. She walks into the kitchen, reaches for Murphy's new kettle and switches it on. But all the time she is sensing exactly where he is, estimating just how far away she is from the door.

'Why are you here, Sheen? That's what I keep wondering.'

She remembers the pink manilla message that was pinned to her door. It had been easy to dismiss – the attention-seeking Boyle, a local kid, a joke. But now 'Why?' sounds more like 'Why the fuck are you still here?'

She dunks teabags in two mugs and carries them back into the living room. And he just keeps on talking. What is it with all the talking?

'Why come to a place where you are immediately obvious, where someone will realise before too long that you're not what you say you are? American? Of course not.' His voice is teasing, sweet with sarcasm.

She turns away from him. 'I've told you why. Some peace and quiet. To find the real Ireland, I suppose.'

He sounds mock-insulted now. 'Oh, come on. You'll have to do better than that.'

'Actually, I don't have to do anything.'

She feigns nonchalance, gathering up the clothes still strewn across the floor, but her heart is racing. Leave. Now. But he doesn't leave, and she has no idea how she will get him out. He is still talking when the picture window explodes. The sheet she'd rigged up billows into the room, twisting and snapping. The wind rushes in, and jagged shards of glass slip from their grouting and shatter on the floor. Meanwhile, Theo is pulling on his trousers, sliding his feet into his shoes as he rushes outside. She hears him yelling. 'BOYYYYyle!'

Boyle is already halfway to the schoolhouse when the Dutchman lumbers out after him like the roaring bull at the end of Sheehy's lane. He didn't think, just grabbed the first thing he could find. So what if it's a stone? He fired it at the window. Smash. She'll be used to that where she's from. He'd forgotten how much fun destruction could be. It made a joyful noise. First, a crash and then a clink clink clink. The only wonder is that he doesn't do this kind of thing more often. But the Dutchman is mad. He's furious. Charging around the garden, bashing at the bushes, stamping and kicking, hollering uselessly. Then, just as suddenly, he uses himself up.

The new one doesn't appear. She doesn't show herself at all. In fact, nothing else happens after that. The Dutchman just goes back inside. They're probably on the phone already. Probably on to the fat Guard over in Skibb, or to Murphy maybe to get someone to sort out the window. And if he could go to Skibb right now, he would. To Jenka, who would comfort him with her luncheon-meat thighs.

Back at the schoolhouse, he starts to feel a bit guilty about the window. To bolster himself, he begins to list the things the Dutchman has that he doesn't have himself and never will. The money, the accent, the ease with himself. The confidence to call those awful chairs that are his alibi works of art, to pull off the gag that he can live on wood alone. And that's before you even get to the confidence he has with women. Boyle has seen the Dutchman on the job with Jennifer – he's watched him sliding in and out of her, her head thrown back, her blonde hair pooling on to the slate tiles. The memory is seared into his brain: the white, white skin, the protruding hip bones, the little breasts. And that fucker of a Dutchman rooting away, then glancing up at Boyle and flattening his face into a smile.

Boyle painted that body of hers into all his favourite places on the island, and those paintings were a comfort to him on winter nights long after the woman herself had disappeared. With his eye on the schoolhouse, Murphy saw a way to make trouble for him. Creep. Weirdo. Perve. When the Guards arrived on Lamb and found the paintings. Creep. Weirdo. Perve. Nobody went after the Dutchman. Boyle was the one they blamed.

The one time that Boyle turned his back on Jennifer was the one time he should have kept on watching. He'd spotted them together, herself and the Dutchman, up on the cliff path. She was making a holy show of herself, yelling and screaming, her face rough with tears. He was embarrassed to see her like that, but he should have forced himself to keep on looking. He should have stayed and watched, but instead he let her down. God only knows what happened to her, pushed or slipped or what. Body dumped at sea. But he vowed right then he'd not be caught like that again.

He wonders if the Guards will bother coming to Lamb for the sake of a window. Will that fat fucker of a sergeant come rapping on his door? Or will they storm the schoolhouse this time – Murphy and the rest of them – and get him out for good? He's getting restless. He raids the music box again and toots and toots away on the recorder. He can't be arsed to light the fire, and his stomach is bitter from eating only flakes of tuna now that he's finished off the macaroni and the Ambrosia creamed rice. He's running low on tobacco and the hash is all gone, and still there is the taste of whiskey bile at the back of his throat. There is no comfort here.

He goes to the outhouse to retrieve the box of Jennifer that always soothes him. He fishes it up from the cistern that hasn't had water in it for twenty years and brings it back inside. He lays the box on the floor and sifts through the items he collected from her. They gave solace once, but now they just make him feel pathetic. The Dutchman gets the real women. All he has are their traces. And anyway, Jennifer doesn't do the trick for him any more. This pile of junk – it's as dead to him as she is. He needs the new one now.

He gathers together the last few geography books and throws on a match. When he has the fire going well, he tips the Jennifer box upside down on the floor and starts to sort through it. He rakes the hairbrush with his fingers. Collects the pale frizz of her hair and lets it float off on the flames. He turns the brush on to its wooden back and tosses it on too – it burns there like a fiery little hedgehog. He has kept the contents of her final ashtray, tied up with a twist in a sandwich bag. He rips it open, tips it on to the fire. There's a pair of her stockings, an apple core, a cup still marked with the bow of her lipsticked mouth. There's a dribble of perfume left in a small rectangular bottle – a greenish, herby scent – but he resists opening it up for one last sniff. Now that he has the new one in his head, there is no need for Jennifer. He is about to burn his boats.

22

Róisín is crouching in the corner of the room. She has wrapped herself in a duvet, and is watching the flapping sheet at the missing window, whipped white by the light-house beam. She jabs in Murphy's number, and tries to stay calm when she tells him what happened.

'The big one? Jesus, you're kidding me. That fella's a bloody curse.' He starts to say that the brother has a yard full of hardboard over on the mainland, that the lads'll sort it out in the morning.

But then the sheet is pulled back. And there is Theo, picked out against the night like a movie baddie. When she puts her ear to the phone again, Murphy is gone.

'I couldn't leave you on your own.' Theo gestures to the window. 'Not with Boyle about.'

He walks towards her, crunching over the shattered glass. Her jaw is clamped shut, her whole body trembling silently.

'So. Here we are again,' he says.

She doesn't reply, because she has no idea what answer he could possibly expect. She waits for him to say something more, but he doesn't. Doesn't speak or touch. Just slumps down on the floor beside her, his back up against the wall. They sit there silently, side by side, arm's length apart. She is hyper alert, wound tight, but she can scarcely even hear him breathe. It feels as if she is the prisoner, and he the guard, and she doesn't dare to test him. And so she waits. She waits for him to pick up the threads of his insinuation. She waits for him to move. But he says nothing, does nothing.

She wants to ask him the obvious question: if Lonergan put him up to this. But in the end she bottles it. Tomorrow, when she walks up to the yellow house, it will be better not to know. She is desperate for sleep, and eventually she musters up the strength to stand and slowly walk towards the back bedroom. He doesn't move to stop her, doesn't speak. When she is in the bedroom, she is weak with relief. She feels ridiculous when she drags the pine chest across the door, but she does it anyway.

She wakes with a start to find that it's light already, that this is the day. She stretches her hand out and sweeps the mattress next to her. It is cold and empty, and then she remembers. She eases back the chest, wincing as it screeches on the tiles. Once through the door she stands and listens. She can hear him, moving about the living room. Slowly, she pushes the door ajar. He has removed the cushions from the sofa and taken out the pads. The rugs have been lifted and the pictures taken off the walls. The material she has gathered on Lonergan seems to have been sorted into piles. She tries to absorb this new out-rage, and then a shaft of sun arrows across the tiles and blinds her for a moment. She squints to locate him, then sees that he is down on his knees, rifling through the suitcase she has still not fully unpacked.

Right away, he senses she's there. Still bent over the case, he turns and mutters at her over his shoulder. A toothbrush. Something. A lie. He stretches, pops one shoulder then the next. 'But since you're awake now, why don't I make some coffee?'

'Oh yes,' she says, forcing the wobble from her voice. 'I'd forgotten. You're quite the expert when it comes to coffee.'

He straightens up and looks hard at her. 'Hey,' he goes. 'Give me a break, yeah? You want water, tea? Because, you know, all you have to do is say.'

He is moving towards her now, and though she knows she mustn't show how scared she is, she can't help step-ping out of his way. He gives a little mock jump, as if to imitate her, then something that is almost like a smile.

She feels sick to think she could have been so stupid.

'I won't be around,' he says then. 'Not for a day or two. In fact, I'll probably not be here much before next weekend. You want to know why? No? Well, let me tell you anyway.'

But her ears are full of noise. All she hears is that someone in Clonakilty wants his chairs.

'So I guess you're on your own now, yeah?'

She gets the message, and she knows that time is run-ning out.

As soon as he's gone, she runs the shower. As hot as

possible, for as long as the immersion heater will allow. Hot billows of sweet, lavender-scented steam. Puffy clouds of fragrant foam. Another world she inhabits for a while until the hot water runs out and the reality of what she has to do now reasserts itself. While she is wrapping herself in the hard greyish towels that come with the house, she spots the hole at the corner of the opaque plastic film covering the window. She scratches at the little torn-off corner with her fingernail. She puzzles over it briefly, but then she remembers what the day is all about.

She pulls on her jeans, her most serviceable top, and drags a comb through her hair. She rubs a little window into the steamed-up mirror and moves her face closer to it. She looks tired, pale. There is a spray of tiny angry spots on her chin. She thinks of Lonergan, remembers his instinct for weakness, and some modicum of pride makes her want to look her best for battle. She has hardly worn a scrap of make-up since she came here – it seems unnecessary on Lamb – but today is different. She opens the bottle of foundation and dips her finger in. There, just below the surface, is a fleshy little lump. She tries to get at it, to break it up, but the neck of the jar is too narrow and it slips away from her. She tips it up, foundation spluttering on to her palm, until finally something emerges. A pellet, a bead. The weight of it in her palm is disconcerting. When she rinses it under the tap, the water browns and then runs clear. And there it is: a deadly slug of steel. Her stomach heaves and falls and heaves. She is sick right there into the basin. And when she has rinsed the bile away, she sits a moment on the downturned toilet seat – her mouth sour, her stomach raw. She gazes at the bullet, glinting against the white enamel, until it loses form for her and becomes only what it is in essence, a threat. And then she lashes out at it and sweeps it to the floor. She is icy cold now, and every rational sense is screaming at her to get away.

She sees their shadows pass across the bathroom window. One, gangly, the other short, thick-set. The bell rings, and for a moment she is too frightened to move. By the time it rings again, she has heard their voices. It's only Murphy's lads, come to fix the window, and so she opens the door and stands back to let them in. They seem to take an age to carry in their tools, and then the sheets of hardboard they say that Murphy travelled over to the mainland for especially. Early this morning, crack of dawn. When she has made them tea, and laden it with sugar, when they have set to work, she stands and listens to the dull thud of their hammers over the jangle of the radio. It is comforting to have them there. It makes her feel like someone is on her side, even if they haven't chosen to be. When she hears the tuneless tolling of the angelus bell, she glances at the clock and notices in passing that it's running slow. But she notices something else, too. Propped up behind the clock is something she hasn't seen before. She takes it down to look at it. A sheet of A4 paper, folded twice. A printout. Black and white. A photograph.

It has been taken in a town. There is a Spar, a line of traffic, a set of lights. A teenage girl is about to step off the pavement into the road. She has a violin case strapped to her back, her light-coloured hair tied up in a messy bun. She is looking over her shoulder, in the direction of the photographer, but past him. As if she doesn't realise he's there. She seems to be checking for oncoming traffic before she makes her move to cross the street.

Something isn't right. Something is familiar. Or maybe it's just that the scene itself is such an ordinary one. Róisín concentrates on the girl. Her high forehead, her small firm chin. And when she realises who this is, the knowledge fells her. This is Ciara, Maura's girl, the niece whose photo she is sent several times a year, but whom she has never met.

The magnitude of what Lonergan is telling her takes her breath away. Whatever happens to this girl, whatever hits her as she steps into that street, it will be your fault. Just as all the other things were your fault, too: the soldier, the shop assistant, the woman.

And in that moment, she realises that what has brought her here is not simply some meagre belated justice for Jacinta. It is rage. The force of that realisation floors her. She never thought of herself as being vengeful before. But the small thing that she asked of him is no longer enough. Lonergan has shrugged off all responsibility for the past, while she has never been able to escape. The injustice of it burns her lungs. It shrivels her heart. And now that she has come this far, she will not let him off the hook.

The boys are standing in the doorway, telling her that the job is done. She is scarcely aware of what she says to them, but it seems to be enough because they murmur something pleasant-sounding back. And then they close the door behind them and are gone.

She is ready for him. It is time. She opens the cold oven and takes out the envelope from between the two black baking sheets. She slides out Ma's letter. Maura had seemed resentful that no letter had been left for her. But maybe Maura knew all this by instinct and didn't have to be told. Or maybe Ma was protecting Maura by keeping her in the dark.

Dear Róisín,

Your da always said you never know what way the wind will turn, and by God did Kenny know all about the wind and how it can change on you. You know a thing or two about Lonergan, Róisín. I realise that. But I know a thing or two more.

I remember when Brian Lonergan first came to Jaipur Street. When old Mrs Fearon died, he moved into her house. He said she was his auntie, though I don't think she had any family at all. Anyway, nobody stopped him. Things were so chaotic then, nobody had the wit to be bothered about who he was and what he was doing there. He was only nineteen or so – a wee fella with a shock of dirty blond hair. I heard he was from somewhere down South originally. He talked funny back then, but people listened to him. God knows why, but they did. Maybe they were scared of him. He was a vicious wee scut, even then.

You were only a wee girl when your da was interned, so you probably don't remember much about it. While your da was being hung out of helicopters and kept awake all night, Lonergan was building himself a power base. When they see someone with that kind of ambition, most people step aside, if they know what's good for them. Soon, there was only one person in his way – a man called Jimmy Kielty. Jimmy was no angel, but he was better than the alternatives. He had a weakness, of course. Don't they all?

One night – it must have been just before Christmas – Lonergan worked on the weakness. He took Kielty drinking. When he finally passed out, they drove him over to the Newtownards Road and dumped him outside a social club, some UDA dive, and let the Loyalists do their worst. He was found the next morning in an entry in the city centre, carved up into pieces.

Later on, it turned out that the two young fellas who were with Lonergan that night felt bad about what had happened. They said they hadn't realised. Had no idea what would happen. They said they wanted to take Kielty home to his family, but that Lonergan wouldn't have it. He was the one who insisted on dumping him by the side of the street. To teach him a lesson, he said. Teach him to hold his drink. Anyway, whether that was the truth or not, they decided to put their version of things on the record. They came to see your da when he got out because they knew they could trust him. They told him everything, wrote out their statements, signed them. It's all here.

Lonergan knows I have something on him, but he's not sure what or where it is. When he arranged to get you over to New York, I suppose you could say he thought he was buying my silence, as well as paying off a debt to your da.

Don't play the hero, Róisín. Make sure you have your back covered. But when the moment's right, make your move.

As she starts to reread the statements, she can feel Belfast close over her again. Cover your back. Don't be a hero. Although she realises that Ma's reasons for wanting to bring down Lonergan are not the same as hers, she will use what she's been given.

Before she leaves, she rattles open the cutlery drawer. The forks are weak, the knives rounded and blunt, and the serrated carving knife is too big to be easily concealed. She decides on the corkscrew, but when she brings it down on her own arm she thinks again. Unless the angle is just right it will make no impact at all. In the end, she takes a pair of scissors – vicious enough, if it comes to it. She puts on her jacket and, opening the scissors to their full extent, slips them into her pocket. The light outside fades and swells and fades and swells. Brief bursts of spring sunshine mopped up by cloud. This rage has made her reckless. She doesn't hesitate. Just sets her face into the wind and heads towards the yellow house.

The steel gate is already open when she gets there, the pale blue rope hanging limply at the side. Silent as a cloud, she moves up the path through the central strip of mossy, daisy-strewn grass. He has his back to her, bending low over a green plastic trough. Planting or weeding, she can't tell which. There is a moment when she has a chance to run at him. Her fingers tighten on the hinge of the scissors, pressing the open blades back against the handles. She takes one step, then another. He stops what he's doing, but he doesn't straighten up and he doesn't turn. She knows that a man like Lonergan will have antennae that don't stop working just because they're no longer in use.

She can tell that he is listening, preparing himself, and she knows not to move, but to prepare herself too. Now that she has lost the chance to take him by surprise, she is keenly aware that no one knows she's come here. There is no one else to rely on now, and she must be sharp. She is tempted to take her eyes off him, to check behind her back. It strikes her that she is like a solo yachtswoman setting out to sea. She should have told someone she was leaving the shore.

In her left pocket is the cell that she has not remembered to switch to silent. She closes her hand over it, willing it not to ring. In her right pocket are the scissors. The back door of the house swings open, and there is Theo, a steaming mug in each hand. She knew, of course, and yet she'd kept some tiny shred of hope that she was wrong.

'Hey,' he says, moving towards her, as if this is the most natural thing in the world. 'Long time no see.'

Lonergan straightens up and turns to face her. 'Who's your lady friend, Theo?' he says. 'If I might be so bold.'

'As if you need to ask me,' Theo smiles, but somehow unpleasantly. 'I don't know what *you* call her, but I call her Sheen.'

Lonergan is looking straight at her, but the sun is in her eyes.

'I see,' he says. 'Very nice.'

A cloud takes the sun, and she knows that he has stripped away the intervening years, the accent and the shiny name. There is no point in pretending.

'We know each other,' she says. 'Brian and me. From way back.'

'So,' he says to Theo, businesslike, not bothered by her at all. 'You can get moving on the other thing then. I'll catch you later.'

And Theo is dismissed. She can't believe it when he simply walks away. Even though she knew already – or should have known – she stretches out a hand to him. But Theo just shrugs. She sees that Lonergan has noticed, that already she is weakened in his eyes. Theo doesn't look at her again, but as he goes she hears him say, almost to himself, 'Over to you.'

As he crunches down the gravel path towards the gate, she feels a sense of desolation. Now that she is alone with Lonergan, neither of them moves. He gestures to the coffee that Theo has left on the plastic garden table. If it weren't for the steam spooling from it, the slight swirling movement of the liquid, this could be a still, the moment in the film when she should decide to walk away. But she shakes her head, and the moment passes. He says it's all the same to him. He ushers her into the house ahead of him, but she is frightened to have him behind her and stands her ground. He shrugs and goes on in himself, and she follows, just far enough behind him to feel safe.

Inside, the house smells musty. But there are daffodils in a plain white jug on the kitchen table, and she finds that oddly reassuring. There is an open packet of Weetabix, a bowl of brown sugar. She follows him into the living room, where some crocheted cushions are propped up on the small sofa. There are watercolours on the wall. Sea and cliffs. A couple of books on the coffee table. Thick, dog-eared paperbacks with raised gold lettering. A table by the half-open window. For a moment, her panic eases. But then she has a glimpse of herself, the house, the island, the great span of ocean between Lamb and New York, and she knows that she should not have come here. Her right hand is tightening around the blade of the scissors in her pocket. She feels it cut into the palm of her hand. And the pain serves to focus her, to keep her alert. She is suddenly so frightened that she can't imagine being able to speak or even to move.

Lonergan sits at the table and clasps his hands in front of him.

'Sit down,' he says, and she does. Just far enough away that he would need to move to reach her. To steady herself, to hone her reflexes, she focuses on his hands. This time, there is no nicotine stain between his first two fingers, but the nails are still bitten. Smelling smoke on his breath, she has the thought that, because she has given up and he hasn't, she is somehow more resolute than him.

It's not much, but it's something. She presses her feet into the ground to try to quieten her knees, shuffles to the very edge of the chair. He leans forward.

'I don't know if I'm supposed to look surprised to see you.' He sounds bored, as if he is constantly plagued by stinging flies – irksome but inconsequential. 'I mean, you all but told me you'd be coming. I knew you wouldn't have the nerve to come to Belfast, to talk to the papers or anything like that. I knew you'd do this in a sneaky back-hand kind of way.'

He taps an unlit cigarette on the table in front of him, still not bothering to look at her, and the action sparks a memory in her. 'Take your hands out of your pockets when I'm talking to you.'

And she does, right away, even though the blade has left a purple indentation on the palm of her hand.

'So,' asks Lonergan. 'What do you want?'

'For you to tell the O'Neills where you buried their mother.' Her voice is high, and she swallows in the middle of her sentence. It sounds ridiculous. She is ridiculous. And her knees, what's wrong with her knees that they won't stop jigging up and down?

He makes a face at her. 'The O'Neills. Really? And you came all this way to ask me that? Have you not worked out yet why I had to shut that woman up?'

This is partly why she needed to come here, she realises suddenly: to have her worst fears confirmed.

'Have you not worked out that Jacinta O'Neill *had* to be shut up? Do you think I do things for the craic? I do things because they need doing, that's why.'

And she can tell that he has told himself this kind of thing so many times that he might even believe it now.

'Your wee Mrs O'Neill, she saw more than was good for her. She saw something and she decided she wasn't going to shut up about it. She saw you and Dolores coming home with me that night. She lived on Rebecca Street, just where I stopped the car. She took down the number plate, of course. And after you did your drama-queen act, she came outside and had a look. She picked up that jacket you threw away. That denim jacket you'd on. It wasn't yours, was it? It belonged to a soldier. And in the pocket, you stupid wee bitch, was a soldier's ID. Mrs O'Neill was stupid, too. She mouthed off about it, down at the launderette. Said she felt sorry for them poor soldier boys who only wanted a wee court. Said she was going to ring the Confidential Number. So don't tell me it's not in your interests that I shut that O'Neill woman up. If it wasn't for me, you'd have been in Armagh jail these past twenty years.'

In that moment, she is more aware of the hum of her own blood than anything else. It is the sound of being alive, and she has done nothing to earn it. Just as Jacinta did nothing to deserve what she got either. The sadness of that is overwhelming. She visualises the daughter who is never off the TV, and her face burns. She would give anything for this not to be her fault.

'What about Dolores?'

'What about her? It's always Dolores with you.'

'Well, it was Dolores for you too, Brian. Back then, anyhow.'

He scrunches up his face in disgust. 'Seen her recently? Christ.'

'I got the calling card. Her mugshot on the wall. I suppose that means you got my email, though you didn't even bother to reply.'

She has rehearsed those words. They are braver than she feels, but she swallows in the middle of a word and gives herself away.

He looks at her blankly for a moment. And then his expression changes, as if he's only starting to remember what all this is about. 'Look here, you.' He's on his feet now, pacing back and forth, and his accent has hardened, his tone of voice too. 'If you want to open this up all over again, go right ahead. Go tell the world you seduced a wee soldier even though you knew it would get him killed. Then tell them all that you planted a no-warning device in a department store one Saturday. Tell them *I* told you to do it all. Aye. That, God love you, you hadn't a clue what you were doing. Even though the world and his wife knows who your da was. You do KNOW who your da was, don't you? Yes no yes? And why were you sent to New York anyway, people will ask, if you hadn't done something the movement wanted done? What made you worth more than a bullet? And even if – after all that – they still believe you, see if they care. Because I'm telling you now. They don't.'

The draught from the window has started to billow the thin cotton curtain. He reaches for the sash and slams it down. She had hoped to conquer her fear of him by now. All those hours spent memorising his face, trying to strip the menace from it. But she is still a teenager, and he has all the power.

'And I don't know where her body is, actually. That's not the kind of thing it's in my interests to know. Anyhow, I'm going to draw a line under this now. Because, nice and all as it is to chat to you, I've business back in Dublin.'

He goes to the dresser and gathers together some papers there, sliding them into a plastic wallet.

She dives her hand into her pocket and grips the scissors by their cutting edge, but she's too slow and he's still too far away.

'Was it worth your while, coming here?' he says, as he turns to face her. 'I don't know why you bothered. All those years, and not a peep out of you, and suddenly you're Jacinta O'Neill's number one fan. Give us a break, love.'

'I know what happened to Kielty,' she says quietly.

For the first time, there is another expression behind the opaque green-eyed gaze. He busies himself again with his papers.

'McGinn and Ryan – ring any bells?' She tries to steady her voice, to fake an air of confidence. He won't respect anything less. 'They were there that night, weren't they? You think because they're not around any more that there's no one left to say what you did? Because they gave signed statements to my da. And I have them. The O'Neills would love to get their hands on those bits of paper, Brian. In fact, I think they'd make very good use of them.' She can hear her own voice. And this isn't her at all. She thinks it might be Sheen.

He doesn't say anything for a moment. And then she sees him switch into politician mode. 'It was terrible what happened to Jimmy Kielty. He was a good man.'

And even though Lonergan's gaze is blank, she can see now that she is challenging his version of himself. She can see that he has to lie to himself too. Every day, she guesses, he is bolstering himself with a whole universe of alternative realities just to be able to do this.

'If you have material that the party should know about, then hand it over.' His eyes falter momentarily. But then he's off again. 'Jimmy's death was a tragedy for the movement. He was a fine strategist, butchered by Loyalists who got off on carving up a Taig.'

'But you gave him to them, didn't you, Brian? Jimmy Kielty, with his armful of Republican tattoos. You had him dumped on the Newtownards Road, where they couldn't fail to find him. Dumped outside a Loyalist drinking club, so someone else could do your dirty work. Mind you, no surprises there. When it comes to getting other people to do your dirty work, you're the best in the business.' She is stoking herself up, and it's getting harder to control her voice. She swallows, tries to gather herself. 'Setting up a comrade? That's low, Brian. Even for you. What will the voters think? And the party, for that matter.'

Her heart is battering now, but she is being bolder than she ever planned to be. She can see she has him worried.

'Don't push me –'

'Or what, exactly? You'll threaten my teenage niece?

Oh, I got that one, too. You're Mr Legitimate now, remember? If you want this to go away, just give the O'Neills their mother's body to bury. That's all I came for. You can rise and rise for all it means to me. Cabinet minister, Taoiseach. See if I care.' She has no more words, but her head just won't stop shaking – it's as if it has acquired a motor of its own.

And then he stands and gives her his politician's smile. 'Hold off till tomorrow, Róisín,' he says. 'I might have a wee surprise for you by then.' He turns back towards his papers, shaking his head in mock sincerity. 'And you came all this way for a tout, for a dirty oul' slapper from Rebecca Street.'

Suddenly, she is overcome by a terrible, helpless fury. Her eyes are on the back of his neck, on the pale line of skin above his collar. She gets to her feet and lurches for him, but he's much too quick for her. He wheels around and knocks the scissors from her hand. He slams her against the wall, his fist in her throat. 'Don't fuck with me.'

The delicate cage of her throat feels ready to snap open under the pressure. He has his face in hers – a cat playing with a bird.

'If any of this comes out, I'll find you. Understood? And I'll fuck you up so badly you'll beg me for that bullet.'

He tightens his hold on her neck. 'Go home. Pack your bags. Take a plane out tomorrow. And if you ever threaten me again, you're one dead fucken bitch.'

When he shoves her away, she loses her footing and slumps to the floor. Her throat feels like it's missing.

Somehow, she gets to her feet, crashing through the kitchen and out into the overgrown garden.

He thinks he's off the hook. He can't believe she'd risk her life to bring him down. As she unloops the blue twine from the gate post, a football whizzes past her ear and thwacks into the hedge in front of her. Out in the laneway, she stumbles into a group of kids. A pair of tiny girls are arguing over a pink scooter while a boy retrieves his football from the hedge. They walk on up the hill, not looking twice at her. She takes in fat gulps of air, but her throat no longer seems to work. Her legs can scarcely carry her, and her body feels deep-frozen. Down at the harbour, she sits shivering on the bench, trying to muster up the nerve to swallow. And then it hits her. Nothing Lonergan says has any meaning beyond its purpose. He is hollow, empty. Lies? Truth? There is no longer any difference. That half-promise he made was only what he'd thought necessary at the time. It had no meaning beyond its own particular moment, which meant no more or less than the next moment, when he took her by the throat. Necessity is all there is for him now, and so it's time for her to go.

'Sheen?' Cat is standing over her, her head to one side. 'What's happened? Hey?' And when she looks harder, the expression on her face changes from curiosity to concern. 'What's wrong? Are you sick?'

Róisín tries opening her mouth, but nothing comes.

'Do you want me to call somebody? There's a nurse lives over on the east end. She –'

Róisín manages to mutter something about bad news, a shock. Her strength is trickling back, and with it the old instinct for the appropriate lie. She needs to pack, to book a flight. She needs to get home. Forever kind, Cat puts her arm around her.

'Look, come and sit inside awhile. Pete can manage without me for a bit. Come.'

The pub is full of strangers. People in brightly coloured cags with life jackets horseshoed at their necks. Men in unseasonal shorts and their wind-burned wives. Cat finds her a quiet corner, brings her tea she can't drink and carrot cake she can't eat. The homeliness of that tea and cake seems freakish and absurd. Somehow, the innocence of it makes her sad. How she wishes it had all been different. If she had been born somewhere else, Lamb perhaps, she wouldn't be like this. Above the excited hum of the yachting crowd on a day sail, there is music playing – some rinky-dink Billy Joel song from another life. But Róisín's head is full of horrors now. She pictures herself beneath a Belfast lamp post, fine needles of rain swirling in the yellowish light. And when she sees Jacinta's face at the window of a Rebecca Street flat, she screams at her across the years to turn away – not to look, not to say. And when Jacinta appears again, trussed up on the floor of a safe house, Róisín reaches for impossibility and cuts the woman free. And in that instant, she is free too.

But then she replays in her head the exchange with Lonergan. A new fear enters her veins and stiffens them so she can hardly breathe. What if he is right? What if she is just like him, and can no longer winkle out the truth from all the lies? She did nothing whatsoever for the truth when she'd had the chance – all she did when she reached

New York was turn her back on it. Jacinta was the one who'd tried to tell the truth. Roísín's head is full of mocking voices now. They whisper all the things she should have known, and maybe did know somewhere deep down. But out of all this comes one clear thought. Now that he knows exactly what she's got on him, she is no longer safe on Lamb.

23

The day is mild as cream. Boyle reflects that you could easily be fooled by such a day. You could start to imagine you're on another type of island altogether. Some place off Sweden, perhaps, with cloudberries and birch trees and little wooden jetties over lakes quivering with fish. A place where seasons take their proper turn and people are prepared to let you be.

With the Easter fete about to start, there are visiting boats in the harbour. Down on the pier, the stalls are in place: plastic guns and stink bombs, home-made hummus and goat's milk ice cream. There is a bunch of metallic balloons printed with Disney characters, a little group of boys in Samba Soccer shirts.

But then Boyle sees someone else down on the pier, and the mood is broken. Lonergan is leaving Lamb already. And the ferry is moving off her moorings towards her berth at the end of the pier. Well, fuck that. Fuckit anyway. When's he going to get his money now?

He starts to head towards the pier, but then something strikes him. Something more interesting, even, than the money. Lonergan has no need of ferries. In fact, he can't remember ever seeing him travel by ferry before. Couldn't the Dutchman bring him anywhere he wants to go? And yet there he is, queuing up with the rest of them. Maybe he thinks it makes him look like a man of the people. Maybe. But maybe he just wants to be seen to be leaving Lamb.

Looking through the door of the pub, Boyle sees the new one sitting there with Cat. She has her back to him, but he'd recognise that terrible pink anywhere. Cat makes a shooing gesture at him, and then he remembers the broken window and how news travels fast. He goes to Molly's shop instead, where she is relaying some anecdote or other to a customer.

She looks up, and when she gives him a half-smile, he can tell that she hasn't heard about the window yet. 'Have you worked your way through that tuna, Boyle? We're doing a collection for the Inshore Rescue – dry goods and cans for the tombola this afternoon – so if you're sick of fish, you know where to come.'

'I see Lonergan's off,' he says.

The customer takes one look at Boyle, then turns his back on him.

'He said he's hoping to get back next weekend. After the vote,' says Molly.

'They'll win that one, I'd say,' says the customer.

'But that family up North, what do you make of all that? Could there be any truth in it, Timmy?' Molly asks.

Timmy gathers his little pile of purchases together on the shiny counter and slides them into his shopper. 'You wouldn't know with that shower.' He gives Boyle a nod, then waddles out the door.

When Molly turns back to the till, Boyle takes his chance. He reaches for the collection box she's been using as a paperweight. Full, this time of year. Heavy. He's due some compo, so he shoves it inside his jacket and closes the shop door behind him. Molly will be on to him soon enough, so he scarpers off towards the pier. The harbour is busy today, but he spots what he's looking for right away. Lonergan is standing at the bow of the ferry like a statue of himself, talking into a mobile. Boyle scans the rows of Easter visitors. RIBs and punts and cuddy-cabined Arvors tied up on the new pontoon. In front of the ferry, a blunt-nosed Bayliner is harnessed to a faded blue yacht. And then he finds the match he was expecting. Theo is on board his own boat, speaking into his phone. Boyle keeps his eye on the shabby hull as it edges its way out of the inner harbour, Theo at the bow hauling in fenders and lines. His boat leaves before the ferry does, travelling slowly towards the mainland. Boyle hasn't worked out yet what's up, but one thing is for sure: there is another story unfolding underneath the skin of this one. Although the new one doesn't deserve a single drop of his concern, he is worried for her all the same.

It is only when Cat comes to clear the untouched cake and tea that Róisín realises there is another thought nagging at her, a connection she should really have made by now. And before she has found a way to frame the thought, it is out.

'That woman, Jennifer. She didn't live in my house, did she? Because I don't feel very comfortable there any more. I just don't feel safe, you know?'

Cat seems to be appraising her. And then she bites her lip. 'Well, yes,' she says, 'she did. But didn't Murphy say? I mean, I didn't think it was my place to –'

'I need to book my flight. Right now. Can I use the internet? I'll be really quick.'

Cat draws back a little, and Róisín can see the little curling strands of doubt begin to settle in her eyes. 'I'm really sorry, Sheen, but the internet's down at the minute,' she says. 'I think it's the Easter. Pete's been on to them, and they say it should be back up in an hour or so. Anyway, no rush, surely,' she says. 'Murphy will take you out to Reen later, and we can always sort out your booking in a bit. And don't worry yourself about the house. It's grand. Just come upstairs and sit awhile.'

The pub is jam-packed now, and Cat ushers Róisín up to the floor above the internet café, to the flat she shares with Pete. A terracotta-painted room, with easy chairs arranged to make the most of the sea view. Róisín just wants to get the flight sorted out, but Cat treats her like an invalid: she drapes a baby blanket round her shoulders, an Indian throw across her knees. And then she notices the wound the scissors made. 'What happened to your hand?'

'I suppose I must have stumbled, getting here. Grazed it somehow.'

'Let me see? That's nasty. It's more than just a graze, Sheen. We'll need to give it a clean.'

Cat returns with a bowl of water, some disinfectant. She sits, dabbing gently at Róisín's hand, but she seems preoccupied, as if she doesn't know quite what to say. She flicks on the radio, and the awkward silence is filled with airily precise music that might be Mozart. But the smell of disinfectant is the smell of crisis. Róisín knows it of an old day, and it turns her stomach.

She hadn't realised how weak she was, how unfit she was to take on Lonergan. His blandness has thrown her. His V-necked jumper and his reading specs. His tatty window boxes and his boring watercolours. His whitened teeth and his bitten nails. He is unremarkable, average. Humdrum, even. But even though she had the means to ruin him, she didn't frighten him at all. She wasted her opportunity. She should have let him have the scissors before she began to doubt herself. Can people change? She doesn't know, but things can. She gazes at the mist that has blown in from nowhere. She knows how quickly things can change.

Later, Murphy arrives and offers to drive her out to Reen. He talks at her, slowly and deliberately, as if she's a child or a very old person, but once they're in his four-by-four his patter dries. He seems to realise she doesn't want to talk about the things they must surely have discussed, Cat and he – her evident distress, this sudden decision to leave Lamb. At Reen, he enters the house ahead of her, although she hasn't asked him to, and she is grateful. He dips his head into each of the rooms, flicks the lights on and off to check they're working now, before letting her go inside.

'Just leave me your details and I'll organise the booking. I'll pop up later with the printout for your flight – we'll get you to wherever you need to go. Don't worry about that.' He stands back from her a moment, shakes his head at her bandaged hand. 'You look wrecked, girl. Get some sleep. No need to wait up – I'll slip the flight details through your door.'

Boyle is almost at the schoolhouse when he sees a small white fishing boat rounding Reen Point. In the summer months it's not unusual for families to anchor in the cove beneath the Marriage Stones, but it's too early in the year for them. The South Harbour has no pier, so the only reason to bring a boat in this side of the island is to avoid being seen. It slows down as it approaches the shore. Even at this distance, he recognises *Marianna*, the Dutchman's boat. He can hear the engine idling, then the throttle churning into reverse. A figure drops into the water and wades slowly towards the strand. And there is no one but Boyle to see Lonergan slipping back on to Lamb.

He crunches his way up the beach, feet sinking into the shingle. He must be soaking, but he doesn't stop. He leaves the metalled road almost as soon as he joins it, cutting across the fields instead. Once Boyle realises that Lonergan isn't heading either for the village or towards Reen, he doesn't even need to follow him. He gives

Lonergan half an hour or so, then makes his own way to the yellow house. He clambers up over a stone wall two fields away and works his way towards it. And, sure enough, there is Lonergan, sitting round the back, calm as you like, where nobody could see him from the road. He has changed his clothes. Changed, too, from cigarettes to pipe. Boyle can smell the sweet tobacco, aromatic in the unexpected sunshine. If you knew no better, you might take this man for a philosopher. You might even take him for a politician. Boyle almost pisses himself laughing, biting hard into the grass. Who's to say it's drugs they're importing out at Goat Point? Who's to say it isn't guns that Lonergan is shipping via Lamb? In case things turn to his disadvantage and he finds the old ways are preferable. Boyle rolls on to his back and watches the sky begin to close itself down. A rush of salmon from the west, the slow dulling of the day.

He gets so carried away by that sky that he nearly misses the moment. It's just the scrape of the gate that alerts him. Lonergan is gone, a streak of army green across the field. He is moving smartly for a man of his age, and his waxed jacket is as good as camouflage. For a while, the patch of pale scalp on the back of his head is a flag to mark him by. But Boyle is struggling to keep up and when Lonergan disappears over the ridge on to the other side of the island, the trail is lost.

Now that the light is fading, the lighthouse starts to silver the grass within its beam. It finds Lonergan, but he is wise to it and, the next time it comes around, he has moved well clear. And in that moment, Boyle wonders if

he's been spotted. In the old days, Lonergan could probably have picked him off from here. What do they do, he
wonders, now that they're not supposed to shoot you any
more? Beat the crap out of you instead? He is worried for
her. He wonders if that feeling might be love. He's had
her in his head before she even arrived on Lamb. But now
that he has her down on paper, she is his, and he will not
let them harm her like they did the last one. The temper-
ature is dropping with the light. There's a skirl of wind.
And there, to the right of Boyle, a movement on the
strand. He can't tell who it is at first. But when he realises
what is going to happen, he knows that he is probably
already too late to stop it.

After Murphy drops her off at the house, Róisín doesn't
even try to sleep. The first thing she does is retrieve the
envelope from the oven. She sticks down the flap, then
stamps and addresses it.

Gemma O'Neill,
The Campaign for Jacinta,
PO Box 1606,
Belfast

She glances up, and spots Ciara's photo. Her heart
freezes when she realises she has forgotten to warn Maura.
She jabs in the number, but the call goes straight to voice-
mail. She tries again, is just about to head out of the door
to the postbox when a young girl answers. She thinks it

might be Ciara, but she can't be sure. It knocks her off her stride and she doesn't know what to say now.

'It's Róisín.'

The girl hesitates. '*Auntie* Róisín?'

'Aye,' she says, though she hasn't used the word in years. 'It's me.'

Maura takes over. She is brisk, businesslike. Ciara and she are on their way back from an Irish dancing competition, and she has pulled in off the road to take the call. Róisín means to say that the danger hasn't passed, that they need to be careful. But that's not what comes out.

'I saw Brian Lonergan today,' is what she says.

'Haven't we all?' says Maura. 'He's never off the telly.'

'I spoke to him, Maura.'

A moment's pause. 'Are you on medication, Róisín?'

'God's sake, I'm not some kind of nutter.'

'Well, you're acting like one.'

'I met him. I spoke to him about Jacinta O'Neill. I think he'll make a statement.'

Maura's voice is muffled, but still audible. 'Ciara, would you get me a pint of milk, love. There's a Spar just around the corner.'

Róisín waits until she hears the car door clunk. 'I wanted to remind him –'

'OK, well, you can stop right there. Nobody here needs reminding of anything. All we want to do is forget. It's over now, you know that. You do know that, Róisín.'

'Thanks for telling me what I know.'

Maura lets out a hard little breath. 'Best to forget.'

'Tell that to the O'Neills.'

'Oh, I don't know about them, Róisín. This witch hunt they're on? Lonergan this, that and the other. Strikes me somebody's put them up to this. Strikes me as convenient timing.'

'You're not telling me you've forgotten who he is, Maura? Because of him, I had to leave school before my O levels. I never saw Ma again.'

'Well, we could argue all day about what you could have done differently, and whether you'd have been better off here or not. As for Lonergan, he's a politician now. He's got a good head on his shoulders. Puts a decent spin on things. And people like him, Róisín.'

'So he gets away with it all? He can lie through his teeth for the rest of his life and people will just accept whatever crap he tells them?' She is so furious she can hardly get the words out.

'What do you want, Róisín? Who's going to lead us out of this? Not people like those O'Neills, that's for sure. Still living in Rebecca Street, with their wee shrine and their interviews and their media campaigns. Still flogging the same dead horse.'

'So the truth doesn't matter then.'

'All truth does is rake things up. We want peace.'

'And it's still peace, Maura, is it? Even when it's just something painted on over all the rot and lies and blood?'

'Oh, for God's sake, would you ever catch a grip. Some of us have to live here.'

'That envelope the solicitor sent me. The one from Ma?'

'What about it?'

'She asked me to do something for her.'

'That's just great, Róisín. Bully for you. You're going to do something for Ma now, are you? Well, I've done a few wee things for Ma, too. Every hospital appointment and boiler service and light bulb, that was me. The at-home daughter. The drudge.'

'She wrote to me about some papers she was given, years back. Statements people made to Da.'

'Da? Spare me. He wasn't Moses, you know.' And Maura lets out a sound she thinks is meant to be a laugh. 'If it was up to Da, they'd still be bombing pubs. At least Lonergan's a pragmatist. He knows there's no sense in war. And people listen to him.'

'But shouldn't they know what he's done? Before they vote for him?'

'Nobody wants to know, Róisín. They really don't. And once you give yourself up to the media, they'll ruin your life, just for the craic of it. Do yourself a favour and go home.'

Home? The word sounds strange to her.

Maura pauses. 'I'm sorry, Róisín. I really am. But you should go home now. Really.'

'Just take care of Ciara, Maura. Don't let her out of your sight. I –'

'Excuse me while I get this straight. *You're* telling *me* how to take care of my own child. Is that it? Well, don't bother your head, Róisín. The kinds of thing you got up to? They don't happen now.'

Maura has rung off, and Róisín feels exhausted, cleaned out. She glances at all the yard-sale, thrift-store props for Sheen that had once seemed so necessary. She doesn't need them now. One by one, she packs them all into the same kitchen cupboard and shuts the door. She is strong enough without them. She imagines Lonergan laughing about her with Theo – stupid wee hoor, her and her scissors.

After the by-election, who knows how far Lonergan might go, how high he might rise or whose interests it might serve to keep him clean? She is almost out of time. She will reach the postbox while there's still light.

24

Down on the strand, patches of daisies shine out from clumps of coarse grass. The bladderwrack fizzes, drinking in brine, and the sea worms are deserting their casts. A whole world is re-forming itself, just beneath the still surface. No moon yet, but soon it will light up a patch of sea like a new island. She thinks of Tom. Gone from her life with a girl called Cally. She thinks of Ma. Disappeared into nothingness. Ma would be proud of her ease, out there in the almost-dark. And not a torch or match in sight. When she reaches the green postbox set into the wall beneath the old school, she hesitates a moment, and then she slots the package in.

She'd forgotten how quickly night falls on Lamb and, by the time she walks briskly back towards the house, it is dark. She is almost at the gate when she sees it. A figure so still it might be stone. When the beam passes over, she realises who it is. His face is turned away from her towards the sea. He must have heard the crunch of her feet on the gravel, and yet he hasn't moved. She feels a little sting of fear. She remembers the neat rows of tools in his workshop, things that gouge and hammer and peel. She remembers the bullet. They stand there, a few yards apart, and neither of them moves.

'Theo?'

'Are you not going to invite me in?'

Her first thought is that at least she has managed to post the documents. But she is frightened by the calmness in his voice, by his stillness. Her heart hangs like a stone in her chest. Her lungs are dry.

'We've some business before you go,' he says. 'Some papers you need to give me.'

She tries to work out how close he is to her. She looks and listens for the dog, but he doesn't seem to have brought it with him. And so she thinks she might be wrong. It might not come to that. But then she sees that someone else is standing in the doorway of her house. A shadow man, the light blazing around the dark contour of his body. She knows now. And when she spots the gap, she goes for it.

Right away, Theo is after her. She can hear him behind her, blundering through the bracken. But she is fitter than him, she is faster. And she has already dodged off the road and into a culvert when she hears the shot ping into the drystone wall beside her.

She stifles her sobs, her urge to scream. Crouching there, she bites her own hand to try to stop the shaking. She hears the trail of something metallic along the road. He is just feet away from her now, heading resolutely in her direction. And she knows then that she's been seen. When she realises her Day-Glo top has given her away, she tears it off, tugging and pulling to be free of it. She bundles it into a ball and shoves it deep into the hedge. She needs to move, to find a better spot. But she has chosen a dead end. She has pinned herself into the long field, the Marriage Stones standing at the end of it like two sentinels.

It has begun to drizzle, and a fine mist is covering her skin. Down below, the tide is gurgling among the rocks. She hugs herself, buries her head in her chest and begins to give up. And just as she is about to let him come and get her, she changes her mind. She will not die in a field. She will not die at the wrong time, at someone else's pleasure. Not like Jennifer or Jacinta. Not like Ian.

But he senses her, hears her maybe. He approaches slowly at first and then, when he has spotted her, he picks up speed. He shoots again. She hears the bullet pinging off stone. And then he seems to trip. Somehow, he loses his footing. He cries out in pain as he lurches against the wall. She casts out to either side and the answer is there for her. The rock is embedded in the soft ground, but only just. It's easy to dislodge and her hand spans it. It gives her strength. She doesn't hesitate. She swings for him and hits him hard. And he falls, heavy as a tree. She hears the clatter of the gun as it hits rock. She doesn't think for one moment he could be dead, that she could be safe. And so she lifts the stone and brings it down on him, again and again. And she is no longer on Lamb at all. Róisín is bashing her way out of a house in Belfast where a soldier with soft lips will not die because of her. She is bashing the door down for Jacinta who will return to Rebecca Street in time for bingo.

She wipes her hands, sticky now, on the wet grass, and then she blunders towards the strand. Down at the sea's edge, she scoops up handfuls of salt water, gritty with sand and sea creatures. She scrubs at her hands, her face. She douses herself free of him. She takes a rock and scumbles it over her chin, on to her cheekbones where she knows it will mark. She makes talons of her fingers and presses them hard into the flesh. Standing there in the sea, her arms and legs deadened by cold and salt, it isn't difficult to jar at them with smaller stones to simulate knocks and punches. She rolls a rock on to her chest and the pain makes her cry out. It wouldn't fool a doctor, but it might be enough to win her sympathy on Lamb.

She is conscious of the need to reach the North Harbour, to get as far away as possible from Reen. But then she remembers the shadow man, who could be anywhere by now. She has just reached the road when she sees the mighty headlights of an oncoming vehicle. They catch her in their beam, and she is overwhelmed. She doesn't even try to run. Just stands there dripping in the middle of the road: head down, arms half raised against the light. A slammed door, the crunch of feet sliding to a halt in front of her. Murphy.

'I could have smashed you into kingdom come there, girl. Where are you going at this hour? The flight's at noon tomorrow, so we'll have an early start. You'll have some stuff to pack, I suppose. Your passport and that – Jesus.' He takes her arm, draws her closer into the beam of the headlights. 'What's that bastard done to you, girl? I swear to God I'll rip his fucking head off. Where is he? Where'd he go?'

She starts to tell him how Theo was waiting for her, how she struggled with him. And then she tells him about the body in the field.

'And here's me thinking it was Boyle all the time,' he says, half to himself. And she knows he is thinking about the woman in the Missing poster.

She points him towards the Marriage Stones, but she can't bring herself to go back there with him. He helps her into the passenger seat and tells her to lock the doors, that he'll be back soon. She watches him move out of range of the headlights, and then she is on her own again. The road ahead is limelit, waiting. The interior of Murphy's car is warm and padded. It feels impregnable, but she knows that's only an illusion. And then she remembers the lifeless sack of Theo's body, his crushed face, and is revolted. She cannot believe that she has killed again. And now that Murphy has left, she can't stop thinking about the shadow man. There is the weirdo from the school, of course, who is never far away. But she knows it isn't him.

Boyle is crouching in his favourite spot, raising his face into the pleasant rain. The picture window is boarded up now, and he finds that strangely comforting. A fox darts along the side of the house and rustles through the undergrowth. There's a heron overhead. And down there in the bay, the moon has shed a little silver on the sea. His head is full of hope. He has reached the house before them – he's confident of that. He'll just stand there and wait for her. He fantasises about arriving on her doorstep and her inviting him in. She'll serve him one of those teas she likes – camomile or mint. And then when Lonergan arrives, Boyle will tell him it's not convenient, that her ladyship's not receiving tonight, and go fuck yourself while you're at it. Oh the joy of it, the pleasure there is in being the hero.

He decides that he will paint her there, against the blank canvas of the boarded-up picture window. The Little Rose of Reen. Once he's been her rescuer, she will do it willingly. He will lay a table out in front of her. Paint in the blue glass bottle he destroyed. And everything will be complete.

The rain is falling harder now, and there's still no sign of anyone. And that confuses him because Lonergan should be here by now. As for Theo, he has no idea where he might be. He might be with the men in leather jackets, halfway to Schull with a boatload of gear. Or he might be here.

He walks around the side of the house. But just before the lighthouse beam comes sweeping back again, a shadow flits across the bedroom window. Oh no. Oh no, no, no. Don't tell me she's in there, after all. Don't tell me she's still hiding from me, and me the Lone Fucken Ranger about to save her skin.

A sadness begins to trickle back inside him. What made him think he'd ever get up close to her? Why would she suddenly just change her tune? Females like her. Sometimes you have to take. He puts his hand on the door and finds it slightly ajar, as if someone is only after coming in or out. He hears the sound of rummaging. And then he peers through the crack and sees Lonergan ransacking the place, but methodically, as if there is something specific he needs to find. Then, just as the lighthouse beam retreats, a car backfires. Somewhere in the distance. Crack. Somewhere to the west. Crack Crack. Towards the sea road.

Back at the side of the house, he selects his weapon from among the stack of rusting garden implements. He chooses his old friend, the shovel, and slings it up over his shoulder. And then he tries the door with the toe of his boot. He waits for the lighthouse beam to light the way. He's just about to go in when he hears the engine, spots Murphy's four-by-four on the road above. The headlamps sweep the hedgerows on the last turn down to Reen. Murphy slows for the gate and his giant tyres crunch slowly across the gravel. The engine idles to a stop, the metal ticking. And there she is. The Little Rose of Reen. Our Lady of the Lighthouse Beam.

And standing there as she approaches him, Boyle is flooded with joy. He has never been a hero before. And for a hero, anything is possible: painting, sunshine, sex. A hot meal in his belly and the new one in his bed. She is walking slowly for someone mad keen on jogging everywhere. When the beam of the lighthouse passes across her

308

face, his heart is wrenched off kilter. She's a mess. Her face is cut, flayed.

He raises his hand to greet her, but she doesn't seem to notice him. Whatever fucker's done this? He feels the satisfying return of hate into his veins. Murphy is following her now and he's yelling for her to stop, that they can get her passport later. That the Guards have been called. He's lumbering along after her, and she turns on him, raises her hand like she's stopping the traffic. 'Stay. Back.'

Boyle makes a fist. Fair fucks to her, putting Murphy in his place. Fair fucks. Boyle's heart has sprung up again, and now it's bounding away in his chest. But there's no stopping Murphy. He lumbers on. Boyle won't let him take the glory. He lifts the shovel down off his shoulder, and brandishes it in front of him. He needs to be the one to save her from Lonergan. And so he walks into the house.

25

As soon as Róisín hears the shots, she knows that they were
meant for her. Four or five at once, and then silence. Nothing. Murphy grabs her by the arm and pulls her towards
the jeep. As they crouch down behind it, her head is buried
in the fleece of his jacket, and she can hear the *rumpum-
pum* of his heart. Murphy doesn't move, he doesn't speak.
And then she starts to say that they need to get away. That
she knows exactly who this is. But he tells her to be quiet
and she knows that if she keeps on talking he might put his
hand over her mouth, and she couldn't stand that. She feels
him reach for something in his pocket, sees the blue gleam
of his phone. When he speaks into it, there is no timbre in
his voice and she has no idea how the person on the other
end could hear whatever it is he's trying to say. The only
words she can manage to make out are 'emergency' and
'armed' and 'Reen'. Nobody else seems to hear the outboard moving off from the strand, but she is sure now that
this is Lonergan making his escape.

There is no way of explaining this to Murphy. They remain crouched down behind the vehicle for what feels like an eternity until a stream of lights approaches in the distance. A convoy of islanders, it seems, making their way to Reen. Their headlights move across the ridge from both directions, dipping down the narrow road. There are tractors and vans and a whole assortment of patched-up cars. Soon, they have filled the gravelled area in front of the house, and are backed up past the old school. She starts to mention the outboard to Murphy, but halfway through she falters. There is no point. No one will believe her anyway. Already, the islanders have decided what happened here.

'There's a history,' Murphy says knowingly. 'The Drug Squad was on to them. Feud with the suppliers, I'd say. Happens up in Dublin all the time.'

The sea is a flat black mirror, and Lonergan will be an old hand when it comes to the crossing to the mainland. She's heard them talk about the rocks at the entrance to the South Harbour, but he must be well past them by now.

Murphy is kneeling beside the back wheel of the car. Head bent, he is muttering into his phone, sending his voice down into the wet earth. 'Grand so,' he says, finally. 'You'll want to tell them to head over towards the lighthouse end. That'd be the best place to land, I'd say. Up there on the ridge.'

The word travels down the queue of people waiting in their cars. She can sense a change in mood to one she recognises: the mood of people who are in on breaking news. Among the heave and scatter of the waves, the purr

311

of engines, there are brief scrabbles of music as car doors open momentarily, then close.

The helicopter is almost overhead now. It is moving closer, skimming lower. It is whipping up the field and shaking out the hedges. The sound of the rotors seems to calm Murphy, but on Róisín it has the opposite effect. This is the sound of trouble – of clashing bin lids and burning buses. It's as if she's never been away.

On a sea as flat as this, Lonergan could be over to the mainland and back twice by now. By the time they reach the house, Boyle has long gone cold and there is no trace of any gunman at all.

Later, at the pub, Cat makes Róisín a succession of hot whiskeys with clove-studded lemons and spoonfuls of thick dark honey. She provides warm, clean clothes. She even takes an anglepoise lamp from the computer room and uses it to examine the scratches on Róisín's face. She lays out tweezers, cotton wool and another bowl of that acrid-smelling disinfectant. She offers a soothing ointment. Serves tea.

The dawn is rising now over the North Harbour, and a small motorboat is bringing in the early stocks: the milk, the peat briquettes, the bread from Fields of Skibbereen. It is also bringing a Dr O'Sullivan from Baltimore. She is a brisk woman in her thirties, dressed in a rain jacket that makes a dry scratching sound as she unzips it and hangs it on the back of a chair. She pushes away Cat's anglepoise and takes out a little stick light of her own. She starts at the forehead, using a pencil to draw back Róisín's hair. 'Would you mind?' she gestures to Róisín's shirt. Róisín undoes it and then she nods again. 'And that as well.'

Róisín takes off her bra and folds it carefully on her lap, one cup inside the other. The doctor murmurs something indistinct, and then continues. 'The abrasions? How did you pick those up?'

'I had to drag myself along.'

'Along?'

'The beach.'

'Ah,' she says crisply, 'I see.'

But it's clear that she doesn't. She begins to write, mouthing the words aloud so that they sound ridiculous.

'Dragging. Self. Along. Beach. Well, that's all, I think. I'll leave you some painkillers in case you need them. But, otherwise, I suggest you get some sleep.'

Outside the door, the doctor is speaking to someone. A man. No, two men. The word 'unexplained' is used, the word 'unlikely'. One of the male voices says there's no reason to think the two incidents are necessarily connected, but she can't hear what anyone says in reply.

Róisín glances down at her watch – only four hours until Murphy will be here to bring her to the airport. When she glances up again, she finds that Cat has returned. She stands in the doorway, just looking. It's as though she is beginning to see Róisín for the first time.

'Can I ask you something?' she says. 'I suppose I'm just intrigued. Pete's been saying . . . Well there's this rumour that the house at Reen is full of stuff. Newspaper cuttings, and the like?'

She says it lightly, but Róisín doesn't miss the real question. She has seen that look before. Soon after she met Tom, they had an evening out with his friends from work. After a while, the others became engrossed in some ball game or other, but Tom's boss wasn't interested and neither was Sheen. The boss was a man in his mid-forties who dressed the way a certain type of East Coast American thinks the English do, in murky greens and tweed. He sat with his legs crossed, relaxed and utterly self-assured. And when the others were distracted by the game, he let her know that he'd guessed an essential truth about her, though he didn't say how.

Pete arrives, and so she has a temporary reprieve from answering. 'The forensic team is working away out at Reen. God knows what they'll do with poor oul Boyle when they've finished. I suppose the family up in Dublin might claim him. One strange thing, though. There's no sign of Theo's boat down at the harbour.'

Their attitude to Boyle is not exactly callous, but no one there will grieve. No one would have grieved for her either. Maura would have got over it quickly enough, and who else is there now?

When Pete closes the door behind him, Cat is still standing there with her hands on her hips.

'What's this all about, Sheen?'

'Lonergan,' she says. 'He's not what he seems.'

It's further than she's ever ventured before, but Cat doesn't take her up on it. She just shakes her head. 'And what about you, Sheen? Are you what you seem?'

The Guards don't arrive for another hour. For a chat,

they say. Nothing formal at this stage, but she can't have access to her passport, no. Not yet. They'll need her to stick around a day or two. They'll want to talk about what happened in that field, about her links to Theo and to Boyle. They don't ask her questions about any of these things. They merely tag them as matters of interest for later, another time, whenever. They sound casual, might even be casual, but from the way the younger of them looks at her a little too long as he leaves the room, she knows that none of this is casual at all.

She spends the remains of that day and the following night in flurries of fitful sleep. She doesn't return to the house: the forensic team is still at work, and no one is allowed past the tape, not even Murphy. Róisín stays on the top floor of the pub, wearing borrowed clothes and lying on a narrow bed in a room whose sea-view wall is an archipelago of damp stains – sea salt seeping through the island sand that was used to plaster it.

She feels like she is underwater in that pale blue room; she is cold all the time. The realisation that her flight would have arrived at JFK by now draws those salty walls in around her, and each time she shuts her eyes she is in the field with the Marriage Stones, hemmed in between old deaths and new ones.

The next morning, a pair of uniformed Guards are occupying the blue benches outside Molly's – caps off in the thin sunshine, sipping at Styrofoam cups. At first she pays them little heed, until she remembers what Murphy said about the police and how they almost never set foot on Lamb. And then it strikes her that they might be there to keep an eye on her. Idly, she wonders what would happen if she tried to take the ferry out.

The O'Neills will have received her envelope by now. She tries to imagine what they could have done with it, then realises she can't come up with anything. Two dead men talking about what happened to another? The more she thinks about it, the likelier it seems that some provenance was necessary, some context, something she hasn't given.

As she changes into the fresh clothes Cat has left for her – someone's oversized shirt and a pair of tracksuit bottoms – she notices that the ferry has docked. New arrivals are walking in clumps along the pier. A group of four or five look like a camera crew – laughing, hoisting equipment on to their shoulders, walking up the pier towards the shop. She senses that, outside the island, the world might have changed in the past couple of days. She is desperate for news, but outside the door to Cat's internet café her confidence falters and she takes a further flight of stairs down to the bar instead.

There is no sign of Cat this morning. Pete brings her some toast from the kitchen. He prepares a cappuccino, making a performance of it, all levers and pistons and steam. When he slides a saucer under the cup and places it on the counter in front of her, they both gaze at it for a moment. Pete is the first to break the silence.

'They're having a press conference this morning,' he says. 'The first since.'

Since Jennifer, she supposes.

'Eleven sharp in the parochial hall. You know where

that is, right? The place where they had the Céilí? It's the only venue big enough.'

Once he has started talking, he seems unable to stop. Pete is usually the silent type, but today he is a talking news site. Two Dutch fellas arrested up in Cork. Seizure. Links. Theo. And then he says it. Lonergan.

'Did you hear the news? Word is that family with the dead mother have got their hands on something big.'

He looks straight at her when he tells her that, and then she remembers her last conversation with Cat. Her stomach shrinks, but she forces herself to try to find out more.

'What kind of thing?'

'Last bulletin I heard, they were appealing for someone or other to get in touch with them again. God knows.'

For a moment, she can track a thought as it almost breaks across his face, but in the end he doesn't quite manage the connection. He taps the bar instead, all business now.

'How and ever, there's sandwiches to make. We'll be jammed later, once the conference is over.'

On her way up to the parochial hall, Róisín passes the old schoolhouse. Boyle's possessions have already been turfed out on to the middle of what used to be the playground. A tatty mattress, a meagre pile of schoolbooks and jotters, boxes and tins, bottles and jars. Right on top, there is a sprawl of canvases bearing crudely painted nudes.

Murphy is there with the same two lads who boarded up her window. They stare at her as if they've never seen her before, and she wonders what they're thinking, what people are saying now. Next to the unruly pile of detritus, there is a dark green metal jerry can. The sight of it makes her queasy, though she isn't sure why. When Murphy spots her, he lifts one of the canvases and waves it in her direction.

'Would you take a look at that. What did I tell you, girl? One hell of a weirdo.' And then he sees the expression on her face, and is suddenly bashful. 'But sure, Lord have mercy on him all the same.'

It feels like the whole island is at the press conference. The camera crew she saw arriving earlier is there, set up to film proceedings. One of the journalists, a man in a brown suede jacket, has wandered over to the far wall to examine the framed photographs of regattas long gone. Two local women she doesn't recognise are serving tea, handing out biscuits from a large blue tin. Rich tea or custard cream? And then she notices, draped heavy on the air, the smell of burning. People are casting around to find the source, and only Róisín knows that it's the contents of the school-house, gone already, up in smoke.

The senior Guard who is chairing the press conference has a thin scrape of hair combed sparsely across his bald pate. Five other people sit alongside him: four men and the female state pathologist. A trestle table from the Céilí has been drawn up in front of this committee of outsiders, forming a barricade against the islanders. Just as they are about to begin, Murphy blunders in from the back of the hall. He approaches the panel, starts pulling a chair up next to the pathologist until one of the Guards gestures at him to stay where he is.

The senior Guard positions his pen horizontally in front of him like a dessert spoon. He takes a little silver-coloured handbell from his bag and places it to his right. When he has laid out a yellow legal pad, and smoothed down the facing sheet, he starts to speak – a reedy, sing-song voice. There is still a buzz in the room though, and he is struggling to be heard. He gives the bell a genteel little shake, clears his throat and starts again. Róisín can't place the accent, having lost her ear for all but the most obvious, but the woman sitting next to her raises her eyes.

'It's far from silver bells the likes of him was reared,' she says.

But the bell does the trick and there's a hush now.

'We are asking all members of the public to assist us in the investigation of the double murder that occurred here two nights ago. One man was found shot dead at Reen Point, in a rented house. Six spent cases have been recovered from the scene – two at the location of the Marriage Stones, four more at the house. Members of the Firearms Squad will be arriving to conduct their investigation this afternoon. The other man is believed to have been battered to death, presumably in the course of a struggle.

'The two fatalities have been identified as Vincent Boyle, of no fixed address, and Theo van der Bey, a local craftsman, who resided at Goat Point. One gun, which was discharged at the scene, was recovered next to Mr van der Bey's body. The weapon used to kill Mr Boyle has not yet been found. Mr van der Bey's boat is believed to have gone missing from its usual berth in the North Harbour and it is thought that this may contain vital clues.'

A door opens at the back of the hall. The Guard glances towards it, and then he seems to lose his train of thought. He raises his hand, but the gesture is difficult to interpret – it could be a greeting or something more defensive. He looks down at his pad, consults his list, and then he is back into his flow again. This time, though, his language lapses into abstraction. Incumbent. Investigate. Procedure. Circumspect. Róisín feels exhausted, and her head has begun to spin. She can't remember the last time she ate anything but toast.

The panel is taking questions now, and a journalist from Cork is probing links to a cocaine seizure near Goleen last autumn. Róisín finds herself concentrating on the cuff of her borrowed shirt where a thread is unravelling from a loosely stitched button. Up in front, Molly is on her feet now, asking what guarantee the Guards can offer that this is the end of Lamb's troubles.

'That's a heck of a lot of funny business for one little island,' she says.

Someone in front sniggers at that, and the tension is broken momentarily. There is a shuffle from behind as another speaker takes the floor. The senior Guard looks up.

'Ah yes, Mr Lonergan,' he says.

Her first thought is that she can't have heard the name right, and then she remembers that the world is full of Lonergans. She has a flash of someone with a cello up Kilimanjaro, playing chess. But it comes and goes within an instant. When the man starts to speak, there's no mistaking who this is. His voice is strong, but unforced. He sounds completely calm. People turn to look at him, and she can see that they are soaking up a kind of comfort from that air he has of being able to sort out anything at all.

'I'd like to offer my support to the entire Lamb Island community,' he says. 'I travelled back down from Dublin as soon as –'

She realises she is about to panic, but she can't help herself. Her pulse thuds in her ears and drowns him out. The rows of heads in front of her dissolve. The room is deconstructed now, just streaks and blobs she can't decipher. She is aware of the back of her own head as if it were the very centre of reality. She is certain that his eyes are trained on it; it feels like it might explode at any moment.

The camera crew are focusing their attention on Lonergan now. Róisín twists in her seat, forcing herself to face him too. She wonders if he even realises she's there, because he isn't looking at her at all. He is speaking to the camera.

'On behalf of the New Republic Party, let me take this opportunity to condemn in the strongest terms the illegal drug trade that's ravaging our society.'

But it sounds formulaic, unconvincing. And she realises then that the last thing on his mind is politics. He has come here to intimidate her, to let her know she isn't safe. He has come to finish off the job.

She glances at the trestle table where the senior Guard is telling Lonergan that of course they'll be searching Goat Point, and the schoolhouse too. They have no idea what they are dealing with. There'll be no protection for her from them. Just as Lonergan is about to take his seat, their eyes meet, his gaze skimming hers. He thinks he's won. He thinks that just by turning up he'll snuff her out.

The pause is just long enough to allow her time to stand. She raises her hand as if she's back at school, but she doesn't wait for anyone's permission. When she opens her mouth, her Belfast accent reasserts itself and she feels a sort of peace. Her ears are singing, but her heart is calm. She is out there on the ocean, no longer able to distinguish sea from sky, but she isn't turning back.

'My name is Róisín Burns,' she says. 'And I was the target here.'

The room is so silent she can hear the herons outside, *ack-ack*ing as they pass overhead. In the haze of faces she sees Cat squinting up at her and Molly, sharp-eyed and intent.

Rushing towards her is the roll of all the years between Belfast and now. Lonergan is a smudge at the corner of her eye, that's all. In the background, someone is murmuring her name, 'Róisín Burns.' Hearing it spoken back to her like that feels reassuring. And though she senses the great wave rearing over her, she is ready now. She turns to face the camera. It has forgotten Lonergan. The lens is all for her.

She can see her story spooling off in front of her.

'When I first met Brian Lonergan, I was just a teenager. Back in Belfast, in the darkest days.'

And though she senses him, moving at the very edge of things, he doesn't frighten her at all. Once the truth has started tumbling out, she feels lightheaded, free.

She won't stop talking till they take her down.